THE GANGSTERS' RUNNER

Jason Cook

Based on the true-life events of a gangsters' runner in
London's underworld.

Part Two of *There's No Room for Jugglers in my Circus*
Part Three is on its way.

All books available at www.amazon.co.uk
http://www.myspace.com/thejugglerscircus
http://myspace.com/thegangstersrunner

Pen Press

First published in Great Britain by Pen Press

All paper used in the printing of this book has been made from
wood grown in managed, sustainable forests.

ISBN13: 978-1-906710-82-8

Printed and bound in the UK
Pen Press is an imprint of Indepenpress Publishing Limited
25 Eastern Place
Brighton
BN2 1GJ

A catalogue record of this book is available from
the British Library

Cover design by Paul Joel
Graphic Artist www.pauljoel.com

This novel is based around a true story line, and some true events. However all characters in this book have been changed and any resemblance to actual persons mentioned, living or dead, is purely coincidental as some have been changed to protect the innocent.

Acknowledgements

Thanks to my Mum, Vivien for being amazing and my brother Gary and his family in Liverpool, for being very supportive and understanding.

A big thanks for Helen and Andy Dennis for all their help and support and patience and for believing in me.

Thanks also to Mr P and Lou, Mark and Claire for their respect and help that they have shown me. Through good and bad times, also thanks to their families too, for making my life that little bit easier and much more eventful and for taking the time to understand me when others have failed.

Thanks to Old School,(aka DJ Mad Al) Mattie the Mac (aka Marcus Delaney) and Mr B (aka Dolly) and his family and not forgetting Ray and Danny from Park wood and his lovely girls for being loyal and a big thanks to some of the most Dangerous Men in England.

Thanks to them and the other faces and villains that let me write about their story in this book and made this book possible. Also a very big thanks to Paul Knight, crime author 2007 and author of the *Coding of a Concrete Animal*, thanks for your time. Also many thanks to everyone that supported me and purchased my first book.

Respect to all those who I have met and who have helped me become who I am today and helped me with my work. Take care of yourselves.

Although Jason Cook has a somewhat insalubrious past, he is now a well-respected member of the Hertfordshire community. Jason now works with local youth community projects, schools and the Hertfordshire police. He educates against gun crime at local schools as well as running drug awareness workshops throughout Hertfordshire. Jason has recently written a piece entitled *Redemption*; a book of short stories in which each of the authors tell of how they've seen the error of their ways and explain how they've turned their lives around for the better. They include Carlton Leach (*Rise of the Foot Soldier*); Joe Egan (Ex Irish Heavy-Weight Boxing Champion); BAFTA award winning author Geoff Thompson; Robin Barratt (author, bodyguard, and owner of *Body Guards and Bouncers* magazine); and several other established authors, Charlie Bronson, Jamie O'Keefe, and Paulie Knight.

This is the story of where that life took him.

Foreword

Jason Cook is a new and exciting author telling his story of a life in the underworld over three books. These books brings to life the diverse characters and follows Jason in good times and bad through a life of crime.

The story of a young man drawn in to the underworld by his habit of The Devil's Dandruff – cocaine. To survive in what he calls the circus Jason has to juggle various dealers and his boss Mr B to feed his spiraling habit. In a desperate bid to help two friends, Jason was forced to take on a smuggling trip to Jamaica. A drug deal that goes wrong puts Jason and fellow villain Old School on the run and back in prison for a second time. Always thinking he is one-step ahead, he digs himself a deeper hole with every scam and deal he takes on. With all other options exhausted, Jason agreed to take out a super grass for £30k, hoping to clear his debts and leave the circus. This story not only shows the rewards and glamour of being involved in such villainous circles, but the darker side also, the innocent people involved and how they suffer.

Where can a gangster's runner run to when it all goes wrong?

About the Author

The author Jason Cook, now 32, was born in Hackney, London. He was the youngest of four. He had two half-brothers and one half-sister. At the age of 6, his parents wanted a fresh start for Jason. They moved from London and settled in Borehamwood. From the age of 12 he was involved with smoking, drugs, and drinking.

Jason Cook from Borehamwood was every mother's nightmare, a bored teenager with no direction but a lust for money and excitement. His distaste for the life of hard work his parents had, and a sizeable drug habit led to his involvement with gangsters, violence, cocaine and rave filled days. Ultimately he realized the precarious and meaningless nature of his life, and that his parents were happy and he was not.

Jason is dyslexic, and during a spell in prison began writing. Since his release, he has admirably gone on to create a new and legitimate life for himself. This book exposes the unglamorous world of someone whose life is dominated by drug addiction and the shady activities that funds such a habit; a life of drugs, thugs, mugs, gangsters and villains. This in turn led him into becoming gangsters' runner for a big firm in London to pay for overdue drug debts and prove his worth on the streets.

Contents

The Ace Card

Well like I said, sometimes you never know when your ace card might be pulled out and you have to make a comeback, even if you didn't want to. Well someone had just turned over my ace card for me.

Before long I found myself back in deep with the Firm once again. It's like a revolving door, once you're in you're in, and you just keep going round and round in circles trying to find a way out. You realise with a weary sense of inevitability, deep within your heart, that the only real way out of the Firm is either in a wooden box or banged up doing a stretch at her Majesty's pleasure! Either that or nutted out somewhere on a paranoid drug psychosis trip, where you can't even string a sensible sentence together. And you're as much use as someone out of the film *One Flew over the Cuckoo's Nest* or even that of *The Shining*.

Of course it's even harder to get out, once you're mixed up with the ways of the Firm – even worse when you're empowered by the Devil's dandruff (cocaine). As the Firm would say, 'if you couldn't play the Devil's music, then don't dance with the Devil. Otherwise you will end up dead.' They say you can only ride the lion for so long before you fall off and it turns round and bites yer... Well I had just fallen off and been bitten, bitten hard.

Remember the heavenly Mandy, Johnny's little sister? Well if you don't, let me remind you... She was a little blonde and a stunner. Looks aside, she had also stitched me right up that night back at the club when the Jewellery Thieves had been released from prison. She had taken me back to her house on a promise, once there she said she would give me some oral, but instead she gave me some home truths about how I didn't do the shooting in Knightsbridge... false advertisement or what? Well what she had said made me stand up straight if you know what I mean and it weren't in the trouser department. She was the one, that her brother Johnny the hit man had said for me to stay away from, and to think of our little meeting together between his sister and I as just a wet dream.

Well that dream had just turned out to be a reality. Because at 9.30pm last night she had phoned me in tears and said, "Cookster. Hi it's me..."

"*Who?*"

"It's me, Mandy."

"*I don't know any Mandys, sorry sweetheart... love to chat, but got a lot to do and unfortunately a great deal on my plate right now, without you turning up again to mess me about.*" (As saying I knew her would mean Johnny the hit man would also be making a comeback very soon. Without anyone or me, even turning his ace card over for him. He would be coming back for me, just like he said he would if I got involved with his little sister again.)

That night when he had taken me for a ride in the £50 grand's worth of Land Rover that he had picked me up in, he had warned me outside Mandy's house to stay away from her and to forget about everything that had just happened between us. He had the gun at my side, then at my head and told me, "There's no room for jugglers in my circus". We were sitting there in the motor with Mr Nice in the back all nice and cosy, smoking his fat Cuban cigar and looking like he owned the place (flash git). Johnny had done all the talking to me. Mr Nice just sat there without saying a dickey bird, just staring at me like I was a rare animal ready to be made extinct, in between taking large pulls on the cigar and breathing out large amounts of smoke. He didn't even move or raise an eyelid when I was told to get in the Land Rover. Whilst Johnny talked to me he just sat there and stared at me listening carefully to what Johnny had to say.

On the same night as the party at the History nightclub for the Jewellery Thieves, the fellas they had shared a cell with had done the robbery on the cash van the day of their release. They had been planning and preparing it. The job was to go off that day whilst they were all banged up sharing a cell together. All the money that they had got had been shared out between the guests that night, and also to all those that were invited to attend the party. Just to give some of us a head start, which was well needed. I had left to go with Mandy, back to hers on that promise she had given me. But unbeknown to me it was a false one and that it had been a big set-up all along by her brother. There was I, thinking my luck was in.

"You have to help me!" came the words from Mandy's sweet lips.

"Mandy, this isn't another one of your set-ups is it, darling? You can tell the person who's sent you this time to stop wasting my time. I'm getting a bit old for all that bollocks now. I'm trying to leave the circus behind me. Know what I mean, darling? I let the boys play at being gangsters nowadays. I'm no longer a little boy in a man's world, sweetheart," (me giving it all the confidence and Billy big bollocks in the world). I was safe for now. I figured that if Johnny did turn up unexpectedly on the scene, and wanted to put a bullet in my nut, just for chatting with his little sister despite his warning, I was safe for now. She had crossed the line to contact me and not the other way round.

"No please listen to me," she said. "I've no one else to turn to or talk to, only you. Something tells me I can trust only you. The others don't want to get involved or just want to for their own selfish reasons. You keep your friends close but your enemies closer in this game, you know that. If they knew what was what and that some people were now out the way, they would think the Firm was weak or falling apart. They could move in and take over the Firm and the Firm's business and there'd be no one to keep them in their place. Right now they are all still minding there p's and q's. You know what I mean? It won't take them long to find out what's happened. You know what they're all like. They're all full of it, giving it charley big potatoes all the time. Thinking they own everything and everyone owes them something, when really they don't. They all think nothing will catch up with them, thinking they're invisible or untouchable or all made of Teflon. Fucking bulletproof. But when you really need them they're nowhere to be seen, unless it benefits them. You were in the game once and saw it for what it really was. There just seems to be no loyalty nowadays and most of the old school gangsters have

3

gone or the ones with the morals and pride have. The rest are either on the run, retarded, on a drug psychosis trip, banged up, dead, or making movies." Well maybe a few have.

Mandy continues, "Cookster. Are you there?"

"Don't worry. I'm still here listening, beautiful."

"You know a woman's intuition is normally right. So it's you I'm trusting with this. Anyway you still owe me and the Firm a big favour."

"What?" I said, quite surprised.

"After all, I saved you that night from getting well out of your depth at the party they had that night. The one that was laid on, at the back of the History nightclub, when the money was all shared out from that bank job they had pulled off, remember? I had kept my mouth shut about the shooting, knowing full well Johnny had got involved and that it wasn't you. You hadn't killed that fella and the Firm thought you had. If I had told them you hadn't they would've probably killed you themselves for knowing too much about their business and taking their kindness for weakness. You would have ended up like some of the other liberty takers. Bought in to the Firm, put on a pedestal and then taken out, shot and left in the woods somewhere, or however else they do their cleaning business. They had brought you right in and told you, clued you up quite a bit about them and the Firm's contacts. They looked after you after that day and just before, when you were about to leave prison. So they would have had to kill you, right there and then, to show a bit of face, for your liberty taking, to teach others not to be so foolish. You would have been made an example of by them, for the other liberty takers that thought they too could take the Firm for a ride, like you have. If they knew for sure you hadn't done it and that you had taken a liberty and all the perks by letting them all think you did, they would have got rid of you for sure. They treated you like one of them and introduced you to the family Firm in London. They made you more than just a Foot Soldier [street drug seller] you were sorted right out because they believed you were better then that. Now you had proved yourself and done the shooting and that you were true to your word. You had done their little favour for them with no questions asked. Just the way things should have been done. So they could move on and up the ladder and bring you with them. So you couldn't have paid your debt back to Mr B. I kept my mouth shut about Johnny and you telling everyone you had done the shooting in the first place. Or getting you out of there before anyone asked too many questions about where Johnny was when they asked me. I just said he didn't get involved in this one. 'OK,' they would say, then I would big you up to everyone I spoke to or met that night by saying 'you know who this is?' when they saw you. This is the man who has made all this possible and for Johnny not letting on to me or anyone else for that matter. Johnny had come to mine and got to you, after he had told me to get you back to mine. So you definitely owe one to Mr Nice and the Firm and you definitely owe me now as the Jewellery Thieves hadn't found out you never done it till now. So that has now put Mr Nice in a bad position."

"So what's special about NOW?" I said, feeling a bit panicky.

"Well now they all know for sure you never done it. So you can see what a big mess it is, not only for me, but for you!"

"You really do want to see me?" I said.

"Yes of course I do. I'm not playing games with you now. I wouldn't have rung you if I didn't think you could help me. It was just lucky I kept your number. I'll tell you more when you come to see me. You will meet me won't you?" she paused then continued with, "talking on the phone would get us all nicked especially with what I want to tell you next. It's best we meet up face to face."

"OK, sweetheart, where do you want me to meet you? Or do you want to come to Borehamwood and meet me outside the Woodcock pub or the Punch."

"No, too many people know you there and they'll start asking questions if they see me. Come to the old East End, to the Blind Beggars pub. We will be safe there. Please come alone, be there tomorrow for about 5pm. Hand on my heart, this isn't a set-up Cookster. I really need your help. You're the one I'm turning to. A lot's happened in the Firm since there was no room for Jugglers in my circus."

"OK, Mandy I'll be there. See you at 5pm then."

"Thanks," replied Mandy as she started to cry again. Then the phone goes quiet, as she must have replaced the receiver. So I put the phone down and went and sat on the end of my bed and started to panic. Well it was getting late by now, but I was well awake after hearing all that news. I sat and thought what all this could be about.

There was a noise of a car slowly pulling up outside my window. I got up instantly flicking the switch off on the lights and moved to the side of the wall, sliding myself along the wall, so as not to be seen if someone looked up at the window. I got to the edge of the window and peered out. I could just see out. It was some uninvited guest sent to come to kill me off now all the news was out. My heart started to race. When I peered out between the net curtains a bit more and looked down into the street below I saw a man looking a bit shady getting out of a car. It was just a cab dropping someone off from a night out, and by the looks of the fella it was a good one at that! He was swaying from left to right and started singing to himself. I sat back down on the bed and thought to myself, fuck. The Jewellery Thieves had now found out for sure that I didn't do the shooting for them in London and that Johnny had. So it wouldn't be too long before the family Firm in London would also come to know about these things and start putting the feelers out for me for the Jewellery Thieves. Come to think of it, it wouldn't be too long before everyone that was connected in some way to the crime world would find out too. So did this mean they had put Mandy up to this once again? To try and get me to them, without them trying to find me, or noising too many people up that they were looking for me. The less people that knew about them looking for me, the better in their eyes. If they were to get rid of me that was. Also, the less that knew the better; just in case someone clued me up a bit, before they could lay their hands on me. They may have thought I would have done a runner or gone into hiding.

This was all going round and round in my head like a record. If this... if that... what if they do this?... what if they do that?... so now what?... was I their number one target?... was I their new

6

man they would want out their way or had they already put a contract out on me for knowing too much about the Firm without me even knowing it? Would they be sending a car round to my address to come get me any time soon? Or let me have it on a drive by? Maybe take me to a warehouse and torture me or any other way they think necessary to teach me a lesson. Were they using Mandy to lure me once again into a false sense of security? They probably thought I was a liability and couldn't be trusted any more with what I knew.

I knew loads about the Firm, and whom they were connected to, and right about now I wish I didn't. Would they just come to London, to the Wood and kick down my door at any given minute and let me have it there and then? Or anyone else that was at my home at the time of their uninvited arrival? BANG BANG and walk back out the house with the gun still smoking concealed in their jackets leaving me in a pool of my own blood on the floor dead, or fighting for my life. Waiting for my mum to find me, just like other unfortunate people that had already paid the price with their own lives for being mixed up in a world of drugs, thugs, mugs and gangsters and all sorts of younger villains.

Those that have also gone wild and fallen foul of the dark side of the underworld or the Devil's dandruff. Where money doesn't grow on trees and we have to hurt the ones we love in the fight for survival in the concrete jungle. Out there where we call the streets the Manors and the ghetto The Wood. There where drugs are for mugs and only the top people made any real money out of them. As the rest are either dead or banged up or trying to make a few quid here, there and everywhere, when they weren't using the drugs themselves of course.

I was very nervous by now so I sat by the curtains for what seemed like an age. Just twitched at them every time a car pulled up or I could hear talking or loud footsteps outside in the street below. That was without doing any cocaine I might add.

As I stared through the gap in the curtains once again, I went off into a trance of deep thought peering out to the empty street below.

7

Would they want their money back? Of course they would, who was I kidding. Wouldn't you? Then they would get rid of me, as I was now no use to the Firm, or was I? What could I offer them? After the money had been paid back that was that. That's if I could make that sort of money now, at least if I owed it, it might keep me alive for a bit. Who knows, I was just small fry to them as they were in bigger leagues than I could have ever imagined.

Did they really think I'd taken a liberty even though I had tried to do the deed for them? Well, they would have known that bit wouldn't they? Well I had taken a small liberty by letting them believe I had done the shooting and walking about giving it plenty of large at their party. Letting them think I had done it and taking all the credit, glory, and money for it. When it was only mine if the fella was dead and I was the one who had pulled the trigger. So he would be out the way and not the other way round. Like it was arranged back in the prison yard, back at Pentonville prison, when I had the first meeting with them whilst walking around the yard with Mr Adams. I should have just told them the truth. That I tried but failed, and given their money back. But how could I, as Johnny had taken the rest of it? Well at least they would have known the true extent of things. I had tried to do it but didn't succeed. Then I wouldn't have been in all this mess once again.

Looking over my shoulder every five minutes if I went out in the Wood or up to London. See, it pays to be honest in this game. Well, as honest as you can be when you live by the sword and die by it. I soon came away from the window, laid down on the bed and eventually fell asleep. After all the thoughts and worries had gone from my mind and the scenarios had stopped going over and over in my head.

I woke up quite late the next day. After all, I had been up all night worrying and panicking myself to death.

It didn't take long for the time to come round to meet Mandy once again. I looked at the clock, soon it would be 3.45pm in the afternoon. So I parked the limo up, back at the yard at Elstree aerodrome and went home. Ran a bath, got in it and laid there relaxing in the hot water, soaking and breathing in the steam.

Submerging myself within the bubbles and letting the Radox do its stuff. I started to think once again, shall I go or shall I stay? Would the Jewellery Thieves be waiting for me there at the pub to put me out of my misery? Could I trust the gorgeous Mandy again after all that she had done before?

I had to go and just lay all my cards on the table and be honest with them. Well that's all they wanted. No stories from me trying to wriggle my way out of it with an excuse. They knew the truth now. I'm sure they had heard many excuses already in this line of business. So I would just tell them how it was. I tried and failed and yes, spent their money that they had given to me, every last penny of it and all. Well it was shared between Johnny, Mr B, and me but I wouldn't tell them that bit. I had tried and failed, took the money and ran and by doing so had taken a big liberty in their eyes.

As you know Mandy was a stunner and would turn your legs to jelly just looking at her and I wanted to see her again, even if it was dangerous, but with some reassurances this time. I was going out with a bang. If I were to get it, then I would try my best to take anyone else out with me who thought they were brave enough.

Right now, I had no choice but to do what I could to stay in the game. If they came out with guns blazing then I would let some of them have it back on my way down. Even if after they had finished with me I had more holes in me then a watering can. Why not try my luck? If I was going to get it then, so should they, after all no matter who we are we're all blood and guts inside! So what made them different? I was getting a bit fed up with having guns shoved at me all the time and being told how it is.

I jumped out the bath, got dried, brushed my teeth and sprayed deodorant on. Put on my black t-shirt and put on my new crisp Armani suit. Put on my platinum and gold bracelet and my diamond ring and done the Cartier up on my wrist. Slid on my Italian shoes, done my hair in the mirror and once again looked back into the mirror and oh boy, did I look good! Well smart and well sorted. In fact I looked the bollocks. I slid on the Armani shades, then slid my finger over the mirror on the dresser to scrape up the charley dust left on there from the night before's binge. A few escort girls, a few close pals of mine and me had partied hard back at mine. Sniffing hard all night long and chatting charley bollocks 'til the early hours of the next morning, 'til the birds started twitting and the "paras" had calmed down a bit.

I then left the house. I wanted to look my best if I was going to see her again. I jumped into my friend's car. He was a proper nice fella. His name was Danny. He owned a little nightclub over in Potters bar. He was doing well for himself and he had worked hard for it. He was a proper gentleman, a right nice geezer, 'e knew the crack.

So whilst he was on holiday I asked him for a little favour. I asked if I could borrow his motor. He said I could and turned out to be a convertible SLK Merc. Result! This would do wonders for my image I thought. All dressed up and in a motor that looked the part too.

I then drove to Roger's house to get some reassurance for the little meeting I was about to have, which was a Glock that Roger was baby-sitting for me for a rainy day, and today it was pouring! I thanked Roger, jumped into the Merc, looked at the gun for a second and then put the gun into the glove box. Then I drove out of Borehamwood, onto the A1 into London, heading off to the East End to the Blind Beggars pub, to meet up with the fine, outstanding Mandy once again. As I pulled up at the lights I looked in the mirror and fuck me it was only the Old Bill, all of a sudden their lights went on and the siren. My heart sank because here I was sitting in the Merc with a gun in the glove box, as bright as day, without being able to hide it before they stopped me, with the Old Bill up my arse flashing their lights at me. So I do the right thing and indicate to pull over and they then overtook me and shot off up the road. Phew! I then sat up a bit sharpish in the car and continued into London.

Meeting in the Blind Beggars Pub
with Mandy

It wasn't long before I was driving down to where the pub was, looking in the mirror all the time to see if I had or was being followed. I pulled up in the Merc about ten yards from the pub. I looked down at the clock, 5pm bang on time. I looked into the mirror, glanced around, nothing. So I done my hair once more, got out some mouth spray and gave it two squirts in the mouth, pulled some after-shave out the centre console, where the mouth spray was. Then patted some drops on to my hands and on to the side of my cheeks. I took out two chewing gums and pushed them into my mouth. Then took the gun out the glove box, undone the safety catch looking down at the gun, then all around once more and then slipped the cold steel down into the front of my trousers. I done up one button of my suit, got out the Merc and shut the door, looking all around me like Knight Rider with eyes moving constantly from left to right as I did so. To make sure I hadn't been followed or to see if anyone was laying waiting for me, ready to ambush me.

Luckily for them they weren't. Well not out here they weren't anyhow. I was even looking on tops of buildings, that's how paranoid I was, just in case Johnny or another hit man had been hired out for me. With my name on their contract or on their bullet, sitting pretty on the rooftops waiting to get a clean shot at me as I walked into the line of fire.

As I got to the door of the pub I glanced behind me to see if I could catch anyone out that might have been trying to creep up on me slowly, but no joy, no one was there. I looked about to see if anyone's car looked familiar, or the Land Rover that Johnny had come and got me in that night, but nothing. There was nothing out of the ordinary. It all looked kosher. They must all be inside, I thought, getting more paranoid with every step.

Even with the shooter in my trousers. It's OK having a gun, but it takes bollocks to pull it out and really use it. It's worth 5 years in prison just for having the gun, let alone pulling the trigger to let someone have it. I was scared. Sometimes that can be the greatest power one could have on their side, as you can do anything if you're scared or pushed into a corner, whether it is good or bad.

All this trouble for a woman, you might think. Well she weren't just your average girl and she ain't your usual good-looking woman. Mandy was outstandingly beautiful. She was "a proper treacle". This woman was gorgeous. She was a proper stunner, elegant in her ways and she would melt your heart with one look. The sort of girl you looked at on the street in passing or anywhere come to think of it, and as she walked close you would mutter under your breath to yourself "core!" Then as she walked past you, you would smile, or raise your eyebrows a little with delight in the hope she would do it back to you. You then would turn your head round as she walks past. Just as you get a whiff of the sweetest smelling expensive perfume that she would be wearing. You would then try and get to look at her again for the second time as she passed you. To see if she was looking back at you, so you could get a quick cheeky smile in and maybe if you were really lucky get her attention and call her back for her phone number. If she weren't looking back then you'd get a sneaky glimpse at her sexy, firm, curvy arse bouncing around like it was chewing toffees and it would be very nice indeed and well worth a second or third look of looking at it. It would give a new meaning to the Worthers Originals as it wiggled on.

Believe me she was absolutely (Bernard Matthews) beautiful. A proper masterpiece! She had curly blonde hair and ocean blue eyes like the Caribbean waters. She was a size 9 and was 5'6 or 5'8 at a guess with her high heels on. She would tower over or be the same height as most men. The clothes she wore were all names and very sexy indeed. They were all Prada, Gucci, Louis Vuitton and a few names off the catwalk that only money-minded people would know about or would be wearing. Oh did she look outstanding! She looked like a fucking goddess, the sort of woman you took home to your mum and sat there with a stupid grin on your face. Or put on your arm to be shown off to your mates in every pub, like she was your trophy while they all sat there drooling over her whilst eating dry roasted peanuts and playing pool. She must have been a 38DD, had an hourglass figure and a golden light tan. She was very high maintenance and took good care of her appearance. She looked so good that it made the girls on the front of *Vogue* and *Playboy* look unattractive. With lovely pert, pinkish lips and a smile that would melt any cold man's heart, and in this game most men's hearts are cold. She was a ten out of ten, and that came from a woman's opinion and I agreed. Men would have died for her and I'm sure a few had, having Johnny the hit man as a brother. She was every gangster's dream. Well nearly every man's dream and a few women's that also like to drink from the furry cup.

She would have made a proper gangster's moll, she was very smart and well clued up, sophisticated, clever, she knew her p's and q's, she was the full Monty and she was a "sort" to go with it. She had everything, the looks, the power, the brains, the respect and the back up from every Firm that her brother was involved with or had been involved with at one point in time.

She was very well looked after by them all, well it helped that her brother was number two for the men at the top, this side of the water. Everyone knew it, and now so do you, and as you know he was in the killing business.

So she was well protected. She was, as *they* were, untouchable. She had the power on her side of every weak man that wanted to do things for her, just for a little hope on their part to try and get in to her pants. She knew the crack, knew men were weak when it came to "pussy" and could be easily manipulated if they thought they were in with a chance of getting some. Only to be blown out by her, once she had got what she wanted out of them. If they thought they were in with a chance, they would do anything for her. Which she would play on and tease and let them think they would get something in return if they did exactly what she asked them to do. It was all done just to get her own way and she never gave it out to anyone. Well maybe a select few that were well lucky and she would truly have a connection with or respect, as she knew men just wanted to get her into bed.

With the gun down my trousers it gave a new meaning to the extension of my penis. The metal felt cold but I felt blessed and larger than life. So much so I walked toward and into the pub with more bowl than a fruit salad bowl and as confident as a Roman gladiator entering the Coliseum, ready to do battle with a thousand men right now.

I was entering the Blind Beggars pub, if I had tripped and the gun had gone off in my pants. I would have been left with just a chipolata. Not much to impress the ladies on a night of passion. Well they say it's all in the tongue and in the way you move your hips, or so I'm lead to believe. So having a big cock is just a myth. Or is it?

To my surprise the pub was empty, apart from Mandy and this big mountain of a man that looked like something out of the Sopranos. He was sitting at a different table looking at Mandy, dressed in a full-length moleskin coat with a black case next to him. It was obvious to me that this man was Mandy's minder and not her solicitor and that he had been told to look after her as if his life depended on it, he glared at me as I came in. I walked over to the bar just like in a John Wayne movie. Hands down my side fingers itching for the trigger. Ready to give someone a good hiding, or to grab for the gun at any false move. I felt out of my depth, I lent on the bar as the bar tender looked up to me.

"What can I get you, sir?"

"Jack D and coke please," he nodded and smiled

"Ice?"

"Yes please, mate"

The bar tender put the drink down on the bar. I pulled out my last fifty-pound note out and handed it to him. The big lump was sitting there and then shouts "It's OK, Don. He's with us."

"OK, Shrek," the barman says. Which must have been this mammoth of a man's nickname. So then the barman walked away from the bar and locked the door and soon came back with my change. I picked up the glass and took a sip. Looking all around the pub and at the bartender locking the door, which made me feel a bit nervous, agitated and uncomfortable. As if something untoward was just about to happen to me. I was well out my depth here and I was now playing with the big boys.

Not just some local dealer on the street or in the boozer that I could knock for his money for a while or 'til I got on my feet again, and make up some excuses why I hadn't got his money yet. But if he ticked me another gram then I would sort him out this Friday definitely, yeah right! You know how it is on the streets. To me this was uncharted waters as it was no normality to me; looking for people for the Firm and not the Firm looking for me.

As I turned round to scan the pub my eyes fixed on hers. There she was, staring, with a sparkle in her blue eyes. She was pleased and looked very excited to see me, just as I was to see her again even if she had stitched me up back at hers that time. I was in love once more like the first time I met her. I looked back at her as if I had just found a diamond. She was smiling straight at me. So I wasted no time in smiling back and walking over to her, kissed her on each side of her soft pinkie cheeks. As she stood up to kiss me back I could smell the fantastic perfume she was wearing, and it felt good to have her in my arms once again.

"Hi, Mandy, how you doing? Long time no see, eh sweetheart?" I sat down at the table and said. "Well my darling now I'm here, tell me all about it."

"Well this is a good friend of mine." She pointed to the mountain of a man, like a Yeti. No wonder they nicknamed him Shrek. I stood up and shook his hands but he didn't seem too impressed with me coming over to him. As he just looked at me with a look that could kill and squeezed tighter than your normal handshake. His big shovel hand wrapped around half my arm as we shook hands. So I sat back down and turned all my attention to Mandy and said, "So, Mandy, tell me all about it, sweetheart."

"Well I was good, 'til all this has happened."

"What's happened, sweetness?" As I took another sip from the Jack D's and glanced at the mountain of a man. Then behind me, then back at Mandy. I then glanced over my shoulder to see if anyone was coming for me out the toilets, but no one was. Even the barman was just sitting eating his tea out of earshot to what was being said. It must be a genuine meeting I thought, so I stated to relax a bit. As I did I looked at the big lump and then looked back at her, once again just to make sure things were OK. I felt the gun in my trousers digging in to me a bit, as I lent forward on to the table.

He was just glaring at me all the time, like he knew something I didn't, which made me feel very uncomfortable and awkward. I then looked deep into Mandy's eyes and listened to her attentively, trying to forget he was even there and concentrated, so as not to miss anything she had said to me. I had thoughts of my own going on in my head as I looked at her and she knew it.

"Well where do I start?" she said, "OK, here goes. The Jewellery Thieves wanted to buy another club in Spain. (*OK not so bad* I thought.) "A Spanish Firm out there weren't having any of it.

"*OK.*"

"So they kept going into Diamonds nightclub causing all sorts of trouble for the Jewellery Thieves, thinking they could do what they wanted when they wanted. They wanted to try and get the club closed down or better still for them to take it over. So the Jewellery Thief said that he had had enough of them coming in and out the club and causing all sorts of drama for him like they owned it. As they were selling their drugs in there and having their women prostitute themselves and trying to get everything put on their tab and not paying for it when it was due. Generally being arrogant to the staff and trying to bring the club's reputation down and push their luck as far as they could. Just being a nuisance that meant business was going bad for them. So they could move in and start running things or get them closed down by the authorities. They could then get on with their own business and make the money for themselves as they had a club across the road that wasn't making much money now Diamonds nightclub had been done up and was now open. So they were losing a lot of money fast, everyone in time wanted to go to Diamonds. I guess it was just more upmarket and catered for a

16

different sort of class of clientele. People wanted to be seen there and the club was the talk of Spain by now.

"If you came to Spain then you had to go to Diamonds nightclub. You should see it, it's very plush. And for those that have been there, then you know what I'm talking about. It's the place to be. Footballers, celebrities and people with a few quid, or anyone that's a somebody would be there or would have been there at some time or another. It was putting the other club under a lot of stress with Diamonds being open. They were finding it hard to make ends meet and were going well out of business.

"So the Jewellery Thief offers to buy out the club opposite, which was where all the trouble was coming from. They had a meeting about it and the fella told him to 'piss off out of it' and that he had a cheek coming in there thinking he would sell the club to him. Even to offer to buy him out was a cheek as they had been there for twenty years. So the Jewellery Thieves had the doormen bar them from coming in to Diamonds. Told them not to come into the club again and to behave themselves. Well they were having none of it and had kidnapped one of the doormen from Diamonds nightclub one night 'til the Jewellery Thief had no choice but to let them in again.

"So they would let the doorman go as his missus was begging the Jewellery Thieves to let them in so they would let go of this doorman and they could be together once again as their son was missing him. They were both in bits and worried for his safety so the Jewellery Thief felt sorry for her and the kid and they were allowed in again once they let the doorman go.

"Then they were still turning up every night, demanding free drinks and fighting with the doormen to come in and being a nuisance.

"Well one night they got in and then came in to the manager's office and put a gun to the Jewellery Thief's head. They had caught him off guard and said to the doormen that they didn't care who he was or who he knew, that he now worked for them and they called the shots for the club from now on, and that they owned the rest of the clubs in Spain. They threatened that The Jewellery Thieves won't be buying any more clubs, not on this island anyway, and that he will do just as he is told when he is told from now on. Otherwise 'we will burn the club down with you in it' and they kept saying they worked for the Spanish mafia. They then said that he would be signing the club over to them very soon and the doormen should do as they're told like his life depended on it.

"Mr Nice heard about it over in Columbia as he was away sorting business out allegedly with a share in a cocaine factory. The Jewellery Thief's wife made a call to him unbeknown to the Jewellery Thief. She had rung Mr Nice saying that they were in danger and that she will be going to the police to sort it all out if things continued. That's all Mr Nice needed. So Mr Nice said, 'Look,' to the Jewellery Thief's wife, 'leave it to me. Don't do anything silly just yet. I will sort this mess out for you. Just give me a day or two, but do not and I repeat, do not go to the police, sweetheart, do you hear me. As you will fuck everything up for me, and for your husband, and in turn for you too. Not only for you, but for a lot of us who are connected in the Firm do you hear me sweetheart?' 'OK,' she said.

"A lot of the money they were making was going through the club for a bit, so getting the police involved would mess it all up. They would want questions answered that we didn't have answers to like where all the money had come from in the first place to get the club up and running. Then Mr Nice rang the Jewellery Thief and said, 'How are things?'

'OK.'

'So what's going on then?'

'What? Oh nothing.'

"Mr Nice then done his bollocks and said, 'Look, don't fuck about with me. I know what's going on. I know you're in trouble and I will sort it out for £100,000. Just get Johnny out there, don't worry, just get Johnny out there ASAP.' He gave him his number, as he knew Johnny would be there and he would be the only one who had the bollocks to come out there and face the Spanish mafia, or these types of people. As they kept saying they were allegedly connected to the Spanish mafia and that the

Jewellery Thief had no choice but to do what they said as they now worked for them.

"So the Jewellery Thief agreed for now with the Spanish Firm but said that the only one calling the shots round here in the end would be him.

"They laughed, 'Senor. You are a funny man. We like this. That's why we will make you our private dancer. Once the club is ours and we turn it in to a lap-dancing place. That's why we are keeping you alive so long, but don't worry your time will come. Once you have signed the club over. I'm sure we could help you have a little accident somehow, but all that in good time my friend. As all good things come to an end sooner or later. But for you I think sooner.'

"So the Jewellery Thief laughs back too and agreed with them and told the bouncers he was OK and to let them do as they like for now in the club. So that the club would still run smoothly even if some of the money was going to them for now. He had done that so they would let the Spanish drop their guard for a second by letting them in to start running his club for now but only on the Jewellery Thief's say-so. Without him having to sign it over just yet. You keep your friends close but your enemies closer. Behind their back and closed doors the Jewellery Thief had called his own shots by calling Johnny, my brother, the hit man to come over from England and shoot the main Spanish geeza. Once he was out the way it would get rid of the rest of them and put a stop to them coming in to the club and giving it charley large about how they ran the island and the clubs on it. Everything then would run as normal with no more upsets once the Spanish Firm were out the way or at least put in their place.

"So a call was made by Mr Nice and in no time at all Johnny was all packed and on the next private jet out there with a V.I.P of course. When he had arrived, the second night of Johnny being there, he had requested a meet with the Spanish mafia boss about what was going on and that someone was using their name. A blacked out car had come and picked Johnny up from just outside the airport. As they drove, Johnny just looked out the window while the driver kept one eye on the road and the other looking at him in the mirror all the way to their destination. Then he parked up outside a restaurant and the driver turned round and grunted at Johnny 'He's inside, Sir.' Johnny opened the car door, slowly got out, and he then walked over to the restaurant.

"The Spanish mafia main boss stood up, pulled out his gun and placed it to Johnny's chest all in one movement as they shook hands catching Johnny off guard. 'Ah, Johnny my friend, you are getting slow in your thinking, coming here to see me like this after our last meeting.'

"Johnny was hired on a contract to come and kill him. But when he got into the room and past his bodyguards Johnny was waiting behind the curtains and walked out from behind them and close to him. He then had him in a neck hold ready to kill him by breaking his neck. When the tables were turned the Spanish boss had said, 'Whatever he or she is paying you, I will pay you double if you kill the person that sent you and I will make sure you are well looked after.' Johnny knew this was an ace card and agreed to take the money so they had made some sort of understanding between them. They had a funeral fixed to look like Johnny had killed him and they even had a Spanish newspaper headline made up to look like it was in the news.

"They took the photos in his restaurant so it looked more convincing and would get Johnny past her bodyguard, the one that had sent him. Then Johnny went and killed the other person that had hired him for real.

"He had just walked into her office, off the street in London, past her bodyguard and into her office as he had said he had some photos and the newspaper with the funeral in it for her that she would like to see. They took a look, then went in to see her, then came back out and opened the door and let him in. She was there bent over the filing cabinet in a black short skirt and an opened blouse showing off her cleavage in a seductive way. She then stood up. 'Hi, didn't take you long.' He then showed her the photos and the newspaper, which she read. She was happy as the Spanish mafia boss had her dad killed. The Spanish mafia boss said if her father didn't put money through his offshore account then he'd have no option but to kill him, and he did.

"He had him shot out at sea as he was on a yacht. Two fellas on jet skis had come speeding over to where the yacht was. They were wearing black out helmets. He was trying to duck when he saw them as he knew something wasn't quite right but it was too late as they both pulled submachine guns from off their backs and sprayed the whole boat with bullets. He was dead but no one found his body. They then took over her dad's food business.

"She went and got a bottle of Champagne out and kissed Johnny and thanked him. She was a looker. Whilst she wasn't looking he had put something into her drink with some other drug which killed her four hours later. He was way, way out of the picture and far away from her bodyguards when they done the autopsy.

"They thought it had been an accident and that she had overdosed on her own drugs on a night out. As to walk in and shoot her cold dead, at point blank range, would have been a bit hard, seeing as the bodyguard would have stopped him from getting close to her. They were hired once her dad had been killed for her own safety. She had them working for her ever since her dad had been killed just in case they came back to kill her.

"If Johnny had just walked in and shot her it might have got a bit messy and her bodyguards would be all over him like a rash, then he would have had to shot them too, and then he would have been left with two more bodies to get rid of. As soon as the bodyguard heard anything out of the ordinary it would have caused a big gun battle when Johnny had tried to leave. They would have checked on her straight away. To do it like this would put him well out the way of her death and with fewer problems for him when he left her and they found her dead.

"So now Johnny had once again come face to face with the Spanish mafia boss but not on business this time but of his own accord, and he found himself with a gun pointing at his chest. Johnny looked at him deep in the eyes, then looked to the side, and quickly stepped to one side out of the line of fire from the gun and at the same time he moved very fast, twisted the gun in the Spanish mafia boss's hand and released the gun into his own hand. And with his other hand twisting the boss round and then placed the boss's own gun on the mafia boss's back. 'Sit down,' Johnny said, 'and behave yourself. Let's talk.'

'Why are you here, Johnny, have you come for your ace card? They say you should never return to your past contracts,' the mafia boss said. As they both sit down Johnny keeps the gun in his hand and smiles at the Spanish mafia boss.

'But this time I'm not here on a contract.'

'OK, let's talk then, 'cos if you were here to kill me I guess I would now be dead, not sitting at the table looking at you. So I guess you're here for the little favour I owe you.' He smiled again. 'OK, what's so important then?'

"Johnny told the Spanish mafia boss about what was going on in Diamonds nightclub. 'I know it well and have had many a good night there, it's one of the best clubs on the island. I hear a lot of good things about it.'

'Why do your men want it then?'

'Sorry, look, we have no interest in it, Johnny. Just that we are given the same respect as we always get from everyone when we go there, that's all we want.' So Johnny explained what the story was.

"The mafia boss made a call and said to Johnny that they knew nothing about what this lot were doing and that they were not connected to the mafia in any way. These men weren't working for the mafia's interest, in any way shape or form and offered to get rid of them for him for the old favour he owed him, and for using their name to inflict pain.

"Johnny said it was personal and that he would like to keep their ace card in his pocket for when he really needed to use it. He explained that this is his business and he wanted to follow it through himself. He wanted to make it a public warning for these fellas, now that he knew they had no involvement with the Spanish mafia.

"So he explained that Johnny could do what he thought best and they wouldn't intervene in any way. He may have some work for him if he was interested with some Sicily mob that wanted to hire his services again if he was up for it. Johnny said he would get back to him once all this had been sorted and put to rest. He then throws him the gun back and says bye. The mafia boss picked up the gun and as Johnny walked to go out the restaurant door the mafia boss turned the gun the right way round and pointed the gun at Johnny's back and pulled the trigger twice.

"The pin on the gun moved forward and back, then forward and back again and clicked in to place. Johnny then turned back and looked at him and said, 'That's why you still owe me.'

"Johnny walked out the restaurant with a pocket full of the bullets he had removed whilst talking to the Spanish mafia boss. He laughed to himself as the door shut behind him. Johnny then pulled the bullets out of his pocket, bent down, and let them roll out of his hand and into the drain plop, plop, plop, plop, they went as they hit the water below. He then stood up, walked over and got in to the awaiting car and told the driver to drive. Johnny had left."

Then the big man called Shrek started to tell me the rest of the story.

"The next day Johnny and I walked straight into Diamonds nightclub. As he came into the doorway of the club, the bouncers that had been roughed up and kidnapped by the Spanish mob, greeted me and Johnny and thanked us for coming as we were smuggled in through the back doorway of the nightclub. They told us The Jewellery Thief was in the office.

"Johnny replied, 'Don't worry about him, just show me this man.' They led us to the man that was inside and the bouncer said to Johnny that this man should be the one to get it. He is their boss and they do what he seems to tell them. Or he is the one giving it all the biggun to everyone all the time saying he works for the Spanish mafia.

"So Johnny and his pal walked straight into the club. Johnny's pal flashed the gun sticking out the front of his trousers to the two other doormen, and then they both nodded and ushered them into the club through the main doors. He looked down from the balcony of the club and they started scanning everyone's faces in the club, 'til the doormen spots him then points the man out to us.

"We then all make our way down different sets of the stairs towards the Spanish man, as Johnny then turns round and gets a quick glimpse of him again between the dancers on the dance floor. He then walks over to the Spanish fella and goes to shake his hand. The Spanish fella sees me approach him out the corner of his eye. He then steps back and pulls his gun out and puts it to my chest before I could move.

"Johnny, with a move like lightning, steps to the side, brings the gun out the line of fire and away from my chest, then twists the Spanish fella's hand, with the gun in it, up towards the Spanish fella's back, pulls the gun out the front of my trousers and brings it up to the fella's neck. He quickly pulls the trigger on the way up, Bang, leaving the Spanish fella to fall to his knees with a hole in his head and me with blood splatters on my face. Then he collapsed onto the table and on to the floor, dropping the gun. The music stopped as everyone started screaming in shock, grabbing their things and heading out to the doors sharpish.

"After witnessing what had just gone on Johnny then turns round and hands me the guns back, so I conceal them quickly in my jacket. Johnny had done it without his gloves on. It had happened so fast, he hadn't known what to expect and had acted on impulse, saving my life. He didn't think the fella was armed otherwise he would have done it all a different way.

"I would have taken him into the toilet, or followed him in, and while I stood in the cubical, I would have screwed the silencer on, walked back out and shot him, whilst he was taking a piss. Then left him propped up on the toilet seat with the door shut and climbed over the door, so it was still locked and would look like to anyone that looked under, that the fella was taking a dump. Then once the club shut we could then pay the doormen, to get rid of the body. Johnny had told me on the drive back to the hotel after we left the club to clean ourselves up a bit, we still had blood splattered on us.

"Not his best bit of work everyone said, but he had wanted to make a statement, and a public warning too. Well he had done just that, as well as saving my life. I would have been shot before

I had a chance to have even pulled the gun out. So some quick thinking from Johnny and a lot of risk had done the trick. But if he hadn't I would have got it at point blank range and wouldn't be here chatting to you now about it.

"With the blast of the gun everyone was now shit scared and running for their lives, ducking and pushing each other over. Falling over each other on their way out. There was a big commotion as everyone was trying to get out the club fast. So it was a very public warning to those that were working with the Spanish fella. He was now lying dead on the floor in front of them all to see; it had the effect Johnny was looking for and wanted. Even at such a great risk with all those witnesses about he had put himself well on offer. The fellas that were working with the now dead man had left sharpish as well, and haven't been back in the club since.

"Now this Spanish fella was out the way and everyone had witnessed it. Johnny then walked straight up to the barman, as if nothing had happened, and asked for a vodka and coke, and nervously, the bartender gave it to him whilst everyone was screaming and leaving the club. Running to the way out for their safety, thinking a nutter had just come in the club and everyone was about to get it.

"Johnny drank the drink down in one. Put the glass on the bar and said, 'Where's the manager?'

'He's in the office,' which he then pointed out to us. He walked in to the Jewellery Thief's office and shook his hand.

'Hi Johnny. Well he's in the club somewhere, mate.'

'I know, he's just got it.'

'What?' The Jewellery Thief stands up and walks quickly to the door and out to be confronted by an emptying club and the dead man lying face down on his dance floor.

'Shit, Johnny, you don't mess about, mate.'

'Do you have my money?' said Johnny as the Jewellery Thief then walks in quickly, opened the safe and handed it to him. 'Here, Johnny, there's £10 grand here.'

'Nice, that should do it.' He put it in his bag, thanks him, and then Johnny handed me the bag. Then as calm and collected as if nothing had happened we both walked back out of the office to where the club fire exit was and where the other bouncers were waiting for us to make a sharp exit. I had gloves on so my prints weren't on any of the guns, I then handed this bouncer the guns. 'Here, mate, get rid of these will ya, sharpish, and while you're there try to get rid of the body before the police turn up.' We could try and act as if it was a false alarm or as if nothing had happened. That we didn't know what they were talking about when the police turned up and said a murder had just taken place. But it was too late for that, the police were already on their way.

"People were still screaming and ducking out the way of Johnny but the club was now nearly empty. We then left the club with a nod of acknowledgement from the Jewellery Thief and the two doormen. As I looked back round before we left, one of the doormen had walked over to Johnny and gave him the security camera tape and hugged him.

'Thanks, Johnny.'

'No worries, mate, it's a pleasure my friend.'

"We then both jumped into the hired Ferrari and sped off down the beachfront. I had given the guns to one of the doormen on the way out to get rid of which meant to bury them or dismantle them, or to stash them up safe 'til they were out on the Jewellery Thief's yacht then drop them in to the sea. But this bouncer didn't have time for all that malarkey, the police would soon be at the club and he wanted them out the way before the police turned up on the scene and found them on him.

"So as I handed them to him, he wrapped them up in some sandwich bags for safe keeping, in the hope the police wouldn't find them. He then also left the club and ran over to a phone box across the way from the club, just before the police arrived. He quickly rang his pal to see if he would collect them. After agreeing he would, the bouncer left them in the bag and placed them in the bin for him to collect.

"So within no time his pal had gathered them, and the bouncer watched him do so whilst the police at the door of the club was questioning him. As he had ran back from the phonebox the police had all pulled up around him and all got out. Once the guns were in his mate's hands he had gone back to his house and met up with his other pal who he knew would be interested in buying them instead of getting shot of them. He knew that his pals wanted some guns for a bank job they had been planning as they had asked him for some tools a few days ago. For this job they were planning on doing they said they would sort him a few quid out of it if he could sort some tools out for them. This fella had said he would try his contacts and get back to him, but couldn't promise anything, but now they were here in his hands. So he had made the call and had sold them on to these fellas.

"The bouncer had come back to the club, thinking the guns were all safely tucked away or gone for good. That night the police had cordoned off the club and took statements from everyone that had been hanging around there and from all the staff who all said false things to try and help Johnny out. The police could smell a red herring, as the stories weren't corroborating with each other.

"The bank robbers got arrested two days later with these guns back at some hotel that they were staying in. When they had got back to the hotel, after the bank job, they had gone rushing about so much to get into their room with the bags of money they had got, the cleaner had saw them acting suspiciously. In their big rush to get in and out of eyeshot they had dropped some money on the floor outside their room and had not noticed the cleaner standing just a few doors away up the hallway. Watching them go in to their room the cleaner walked quietly and carefully up to the room and sneakily looked through the keyhole. There she saw one of the men walking about with the gun in his hand, shouting that he should get more of the money as it was his job and he had planned it all and some other stuff, she couldn't quite make out. So she came away from the keyhole, as quickly as she had got there, just in case she was caught looking in. She then bent down as fast as she could, picking up the bundle of money that was dropped and just lying there outside the door. Which would have been the biggest tip she had ever got in her life.

"She then ran off and raised the alarm by telling the manager of the hotel what was going on in the room and what she had seen, but not about the money. Once he heard her he phoned the police. In no time at all they were at the hotel and outside the robbers' doors all armed and ready. They had come in and waited for a bit outside ready to do their bust.

"Just as they were all in place, one of the robbers opened the door to the room to come out and that's when the police had acted, and come in, had got them all on the floor and arrested them. The guns that Johnny had used were resting on the table with 3 balaclavas and bundles of Spanish notes and a bag with notes sticking out of it. There were notes neatly stacked in piles with the bank seals still around them. Some were sprawled out all over the table. There were some in neat bundles that had elastic bands put round them, ones that had been counted out. There was a small bag with some more elastic bands in it on the table too, next to all the cash.

"They had been caught, bang to rights. There's no story to say only we must have checked into the wrong room by mistake and this stuff was here with the balaclavas when we came into the room. We were going to complain to room service and then call you, but the police wouldn't swallow that one, or the jury come to think of it once they were facing them in court. So they were caught money and guns, the lot. They had entered the bank and had been seen on C.C.T.V cameras. Seen outside as well in a nearby car park where they had parked the getaway car. Just as they had pulled up the camera had turned and watched their every move, unbeknown to them. It filmed them putting on their balaclavas as they got out the car ready for the job. The cleaner at the hotel had also seen them so it wasn't too hard for the police to see who had done it once they had got to the bank they were gone. One of the robbers wasn't even wearing a mask fully over his face when he walked into the bank. Then he decided to pull it down over his face when he saw the camera. It's too late then, normally you have it on when you come in, not the other way round. So now they had been caught with this gun and the dough. That also meant they had put Johnny right in the frame for murder. As now the police had the gun with Johnny's fingerprints all over it as well. That's when the message had gone out to all the forces and the Customs and Excise to hold Johnny for murder if they come across him. They knew him already and they now had a dead body and the murder weapon with his prints all over it.

"So Johnny was the number one suspect for murder. The police now had the weapon and the body and now all they needed was Johnny, the last piece to their puzzle. So he was now fucked and well in the frame, as they would be looking for him by now. The prints were a perfect match on their computer for his. They did catch up with him trying to leave Spain as he was intending to go to Morocco. He was on his way to see the other Jewellery Thief's brother with some bird, who was to smuggle 50,000 Es over there, to be sold in the other brother's club.

"He was caught at the airport as the passport reader had let him pass. It had flashed up as 'wanted' but had tried not to make it look to obvious to him, and this way made it easier for the police to do their job properly without causing too much alarm to other people around. She was arrested too, but Johnny denied all knowledge that he knew her, or that he had anything to do with the smuggling. Although they tried to get it to stick on him as well but he wasn't charged with that as they now had him for murder. The smuggling charge was nothing to the charges he now had to face, so they dropped them on Johnny but charged him with the murder and her with the smuggling. Just before he stepped on to the plane to freedom armed police were sitting on the plane waiting for him and her to board. They grabbed him and that was that. He and this bird were carted off to a Spanish police station and then off to prison, on remand for murder."

I looked at the big lump as he talked. He just looked back at me with a cold stare, he was summing me up and then he smiled. I looked back at Mandy, she continued saying that news had also got out all over Spain that Johnny had done this to this fella who was or said to have been connected to the Spanish mafia. He was just using their name to scare people but the rest of them didn't know that and thought he had balls of steel to mess with them. So this news meant the Jewellery Thieves had just stepped up a notch or into even bigger leagues in the realms of gangsters and villains now their man had been taken out the way. No one else would mess around and definitely not with the owners of Diamond's nightclub. It had had the effect Johnny was looking for. A public warning, at great cost to Johnny's future.

"No one else would mess about with the Jewellery Thieves now, and like he had said, he was now the one calling the shots with Mr Nice and they would look after him when he came out. Or they would sign one of the clubs over to him, for doing time for them and this job. So that meant he could retire when he came out. Well he would be an old man by then so he would have no choice.

"It wasn't Johnny's best bit of work. It wasn't well thought out or planned as he would have been wearing gloves, or had someone else do it for them but it was a spur of the moment thing. If he had done it properly, or done it a different way by not bringing too much heat upon himself then things might have gone a bit better. He would be here and you might not have been. Johnny was paid well for his work, which is what I now have with me." She pointed to the sports bag that the big lump had.

"This is Johnny's pal, Shrek, the one that was with him that night as you now know. Johnny had put him in charge of the money to make sure it got back to me once he was banged up." I turned and looked at the big lump again. He was looking back at me and listening very carefully to every word that had just been spoken. He looked back at me with the same cold glare as when I first came in to the pub and sat down at Mandy's table.

I turned back and Mandy continued. "There is near on about £100,000 in the bag. The money is no good to Johnny in the nick. You can be the richest man alive on the out but in there you're all the same. You can only spend a tenner a week in the canteen, so it don't matter how much you have in there really. It's the people outside that count. Everyone is begging for something in the nick like a match or burn, stamps or paper. In there where everyone is your brother, all they have is a phone card, pin chips or double bubble from some deal that went well one week on the cards. Not forgetting some burn and a few Mars bars they may have won at backgammon or chess while sitting there bored stiff playing games in their cells, or building things out of matchsticks just to pass the time away.

"He had left the bag of dough in a very safe place so it could be brought over here to me by Shrek if things had gone wrong, and before it got in the wrong hands."

Then Shrek the big lump says, "The Spanish police were called to the club and before I had a chance to get Johnny and me in hiding or off the island, he got himself caught. He was picked up and arrested by the Customs officers trying to get to Morocco with some silly tart at the airport. A photo fit of him had been passed around to all the police forces, Customs and Excise just minutes after the shooting had gone down. They had got their first piece of evidence of the person that had done it once the gun was in their hands. They had Johnny's prints and the photo of him on the police computer once they were put into it. I bet the serious crime squad were rubbing their hands together when that photo of Johnny had come up, they have wanted him for a long time no doubt.

"He was now being held in a Spanish nick once the news had got out. I got the money and flew straight to England, it didn't take them long for them to pass the info to the English police at Scotland Yard and they then put two and two together and came up with four. As the gun that was used in the bank job matched the one in the murder in Spain. And believe it or not also matched the one that was used to kill the man you were supposed to shoot in Kensington, London. The one that everyone was led to believe that you had done, even though you hadn't which we now know about. It's all out in the open now this has happened.

"The police found the gun even though the robbers were going to get rid of it the next day after their little withdrawal from the Spanish bank. The gun should have been looked after better and got rid of straight after Johnny had done the job. It should have been buried, dismantled or taken out to sea or even smuggled out the country the next day. Well I guess there's no use in crying over spilt milk, it was too late. The police were on it like a rash, which was a bit of bad luck on Johnny's part as now they had the gun in their possession with his fingerprints all over it. Which now meant in no time at all Johnny was in custody without being able to slip through the net. He was caught. If his prints hadn't been on there then he may have got away with it. The robbers of the Spanish bank could have got charged as they looked a bit similar and the gun would only have had their prints on it.

"He should have just let me do it as we had planned, but he just grabbed the gun and done it himself. Johnny now thinks that the serious crime squad was watching him and reporting his every move back to Scotland Yard back home. That's how the police in London picked up the gun so quickly. He didn't know until now that the doorman had sold it on instead of getting rid of it like he should have. If he had, it would have put an end to all this. That's why Johnny was caught trying to flee to Morocco so fast. If he knew what the bouncer had done and he was out, then he would want the bouncer taught a lesson for not doing the right thing. Silly cunt. That's why I still have the money, it was my job to take care of things if things ever did go wrong an' I was out of course. That's why I've brought it to Mandy, that's what Johnny would have wanted."

Mandy then says to me, "You know why the Jewellery Thieves now know you hadn't done the shooting in London for them and that Johnny had."

"If you had, son, things might have been a little different," said Shrek.

Mandy continues, "Soon the English consulate will be extraditing Johnny to England to face two counts of murder in a trial over here at the Old Bailey. One for here, and the one he did in Spain allegedly. So *NOW* you see why it's such a mess. The Jewellery Thieves paid him £10,000 to sort all their mess out for them. He was going to give Mr Nice some of it for getting him the work as agreed. Now Shrek has bought it over here to me, so Mr Nice will want paying soon too."

"OK," I said.

"Also, Shrek has a note from the Jewellery Thieves to give to you which is in the bag. So it has all backfired you see. It's all been left in such a mess, and now Johnny might do life in the nick for these two murders. If we can't help him then I'm really on my own, with no family, no one."

Mandy now had tears rolling down her cheeks. I listened intensively to Mandy's words and now and again got lost staring in to here lovely foxy blue eyes. I pulled her close to me. The big lump stood up and looked like he was ready to tear my head off with one false move.

She said it was OK and that she had tamed the beast of a man that was sitting there guarding the money and her. He sat down again. She smelt fantastic as I got a quick waft of her sweet expensive perfume. I lent forward across the table to comfort her.

"It'll be OK, mate." I gave her a tissue from my pocket and told her to wipe her eyes. "You'll see. You have me now."

I was trying to reassure her even though I was in a right mess myself after hearing all that. The Jewellery Thieves now knew what I hadn't done, so that's what all this was about. "Where's this letter then from the Jewellery Thieves?" I asked.

She put her hand out and the big lump placed the bag on to the table and pulled back the zip of the sports bag revealing what was inside. There it was, money, a knuckle duster and the envelope which was the letter for me. He pulled out the knuckle duster and placed it in his pocket. Then he pulled out the letter and placed it in Mandy's hand. After seeing the duster, I felt nervous. I thought that soon I would be getting it. But hey, I had some reassurance in my pants that I thought might tame the best of a man. Or at least get him to sit down whilst I ran out the pub. Then he zipped the bag back up and sat down, bringing the bag next to his chair.

I turned round and said to the barman, "Can we both have the same again?" Now I had witnessed him putting the duster out and placing it in his jacket pocket I was feeling nervous and put me right on edge. I thought I could be getting it myself some time very soon. Right now I really needed a drink, my mouth was dry after hearing that I was once again now deep within the Firm, whether I liked it or not. He nodded and within seconds the drinks came over to our table. I asked Shrek if he wanted one, to try to make it all friendly, but he said no thanks. I went to pay the barman and he said being with Mandy meant they were on the house, free. "Thanks," I replied. Mandy handed me the letter. I slowly opened the brown envelope and pulled out the note.

It read like this.

Well well well, Cookster my son, it's been a very long time. We now know you didn't do that little job for us in Kensington. The one you had us believing you had done. The one we praised you for. So now there's just a small little matter of us wanting to see you once more, for your liberty in letting us think you had. Also for you to explain yourself as to why you didn't do it in the first place. You can tell me where my £30,000 has now gone. Now I know the truth it seems it belongs to me. I want it back. We aren't very happy with you taking our kindness as weakness, son. If your balls were as big as your brains, then you'd be a fucking genius. You should have thought twice about crossing us. You weren't working for monkeys and you weren't getting paid monkey money.

I think £30,000 to put a hole in someone was way too much. In fact it was very fucking generous of me. I knew you were coming out of the nick and you would have been on your arse without a penny to scratch it with. Either that or Mr B would have banged you to a pulp till the £10,000 that you owed him turned up. So I thought I would help you out a bit by giving you money. Help you get back on your feet. I would have done it myself if I was out but I thought you wanted your debts paid off to Mr B and this little favour seemed the answer to this little problem you found yourself with. So really I done you a right favour, my son, by giving you the £30 large in the first place and by putting you in a good position in the Firm. In fact you were well looked after by us all if I remember rightly. That's because I liked you and thought you could be trusted, and this is how you repay me. By mugging us all off. Son, you now owe me my money back 30,000 large and I'll be mugging you off from now on 'til it's all paid and up to date. If you don't come up with it

very soon we will be coming to you, mark my words. We can assure you it won't be very nice. You won't be able to hide, we'll have every man on the Firm and payroll looking for you. Like bloodhounds they'll be looking in every club and venue and in every nook and cranny. Smashing every fucking door off its hinges in London and Borehamwood or anywhere else. Don't think you can hide from us. 'Til they find you or 'til someone tells us where you are, I will be putting interest on the money. You now owe me 'til every last penny is all paid back and I will add a little extra on to the bill for our time. Time is money, son, and right about now you're wasting my time. *Your* time is now *my* money and your time is running out fast. And by the looks of things I bet so has my money. Unless you have been spending wisely and not *putting it up your nose, which I very much doubt.* So, son, there'll be no hiding under the bed for you, Mister, as we've just been speaking to Mr Nice about all this mess. He ain't over the moon with you either as you have now put us all in a little predicament. From being Mr Nice he has now changed into being Mr Very Fucking Unhappy Indeed. His nasty streak has just come out and he ain't coming across very Mr Fucking Nice any more. In fact he is very Mr Serious now whenever your name is mentioned. Right about now he is a bit like Jekyll and Hyde. As he said he now wants to pull your toenails out with a pair of hot pliers and put a cut on your arse cheeks so that when you sit down you will remember the liberty you took with us. He said you'll need more than fucking Andrex for that one, son. Either that or he is going to take you out into the desert with a few of his henchmen and get them to hold you down naked, bend you over a tree stump and whack a cactus up your arse with a cricket bat. As you scream from the pain one off Mr Nice's henchmen will pop an apple in your mouth to muffle out your screams. Then he will leave you there for the buzzards to start pecking at it once they see the blood running out. Or he said the only other way to get the money back will be to put a blonde wig on you, some make-up and a skirt and pimp you out up Kings Cross in some gay bar 'til all our money is paid off. And you'll then be walking around like Robo cop as your arse will be so sore and stretched it will be hanging out like a windsock or a wizard's sleeve, one of the two once they have all had a go on it. As right now he is saying you're as much use to the Firm as a sore throat is to a yodeller. Right now he said he could cut out one of your kidneys and sell it on the Russian black market as he thinks for a kidney you can get near on £5,000.

He also says if you know what's best for you, son, then you will book a flight for you and Mandy to come straight out here to see us. So we don't have the trouble or drama of coming to you, or the added cost. So my guess is you'll be on the next flight out to Spain if you know what's best for you. So we can have a proper chat face to face about all this mess you now find yourself in once again. I want to look deep into your eyes to see what sort of man you really are and to see if you have the balls, son, to be a real man. Come out here and face your fears. Explain or redeem yourself as to what happened and why you thought you could take a liberty with us by pulling the wool over my eyes. Boy, it better be good, as it seems we have so much to catch up on and you have a lot of explaining to do. Now it's all out in the open and all your cards are laid out in front of me on the table. And unlucky for you there seems to be no ace card in your hand to pull out this time. You're now sitting there with a handful of Jokers, my son. You have just wasted your ace cards by trying to fuck me and Mr Nice over. My arse feels very fucking sore indeed, son. I can feel you was trying to slip something up there whilst I wasn't looking and by the feeling of it you weren't even prepared to use any Vaseline whilst I was bent over with my eyes shut. You were taking my kindness for weakness. I don't bend over for no one, son. So my guess is Mr Nice and I will be seeing you. Some time very soon.

I'm looking forward to it.

Signed
Mr Nice & the Jewellery Thief

I put the letter back into the envelope and chucked it on to the table then swallowed hard. The end was near but I had to stay as cool as I could for now. I took a deep breath. I was once again now well in the deep of things. It's amazing how your life can change round in just a drop of a hat. I realised the only way out of this sort of life I had created for myself would be in a coffin. As right about now I was going nowhere fast. One minute you're charley large potatoes with loads of respect being thrown at ya here, there and everywhere. Being put up high on a pedestal and having no cares in the world. Sitting in most of the clubs and pubs and the strip bars with all the boys looking and behaving like you fucking owned them all with as much free sniff as you can get up you nose. Looking at more tits and pussy that you have ever seen in a pet shop, having women hang off your arm like a cheap suit, sniffing hard at your Devil's dandruff. Thinking you're the next best thing since sliced bread.

Then the next moment your Billy no mates. All dressed up, nowhere to go and no one to go with. Even your acquaintances have left you just sitting there with just an empty cocaine wrap in your pocket. With a sore nose, a screwed up crumpled five-pound note and an empty packet of peanuts still lying on the table in front of you. And now all you're left with is a big debt for 150 quid for the 8th that had just been ticked for the gear in the first place. Everyone else had conveniently sniffed it all and was now all gone. So where were they now? No one wants to talk to you or come near you. So you might as well be sitting in the pub in just your boxer shorts for all they cared.

For me I was now sitting in the Blind Beggars pub. From two nights ago, sniffing at Columbians finest, I was still a little paranoid. With a debt of 30 large that had just been put back on my head and with a contract all ready written up with my name all over it. I hadn't even been able to tell my story of events. If you thought Mr B was bad, you ain't met Mr Nice yet. If I couldn't find 30 large very soon I was in trouble, big trouble. Nowhere to run or hide. Every cunt that's in the know knows you, knows where you go, where you live and will also now know that you had fucked up.

So I was now on my own sitting there with just the change of the fifty-pound note in my pocket from what I had spent back at the pub. It's like you take two steps forward and then ten steps back in these sorts of circles you mix with. The only thing the gun that I had concealed was going to do for me, was put myself out of my own misery. But that would have been too easy. Too easy for everyone. I was now bang in trouble and going nowhere fast with not a lot of options but to go over to Spain to deal with the matter, he was right. These fellas, over here in England, the family mobsters were my ace cards and now I had just passed them on to the next dealer.

If there was any trouble here in London with any other firms, or if someone steps out of line, or got out their pram a bit, or didn't pay me, then these fellas were my ace card. They would take control of the situation and step in to make sure it was all sorted and above board or enforce at the right time. Then the payments were paid, as they would make sure of it one way or another all on the Jewellery Thief's say-so. Any trouble then the Jewellery Thief would get straight on the blower to the big family mobsters, who would then come down on the people it concerned like a ton of bricks. Any trouble that I might find myself in, or problems caused whilst working for the Jewellery Thief's firm's connections they would make sure they got sorted out for me. Well I was making them all very good money, near on seven grand a week sometimes. So it was in their interest to look out for me.

But now they had found out I had taken a liberty with the Jewellery Thief, I was on my own and would have no one to fight my corner when things went sour. All eyes would be on me now, from every firm that they were connected to. If things got out of hand and I couldn't deal with it myself directly then I would be fucked. I would be on my own now making them money or not. Loyalty meant more to them then the money. As they would say, if you can't be loyal then you can't be trusted to make money. Mess up a little and you have fucked up a lot, simple really when you look at it closely. The money to them was just an added bonus with people like that. The two came hand in hand in their eyes, and they had made shit loads of it but still wanted more. As once you're in the game, you're in the game. There's no making a quick buck then getting out when you're mixed up with these people, as I was to find out later on. Once you commit yourself, you're in and in for life. Otherwise life expectancy is very short in this game.

So that meant money or no money I was a dead man. I was bang right in the shit of things. In their eyes they would now think that I had taken a right liberty with all of them, by taking their kindness for weakness, by doing that to their true friends. Even if I could or had paid them, it wasn't about the money any more. It was about the liberty that had been taken and the wool that I had tried to pull over their eyes just as the Jewellery Thief had said in his letter. I knew there was no point in running, they would find me eventually. Then it would be ten times worse for my family or me. I would have to look over my shoulder for the rest of my days. In every manor, in every club or pub I went to around the West End and other parts of London, well to be honest all over the U.K. Or an ounce of heroin would be put on my head for some junky to come and kill me off. Or maybe a contract would be written up that was worth a few hundred to the person who would carry it out. As life was cheap nowadays to this mob, it was worth peanuts. They would just do me themselves in no time seeing as I was now their weakest link. It was less time and money for them, I was nothing right about now, just another headache or stress adding to their problems. They would all be out trying to get me and chop me up and feed me to the birds.

I took a deep breath then smiled. Mandy looked straight up at me and asked, "You OK? What did it say?" She must have seen the look on my face and knew by the silence it was bad news, or by the way my jaw must have dropped in to my lap. I was gobsmacked that they knew, wanted to see me and probably wanted me dead. Getting a good night sleep was a thing of the past with this hanging over my head. I would now have to sleep with one eye open just in case. I was in big trouble and I knew it. You see the skeletons in the cupboard can always come back to haunt you. That's why it's best to be honest and put the skeletons to rest. Well it's best to be as honest as you can be in this game with these sorts of people, they don't tend to fuck about.

"We've been invited to go over to Spain, for a short break by the Jewellery Thief, to see some old friends of mine whilst we're out there." Me putting on a brave face and pulling myself together from the panic I was now in after reading the letter. I took another sip of the J.D.

"OK," she replied. "That will be nice. I could do with a break."

"This way you can get the chance to see Johnny in the Spanish nick before he comes to England. And I can get a chance to have a chat with the Jewellery Thief and a few old faces. I could maybe see some old friends of mine that are out there, that's if they also haven't been nicked by now. While we are there we can try and have some fun too even if we both don't feel like it right now, eh Mandy?" She smiled and wiped the tears off her cheeks.

"The break will do us both good."

She smiled again and said, "Thank you." As she touched my hand there was a bit of hope in the sound of her voice.

"So we need to book the next flight out there," I said. "Let me go home and pack a bag. I'll come straight back to yours. We can then chill out and look for the next flight if that's cool."

"Yes," she said. She then moved her hands from mine, pulled a pen from her bag and wrote down her address on the back of the letter for me. I'd forgotten how to get there after that night when she took me there and Johnny took me away again to the Hilltop on Organ Hall. She pushed the letter back to me with the address on it.

"OK, Sweetheart, see you there soon. By the way, all my money's tied up in the Firm," I blagged. "Couldn't sort out the flight money could you and when we get back I'll square you up."

"Not a problem," she said. "I understand."

The truth is I only had £40 and right about now times were hard and they had just got a little bit harder. Now that I was in this much trouble and I owed 30 large once again. I picked up the JD and swallowed it in one gulp, put the glass down and then stood up. I kissed Mandy on the cheek and shook the big lump's hand but this time I tried squeezing his hand back a bit harder, but it was so big he probably didn't even feel me doing it. I then walked to the toilets to adjust the gun in my trousers as it was becoming a bit uncomfortable. I looked in the mirror and then left the pub and went back to mine.

I put the gun on the table and packed a suitcase. Then picking up the gun from the table I concealed it in my trousers once again. I left mine, to drop the gun back to Rogers for safe keeping, after wiping my prints off it and putting it in a shoebox ready for Roger to bury it somewhere safe again.

Back at Mandy's

Smooth I thought, I'd just invited myself to stay at Mandy's and she had said yes! What a result.

I got back to Mandy's within no time at all. For some reason I liked being in her company, it felt genuine. In fact I couldn't wait to be back in her company and more so in her bed, if luck would have it. In this world if you don't try you don't get, I thought. The minder wasn't there at Mandy's house, which was a big relief. Maybe he would only be with her when she went out and about. Or had he overseen his job by making sure she was with me and that we now were both going out to see the Jewellery Thief over in Spain.

We got a bit cosy on the couch and had a coffee while we looked up the flights we needed on the teletext. There was one leaving at 6am from Gatwick. So we booked it there and then. Mandy put it all on her card, as I was skint.

"Well Mandy. We best get some sleep darling" We cuddled up and finished off the film that we had turned over to watch after booking the flights.

"Yes," she replied. "It's getting late and we need an early start tomorrow if we're going to make it to the airport on time. I phoned Shrek to arrange for him to take us to the airport tomorrow."

Mandy had told me he'd said he had managed to get the money into her bank account. He told her more about it on the drive to the airport. He had managed to get the money into her account with no problems. Something to do with an estate agent that he had a good relationship with and a bent solicitor that had worked with the Firm before. He was able to draw up snide papers and deeds for sale of a house. They had managed to get all the money in the bank without any questions or investigations being made into where the money had come from. Lucky I

42

thought, as it was put in there on a false sale of a property that didn't even exist.

"OK, you can sleep on the couch." What? I thought.

"I'll get you a quilt and a pillow."

No! Not the couch. I wanted to be next to her, in her bed entwined in each other's arms, caressing every curve of her lovely well-developed body. Kissing it and making it tingle with every caress and then building up a sweet togetherness. As we grinded and moaned with the pleasure we would be giving each other all night long. Before we got down and done the wild thing. Well I was half way there.

So the couch it was for now but I was sure she liked me and was just playing hard to get. Who knows, women can be very strange at times. Maybe she just wanted some comforting and reassurance that things would be OK in her moment of loneliness. She must have felt a bit alone now her brother wasn't here to protect her. I was now on the couch much to my regret and all my dreams of being next to her in bed had been shattered by the couch treatment. The more time I spent with her, the more I felt I was falling for her in a big way.

I felt the way I did that first night I saw her back at the club when the Jewellery Thief had come home from prison. Even if the way she had come on to me was under false pretences, it was still nice and an experience not to forget about. I kept it to myself that I liked her though. Even if she had an idea that I did. After all I had business to attend to in Spain and my mind needed to be focused on that. Not on women for once! "OK, the couch it is then." She smiled and handed me the quilt, then walked back into her bedroom in just a see-through slip that she had put on which for me was just a little teasing.

She then turned back, "Cookster?"

"Yes?" I said. All hopeful that I was just about to get an invite into her bed and that she had seen the light. I was now just about to feel what heaven was all about.

"Night mate," she said.

"Night beautiful." As she let down her hair, then she closed the door behind her.

Before long I was asleep, after my mind had stopped racing with thoughts of how Spain would go. And whether in the middle of the night Mandy might come in to the front room with just her knickers on to invite me in to her bed. Better still slide in to mine on the couch, whilst I was asleep, whilst sliding her knickers off or better still letting me slide them off for her once she had woken me up a bit. Yes I had fallen asleep and was dreaming. I woke up and could smell cooking. The couch wasn't that bad after all. I had still managed to get a good night's sleep even if at the start of it I had been lying there all night hoping Mandy would jump in with me. Or at least her inviting me in to her bed, which would have been a dream come true.

Mandy was up first, she had made breakfast for the both of us. Good girl I thought, I was just sitting there in my boxers and she was there still in a pink slip nightdress and looking like a priceless painting. I was bending my neck a bit more to see her every now and then, bending over the table as she put the plates down and laid the table.

We ate breakfast at the table, she then went and got showered and changed. Once I had finished my breakfast I showered and got dressed. We were all ready to go. Now we were all refreshed I asked Mandy if the big lump was coming with us.

She said he ain't coming over to Spain and yes he was employed by the Jewellery Thief to look after her now Johnny had been banged up, but now his job was done. There was no need for him to be with her as he had fulfilled everything that had been asked of him, as Johnny would have wanted. So he could go back into hiding as the police wanted to question him as a witness. The club had put his name forward and saw all that had happened there with Johnny and him doing the shooting. So he was with us yesterday just to make sure the money got into the right hands and that Mandy had met up with me. Also to make sure things went well, but now she was with me they knew she was in good hands and that I would look out for her and not let anything happen to her from here on. So there was no need for him to come along for the ride, anyhow if he did he would have put himself on offer to the Old Bill. So he would be just here with us today to take us to the airport then he would go back on the run. Before long we were at the airport.

We said "Goodbye."

"You best take care of her as you're already in big trouble."

"I will," I said. We then boarded the plane heading to Spain, to see my amigos, the Jewellery Thief and even unluckier for me Mr Nice once again.

The Trip to Spain
to See Some Old Faces and Villains

We arrived at the Spanish airport. I could feel the heat as we left the plane and walked down on to the runway to wait for the bus to take us to the terminal. Boy was it hot. The Jewellery Thief must have anticipated that we would have gotten the next available flight out there, like they had told me to in the letter. Well I thought, they didn't get to where they are by being stupid.

I would have been foolish if I hadn't come over. They would have sent their people over on the next flight out to England to come see me, or got their contacts in England to do so. Believe me, if they had it wouldn't have been a happy greeting once they had caught up with me.

I had once heard them talk and planning about the bad things they had done to others that had been unlucky to have crossed them. One was held over a balcony and one had his hands tied together on a meat hook and hooked up in the back of a chiller lorry like a piece of meat. He was then wrapped up in cling film and used as a punch bag to train the local lads up before they went on to their underground boxing matches that would get arranged with some local travelling chavvies. They were organized in some old skips or in some underground car parks or a warehouse that had been left empty. They were done out the way of prying eyes and the police. They were kept low key. That's where different firms put on some bets, when they weren't at the horses or the dogs betting. They would be here to watch and lay a few guided down on them.

The Firm would say "This is what happens to liberty takers so best you all learn fast," as they lift the door up on the back of the chiller truck to see a man there hanging off the hook, half chilled to death. I guess it was all an education in the ways of the Firm for them and for me as we would watch the man moan and groan and wiggling around a bit. As the fella they were training would give a left and a right to the fella and you would hear a muffled shriek of pain coming from the cocooned man hanging up on the meat hook in the back of the lorry. He was there for payments long over due or 'cos he had taken the Firm's kindness for weakness.

The Firm could make some good money betting on them underground fights back then. Some of them they would fix and make the other fella go down in the 2nd or 3rd round, whichever one was told to take the drop so they could guarantee the cash coming back in on their bets. I was just a young boy and just saw the money pass hands from one to the other, after two fellas had smashed each other to bits in these underground fights whilst everyone was cheering them on, waiting to win their money.

We came through the arrival gates into Spain, past Customs and the bag in place, past the queues of people rushing off to their destinations. Quickly grabbing their bags as they come through on the belt and pushing past so they could then get on with the rest of their journey. Then finally we came out to the arrivals lobby where there were two people ready to greet us. One was the Jewellery Thief's minder, his name was Big Carlos and the other minder was Big Wheel Will from Potters Bar much to my surprise.

Don't get me wrong it was nice to see a friendly face once again after all this time. The bigger firms had Big Wheel on loan for me once or twice back in the day. That was when things were good and everything was running as clockwork back in the Wood, Potters Bar and other parts of London. Big Wheel had also been employed by Mr Nice as one of his minders. Now he was living it large out here in Spain in Porterbanos. Well he had no choice after he had been employed by the Jewellery Thief to rough someone up real bad back home in England. He had to come out here to hide from the police and the criminal system, before he ended up doing a long time in Pentonville prison. He had made a right mess of this fella outside the pub, who had tried to knock this Scottish Firm for three keys of Columbians finest. Not knowing that it was or had ticked off this Liverpool Firm we were working side by side with, and they had sold the debt on to the Jewellery Thief. That's when Big Wheel was given orders to find the fellas that had done it and get the money or drugs back dead or alive. It really didn't matter to the Firm. They would have wiped their mouths of the dough. As long as he had got hurt for the liberty and the money was back all safe and sound then it didn't really matter what happened.

So Big Wheel had left this fella half dead outside the pub, after giving him a good hiding. Then him and a pal had kidnapped this fella and his brother the next day and had held them at ransom down in a mobile home in Wales for payments that were still well overdue and 'til the money for the cocaine had turned up. Their mum had to arrange by remortgaging her house to pay for their release. But they still owed £50,000 and the rest of their family had found out what was going on and went to the police for their own safety. They were all then put on to the witness protection programme. Otherwise they may have been Big Wheel's and the Firm's next victims, hurt or killed for money that was outstanding and didn't belong to them.

It's always the same when people owe money for drugs, they say they are skint but the next thing you see them in the pubs drinking and sniffing hard or buying it off another dealer. So they must have got some money from somewhere. The mum had paid some of the money the two brothers had owed back but not the full amount had come in. So Big Wheel had to let one of the brothers go on the understanding that the rest would be paid once he had got home. But like I said, they went straight to the Old Bill and grassed everyone up that had got involved with the kidnapping.

Our firm had bought the debt off another firm up in Scotland and our mob had hired Big Wheel on the front line to go and collect it in. Big Wheel did pay what he got back in to this Liverpool fella instead of the Scots; well it was them the money belonged to. The Liverpool fella was right cocky about it all. Well half the money was his and the rest belonged to the Jewellery Thief. Now as Big Wheel had got it back in he was over the moon about getting some of his money in as he thought they had lost the lot. Thanks to Big Wheel some of it was now back in and a bit of respect had been made between both firms now. Even though they had to do what they had to do to get it back in the first place.

Sometimes it has to get a bit unfriendly for people to start to stand up straight and really realise who they were dealing with. This cocky fella from Liverpool was allegedly well connected with two brothers over in Columbia, and had a lot of clout with most firms here in England. Well most of the money had come back to the Liverpool Firm one way or another and a little bit came back to the Jewellery Thief. After all they had taken on the debt to get a cut of the money themselves. It was all going very well until Scotland Yard got involved from the info given to them from the brother that was let go. The police told the family that they were now safe on witness protection, the ones that Big Wheel was trying to get the rest of the dough out of any way he could.

It had all gone wrong, terribly wrong, now they had gone to the police. The brother had grassed them all up. He had told it all to them, seeing as the police had said if you don't tell us everything then they couldn't help him. So the brother told about the debt they had got themselves into with the Scottish mob and that they had passed the debt onto the Jewellery Thief, who had taken it on board to collect it all in for the Liverpool mob. That's where the cocaine had come from in the first place. They said that this cocky fella had been organising large shipments of cocaine to come over to England and that they had fallen in debt with the Scots and the Jewellery Thief.

He explained how they had tried to knock another Scottish firm for three keys to pay their long overdue debt back. Not realising the cocaine had also been ticked off the same Liverpool Firm. So the police left no stone unturned until they managed to find the other brother. Luckily Big Wheel had popped out for a McDonalds for them all and when he got back there were police everywhere around the mobile home. It was surrounded. So he just turned the car around after seeing his mate being pulled out handcuffed up and being placed in the police car. He watched as the brother walked out with the policewomen, he drove straight home, grabbed his passport and was gone.

So once the police had all this info from the brothers, it didn't take them long to have this Liverpool fella in custody. They had uncovered some details that had opened a can of worms and gave spring to a new lead for their enquiries, which had nothing to do with the kidnapping itself.

It had changed their enquiries, well away from the kidnapping and they're attention was more on this cocky fella. The more the police started digging and questioning and pulling in people, the more it had led them to one of the biggest busts in English history. With five men and this cocky Liverpool fella on a big conspiracy charge for 85m pounds worth of cocaine that they were all supposedly trying to smuggle over on a submarine. If they hadn't tried to get their money off these two brothers, then the sub would have come up from the water unnoticed and everyone would have been singing "We all live in a yellow submarine." They would have all made millions of pounds and brought over enough cocaine to see London sniffing hard at Colombian's finest for the next four years or so.

But it was a lot of money to keep your mouth shut about and a lot of bird riding on someone's head. Once you're sitting there looking at ten or twenty years, people that you wouldn't think of start to think who they might be able to point the finger at and grass up just to get themselves off. Well some of them might but others would take it on the chin as we know that one day the police will soon be knocking on our doors in this line of work. Once they had got this bust their attention had been taken off the Jewellery Thief who was just put on 'obo' for a little while.

Big Wheel had managed to escape to Spain before the police caught up with him. It wouldn't be too long 'til the police enquiries led them to him for the kidnapping. So he had got on the next plane to Spain for his own safety, and England would now be a thing of the past for him. Otherwise he would be doing at least a ten-year stretch for her Majesty or birded off at her pleasure. So now he is a fugitive in Porterbanos, and the Liverpool fella's boss had got caught and now is in Belmarsh prison banged up doing 12 years. Big Wheel has no choice but to stay out there or come back and rot in jail for at least 10 years or so. Time for his part he played in the kidnapping and the conspiracy with the shipment of cocaine along with other villainous things that are best not talked about that he was involved with. So that's why Big Wheel had to get out of England sharpish and away from it all before the serious crime squad caught up with him. Bringing him and the rest of the Firm down too with charges of conspiracy to smuggle large quantities of cocaine, charges of kidnap, demanding money with menace and not forgetting a few threats to kill. Not to mention some money laundering and fraud jobs that they were doing with a diplomat that was flying refugees over to London on a private plane, sorting them out with bent passports for £500 apiece. Along with any other charges the police could think of to hold the Firm down and throw away the key. That's before they got bail and skipped the country.

When we came through to the arrival lounge Carlos was standing there with a board saying 'Mandy' on it. Big Wheel and Carlos were very big men indeed. They were both body builders and they must have weighed about 21 stone each. They looked very menacing. So much so they would have scared Mr Universe in a body building comp. They were that big, even Hercules would have been a bit scared if he saw them. They were all full of steroids and pumped up on pure adrenalin and wouldn't think twice about ripping your head off whether they were told to do so, or if you got on the wrong side of them. Road rage is a very powerful thing.

They had both been sent to pick us up from the airport by the Jewellery Thief. They were told to drive us to a lovely Spanish villa that was overlooking the sea and a bit out the way from the main stretches of Spain. It was away from all the clubs and bars much to my regret, as I loved to party hard back then. They had been told to make sure we were well looked after and very comfortable while staying out there. It was good to see a half friendly face coming over here. After all I wasn't here on holiday or business and I hadn't been out here for years. I was here to see what was going to happen to my future. That is if there was one, as right now it didn't look promising.

The villa had its own swimming pool and private Jacuzzi, which was very inviting indeed. A balcony you could have breakfast on whilst looking at the sea as it lapped at the rocks below. It also had its own stretch of beach that the villa's occupants only used, which I loved the idea of at first but then came to dislike later on. No holidaymakers were allowed on this part of the beach, and only if we, the occupants of this villa, had invited them.

I had arrived in Porterbanos with 40 pounds in my pocket, the change from the J.Ds, back at the Blind Beggars pub. I didn't have two bob to scratch my arse with now once this was gone. I was skint. Luckily everything was laid on or paid for by Mandy, which I would see her right for again once all this mess was sorted out and I could start to make a few quid again.

Carlos had said we could stay at the villa whilst we were out there and to make ourselves comfortable. Once again the Jewellery Thief and Mr Nice had laid it all on. Mr Nice must have a never-ending pot of gold or shares with the royal mint with all this money and assets he was throwing around or had around him now. Well as the story goes I know his ex missus had a few quid out of the royal mint once when she worked there. As she knew a few cleaners that were on the fiddle and she would take a cut if she left a certain door open for them in order to get through and steal a few notes here and there. So I wasn't far wrong. Also he allegedly had shares in a cocaine factory that was hidden somewhere in Columbia.

Carlos helped us in with our bags and said that the Jewellery Thief would like to see me after 5am that next morning, after the club had finished. He did a few lines up of Colombian's finest then left them there on the table for Mandy and me to help ourselves to. He then shook my hand and kissed Mandy on each cheek. Then said that it was nice to meet us both and that he had heard so much about us from Big Wheel. Even though he had never seen us before or hadn't been to London. Big Wheel had told big Carlos what nice people we were, and that he had done some work with the Cookster before and that Mandy was Johnny's sister.

And by now Johnny was a legend in these parts. Well he was the talk of the town out here, so everyone knew who he was before they even had the chance to meet him. As if his reputation now came before him after shooting this Spanish fella. It was all over the papers what he had done; he was getting to be well known all over Spain. So now the Spanish fella was out the way and Johnny had talked with the Spanish mafia. This had now put Mr Nice and the Jewellery Thief in a much bigger and dangerous position. The paparazzi was all over them now for a bit and was following the story in the magazines out here about Johnny's arrest.

Other firms knew not to be so confident. The Jewellery Thief was well connected in other parts of the world, and now they knew that they had a few men on their payroll in different countries that did as they were told when they were told. It meant they knew when they had said something that they really did mean business. Which meant the Jewellery Thief was now nearly at the top of the ladder and now they could say what they liked to influence the papers out here. So Johnny was sort of a legend now within the firms.

Big Wheel then said bye, left the villa and went outside. We followed them out and waved goodbye. Mandy and I then went back inside and made ourselves comfortable as it was so hot.

I sat down in front of the lines and rolled up a 20 note, and said. "Here, darling. You can go first." Mandy refused to my surprise and told me she didn't do it.

"It turns real men into mice and had made many a big time gangster hide from his own shadow." She said I could have it if I wanted it. With that I wasted no time at all and lent down with the note hanging from my nostrils and sniffed hard at both lines, straight up my hooter. A moment of weakness you might think and a moment of glory that followed.

The cocaine shot up my nose and melted on the back of my tonsils, numbing the back of my throat for a split second. Then all of a sudden my heartbeat began beating slowly and then I took a deep hard sniff as my heart kick started itself. I felt like a Trojan horse charging into battle as my heart started to race and my pupils got bigger and bigger. I then needed the toilet as my stomach started to quiver as the paranoia kicked in a bit. I did start to feel a bit scared like a mouse after about 20 minutes of doing it just as she said. Well that is after you had talked charley bollocks for about 10 minutes.

Well I hadn't done it for some time. So now and then wouldn't hurt, or so I thought. When it's put in front of you like that it's hard to say no. Absence makes the heart grow fonder or when there's cocaine around it starts to scramble your mind and your thought pattern goes out the window once your nose has stopped running. Then the old demon turns up on your shoulder and says. "What you waiting for, son, go on. Get that lot up your nose. You know you want it. You have worked hard for it. So why not indulge every now and then?" Then the angel turns up on the other shoulder and starts fighting with you in your head with all the other voices going on. "You're an addict; look at you, you junky. Why did you do that? No more. Sort yourself out; fix up, look sharp. You said you wouldn't do it no more, only on special occasions." Then you shake it all off and start to get your scruples back in to some sort of order as you come down a bit from the line. Then once again you find a stable sort of mellowness. That's when all of a sudden, hey presto! You're bending down with a card in your hand, with an open rap of charley spreading out the lines, ready to go through the same thing all over again. Just for that 20 minutes of rushing off your nut and then 3 hours of paranoia. Maybe a bit of wild sex. That's if you're there with some woman company who at the time of buzzing you both feel game and up for it. It hardly seems worth 50 pounds or however much you pick your charley up for.

After one line you now want another line and you go round and round in circles 'til the line; half a gram, gram, 8th, oz. bar, key is gone. Then you wake up in the morning in debt and with a sore nose. You had ticked it from every dealer you know, whilst you and your pals were buzzing off your nuts.

As I was getting a bit agitated, I turned to Mandy, "We should go to the beach and chill out for a bit." My heart was now racing; I didn't know what to do with myself. I was now buzzing, buzzing hard.

"Why don't you go? I'll make some enquires as to where Johnny's being kept. So I can go see him in the morning. I'll stay here and unpack. You go. I'm OK here."

"OK," I replied. "You going to be OK?"

"Yes," she said. I changed into my Ben Sherman shorts and half-sleeved Hawaiian shirt; got my shades and sun block on; slipped into my sandals and kissed Mandy on the side of her lovely cheeks once again then headed off to the beach where all the tourists were.

It was no good sitting on our part of the beach outside the villa as there was no fucker around, and I'd just be sat there on my own like Robinson Crusoe. Twiddling my thumbs and mumbling to my imaginary friend Man Friday. I was still buzzing hard from the two lines I had just had as I walked down to the beach.

I remembered when I was young, I had come out here with Mr B one summer. He had taken me to a gym called Monsters Gym to see a good friend of his; an old boy called Mike the gangster. He was the owner of this gym. Mr B told me to go see him and spend some time training in his gym. To see if I could put some muscles on my chicken frame that I had back then, whilst he attended to some business with some Jamaican friends of his. They hadn't seen me before so Mr B said it was best for me to be out the way for a bit being as young as I was. They only like to see who they knew and would only do business with people they were familiar with.

That's where Mike had shown me my first gun. Well he hadn't shown me it at all, I had stumbled upon it by mistake in a sports bag under the till. As I looked down I could just see it poking out a bit. The sports bag was half open and curiosity got the better of me. Mike had a big scam going on the island with some time-share business. He was selling apartments that had all ready been sold and wanted to borrow some money off Mr B to make the scam work better. That's why we had also come out there. I had stolen the gun one day after my workout which had caused them all so much panic. I had left there with it unbeknown to Mike, until he looked and realised it had gone, and so had I. This made his arsehole start twitching like a rabbit's nose. He was worried sick, a 16-year-old boy with a gun did not add up and could only mean one thing, big trouble. And unwanted trouble at that, coming his way.

I just wanted to see if what Mr B had said to me was true. Back in London one night, we were out in some wine bar on a night out. His good pal Ray who used to own the security firm that looked after Bagley's nightclub had picked us up. We met him outside the Cross nightclub in his limo after the clubs had finished, and they were talking. Then Ray said that he had some of these and pulled out a shooter. I heard him talking saying it gave you a sense of strength and power holding one of these and you also felt a bit scared with it once it was in your hand. He said. "If you pull one of these out you should be prepared to use it. Otherwise they will come back for you and use one on you. You must have balls of steel to use one of these as you could be looking at 10 years or more in jail."

"I don't need any right now, Ray. I have my own one but I'll keep it in mind and put the word about. If anyone wants one I'll be in touch, and if they're cheap enough, then we may have a deal." Then Mr B got out the Limo saying goodbye to Ray and his minder as he moved out the way of the door. As I followed to get out, his minder got in the way for a bit and Ray said, "Listen, son, if you ever want to work for us you just let me know. You'll be able to get in touch with me at Bagley's nightclub in London. Just come to the entrance and ask any of the doormen for me, and I'll get the doormen to let you in and bring you to where I am, OK?"

I never did work for him, as my loyalty was with Mr B, and they were good friends. So it was all OK and may have been a test. I did see Ray again and we too become friends and got to know each other on a better level. I did go into Bagley's nightclub with Donna and Nick a few times, met up with him and got in without paying just like he said I would. He was kind enough to let certain people in that were close to him.

I remembered lying on the beach with no money, just the gun under my towel. Then the ice cream man pulled up and I thought this was it. This would be a good time to see what this babe could do. I was excited and it was very stupid of me I know, but hey, we all are when we're kids. Some of us have no fear. So I walked over, as fast as I could, with this gun in my hand wrapped up in my towel. I looked around and saw no one was about, a perfect opportunity I thought. I let the towel fall to the floor leaving me standing there holding the gun to the window of the ice cream van. As the ice cream man looked up and said, "Yes?" He nearly fell over backwards when he saw and realised what was happening.

"Shit kid! Put that away, son. You'll hurt someone or get nicked." Then he pulled himself together rather sharpish when he knew I wasn't messing about.

"Yes, son. Please tell me that's a fucking water pistol," he joked nervously.

"Quick, give me two fucking ninety-nine's and be quick about it," in the deepest voice I could come up with. The ice cream man was only fucking English and turned round.

"Fuck me, kid. "I suppose you want two fucking flakes as well with that."

"Yes please and while you're there some strawberry sauce and some sprinkles. Now get a fucking move on! Some bubble gums too while you're at it, and a can of lemonade."

He pressed the two flakes in the two ice creams, and passed them over to me. I put the gun on the side of the counter to hold them. He then picks up the gun and says, "Now fuck off and don't come back. Otherwise that'll be two pesatas 50 you owe me, and I'll be giving you a kick up the arse for your cheek. Now sod off and don't come back. You cheeky little bugger." I ran off, as the ice cream started to melt. So as I ran off back up the beach, I thought where was the power in that? Licking the ice creams as they melted from the heat without the gun.

Mike and Mr B had shown me how powerful the gun was the next day when I had thought things had calmed down a bit. I had forgotten or tried to forget what I had done, and they had found out what I did with the ice cream man. As it turned out the ice cream man was Mike's friend. Which was a bit of luck on my part. Well at least I knew he wouldn't be reporting me to the Old Bill and the gun was in safe hands once more. Apparently the ice cream man tried to sell it to Mike the gym owner. He knew he would be the one that would want it. But as he was looking over it to pay the ice cream man for it he said, "fuck me, mate, this really looks like the one I have, as he lent down to the bag behind the till only to find it missing.

Then Mike asked, "Where did it come from?"

"You ain't going to believe me, but some ginger kid only tried to rob me with it." That's when Mike twigged it was his one in the first place at which point had a much closer look. He knew I had stolen it. He gave the ice cream man a drink for its safe return. I was only 16 at the time. You learn quickly from your mistakes, especially when you're black and blue from the beatings you got if you mess up and I had messed up real bad that day.

When I had come into the gym the following day Mike asked if he could have a word with Mr B and told him all about what had happened out of earshot of me. So I started to train with the weights as normal.

Then they both come out and Mr B said, "Get into the ring, Cookie. I want to see what you can do, son, it's about time you learned how to look after yourself. I won't be here forever, son. So here, put on these gloves and get in the ring," as he throws the gloves to me.

Next thing the minder comes out of the changing room in his boxing shorts, slides into the ring and gets up and starts boxing with me. I was all over him like a rash, with my left and rights and a few hooks; bobbing and weaving all over the shop thinking I was Mike Tyson, giving it all I had blow after blow.

Then all of sudden Mr B says, "Go on, Terry, teach the little fucker a lesson, the little thieving bastard." With that he sprang into action and I was being boxed around the ring like a ragdoll. I could see stars with every punch that the 18 stone minder was giving out. They was now raining down on me, punch after punch and every one was connecting 'til I was laid out cold on the canvas of the boxing ring with my eyes closed. Sleeping like a baby, yes I had been K.O'd.

When I came round Mike and Mr B were laughing and said, "That will teach you not to nick things that don't belong to you, ask for things before you borrow them, and for taking a liberty. Now get up and get dressed we have work to do."

So messing about with the gun only bought me two fucking ice creams and two black eyes and very sore bruised ribs. I had learnt a valuable lesson that day. Respect is learned not demanded and in future you pay for your fucking ice cream otherwise you go without. And never step in to the ring with an 18 stone man that has fists the size of King Kong's unless you have a tool hidden in your shorts to finish him off with. I learned you never take things that don't belong to you.

I stopped thinking about when I was young as I walked on to the sandy beach in front of me. The sand was scorching from the sun. When I stepped on to it I could feel how hot the sand was on the fronts of my toes. My sandals kept flicking the loose sand up, burning the end of my toes as I walked. I looked up and down the beach, I could see women with their tits out. There were women in small bikinis everywhere. It was all very nice, men and women of all shapes and sizes with thongs and bikinis on. The sea was blue and clear; it was gently lapping at the shore and sparkling as the sun's rays flickered off the waves as they came rolling in. I found my spot and took my top off. I asked the lady next to me if I could use her sun cream. She got up, put her book down, then smiled and said only if I could rub some on her back for her. What a result I thought for just a second.

I then winked and said, "Yes of course. I can do that." I had the biggest smile on my face you could have ever imagined. I then said, "I could do the front too for you as well, darling, if you like." She laughs.

"No, cheeky. I can do that bit myself." I put some more cream on me then rubbed some into my hands and onto her back as I asked her name.

"Sarah, and you?"

"I'm the Cookster, darling, very nice to meet you, sweetheart. She then laid back down flat on her beach towel, pulled her hair to one side and shut her eyes. So I then squeezed some cream on my hands and started to massage it into her browning skin, it was very soft so I really took my time about it. She then said. "OK, that's enough don't be getting too carried away."

"OK, thanks for the cream." She laughed.

"That's OK." So I stopped.

I then went back and lay down on my lounger, soaked up the sun and relaxed. Watching the babes play bat and ball about five feet away from me. Every now and again I would glance at her, but she must have gone to sleep. I could see the banana boat fly past, the paragliders going up and down the beach and the jet skis skimming past me when I looked out to sea. Sometimes the nice arses of some of the women walking up and down the beach along the shoreline, all undercover of course with Armani shades on. If they had fallen off I would have had one eye looking to the left and one to the right, with all the left and right looking I was doing. My mouth was dry and my thoughts were warped from the come down of the cocaine I had had back at the villa. I had to get a drink. The barmen were coming round with trays and taking orders from the bar next to the beach. So I called one over to me. "Señor. Hello, one beer please my amigo."

"OK, my friend, no problem," he replied.

The beer arrived and I lay back more on the lounge chair and got myself comfortable. I looked to my left and the lady that I had borrowed the cream from had now turned over on to her back. She was topless and looking very nice. She was reading a book with her shades on. So I smiled at her. She smiled back; her eyes weren't on the *book* they were on *me*. Otherwise she wouldn't have known I had smiled at her I thought to myself. She must be doing the same as me under her shades, eyeing up the men but pretending to read or glance at the book. She smiled a 'you know you want it' sort of smile but nothing happened. That must happen a lot, just too scared to do the communicating. Or she was just being friendly and the cocaine had twisted my melon man with the heat of the sun and the cold beer. Who knows if she did want it or not and I never got to find out.

I then looked away and took a sip of the cold beer and once more drifted off into oblivion or some other part of the world my messed up coke head took me. The beer was cold and it hit my head straight away. I never really drank beer but it did the trick for now. I felt a bit pissed from the heat of the sun and the coldness of the beer. It tasted like gnat's piss. Well I ain't really a beer drinker so to me it did.

Then a voice said. "Hi, you English?"

"Yes," I said as my eyes squinted to look up at a Spanish dude, wearing a big straw hat and a bum bag round his waist, "as a matter fact I am."

"OK, two euros please."

"What for being fucking English!"

"No señor, the sun lounger."

"Sorry, mate, two euros for the sun lounger, Oh yes here you go, mate." He left and hassled the next person that was English. Fuck, I wondered how much it would be if I weren't from England. He had just got two euros out of me for the sun lounger. I felt a bit robbed and he weren't even wearing a mask. Things had changed since I was last out here. Now everything cost and had become all commercialised. Even the peseta had now turned into the euro. I leant back into the chair got myself comfortable, pulled my cap down over my eyes leaving the hot sun beating down on my chest and put my sunglasses back on.

It weren't too long before I had fallen asleep. When I woke people were picking up their stuff and heading to the nearest restaurants. Shutting down their umbrellas and the beachmen were now coming round grabbing the beds back, piling them up neatly at the side of the beach ready for the next day. I was going to be cheeky when he asked for the bed back, and ask him for my two euros back. They were stacking the beds ready to start getting them out again early in the morning, ready for the mad rush. The tide had started to come in and was now just about touching my toes, cooling them off from the heat. So I put on my top and headed back to the villa. I wanted to know how Mandy had got on with finding out where Johnny was being kept.

When I got back to the villa Mandy was there in her white short summer dress and her golden blonde locks were all down and hanging just off her shoulders. She was wearing her Chanel glasses, Prada high heels, and if you looked carefully you could just see a glimpse of her thong through her white dress, as she turned round. Ooh she looked hot and very attractive as always.

"Hi sweetheart, how did you get on?" I said. Pulling my mind away from my thoughts and my eyes off her arse and her thong. As she turned back round to face me, I slid my glasses on to the top of my head and listened to what she had to say.

"Well he's being kept in Delmont prison and I can go see him around 12 noon tomorrow. I've rang and made the appointment, it's not that far from the villa and I have booked a cab to take me there. So it's all organised for me to go, so one less thing for me to worry about for now whilst I'm out here."

"Do you want me to come with you, when you go?"

"No, if he sees you he will get angry and do his nut and we don't want that do we?" She was right.

"Mandy, I'm hungry, darling. Shall we go to a restaurant and get some food?" Now that I had come down from the cocaine and had had a nice rest.

"That'll be nice, let me shower and change," she said. "Then we'll go."

"I could do with one too before we leave."

So we both showered. Not together though which would have been nice. Once ready, we headed off down to the seafront where all the restaurants were paraded along the beach and the people were trying to get us into their club or restaurant as we walked along. Mandy and I started opening up to each other about our past as we talked on the way down to the seafront to look for a restaurant we could eat in. I felt like I had known her for years as she opened up to me more and more about herself and her past. Mandy told me about her mum and dad, and how she'd moved from Essex to the East End in London. She spoke a lot about her brother.

She said how Johnny had left the Marines a gentleman, and then got in with this door firm and became a doorman at the local clubs in Manchester and Liverpool. Before long his reputation started to get around by firms in London and other clubs' management. He was forever making the clubs clean of any trouble and getting rid of the drug dealers and the no good that were in them making the clubs bad. He was smashing up big time drug dealers that were supposed to be hard men or had a reputation for being able to handle themselves. He could and had made many a club that was being brought down by drugs or villainy, clean again. As he took no shit and had heard it all from people on the door who he had barred many times, they would come back for him. Some did and some were all full of it. *I'll kill you. I know where you live. I'll be out here when you come home waiting for you.* You name it he heard it, but it didn't scare him one bit. He buzzed off it and if they tried it on he made sure he finished it there and then. He would say he hated bullies. They would say he was the man with no fear, as he feared no one and didn't care who you were or where you came from. He had said you can tell a man by his words and promises, if they stick to their word then they are half reliable and if they do what they promise then you can't go wrong having them as a friend. Names or reputation didn't mean a thing to him. He made his own mind up when he met you himself, or after he had smashed you all round the gaff.

He would say after seeing what he had seen in the army, that this life was a breeze for him. He didn't care who you knew or who you were or whom you thought you knew. He would say they ain't here now so it's just you and me sunshine so you're just about to get hurt, and they did if they pushed him too far. If you're going to get shot or hurt then stop talking about it and come do it he would say, as talk is cheep and actions is what this life is all about. So unless you have the money to fight me stop wasting my time giving it all the biggun, I will only fight you for a few quid to make it worth my while. If you haven't got it then stop wasting my time and jog on. The paper named him one of the hardest men in Manchester once. Word got out that he was quite handy with his fists. He was well respected by most and had made lots of friends whilst on the doors and a lot of enemies too.

He started to get hired by big-time criminals and debt collectors and other villains. Not the small fry, he was throwing them out of clubs and confiscating their drugs. He would get the big firm's money in and a few loan sharks and before long he was collecting money in for a big firm in Manchester. Bodyguarding a few old school mobsters and some Italian men that allegedly had set up a big protection racket over here in London. Working restaurants and club doors involving the 'K' brothers whilst they were still in prison. So it wasn't long 'til a family firm heard about his reputation that he had built up for himself in London and they had sent some of their best men to see what he was all about. Also to sort him out and to tell him to mind his p's and q's, but they came unstuck and he was the only man still standing. So he was hired to be a mercenary for this big firm in Manchester. Whilst working close with them, he had met and been introduced to a well-known and very dangerous family firm in London. He had become their head doorman in six clubs that they owned.

He was working with them closely as one of their henchmen and had now turned hitman for them and had started a war of gangland shootings which started to put people in their place. He was now in with the top boys in Liverpool, Manchester, London and parts of Essex. There was no stopping him or them, with someone on their side like this they couldn't lose. Also he was well in with Mr Nice too. It was all hush hush what he and them got up to. Mandy said the Liverpool fella ended up inside but he was well connected allegedly with some brothers in Columbia. Then through this London firm he was introduced to the Jewellery Thief and Mr Nice who was also connected to a firm in Colombia. He worked closely with the family now running parts of London, and they had made him what he is today; a loyal respected gentlemen and womaniser on the outside, but a raging wild animal on the inside. They would pay him to kill or do what was necessary without batting an eyelid for the two firms, keeping them and everyone that worked alongside them all in order. Sometimes it was done just out of respect for this firm as they had looked after him and put him where he is today.

They had also put a few zeros on the end of his bank account with all the drugs they were selling. It was coming over to them first before it was getting cut and going back out again to other big time dealers. The money was shipped around the country to try and avoid the paper trail. Businesses were popping up all over the shop that were now willing to help put the dirty money through their books to clean it. With his handiwork he had put them in the position to be able to do what they like when they like. Seeing as they now rubbed shoulders with most if not all of the untouchables in the underworld. Now he knew all the families and the faces in London or who was in the know. If you said do you know such and such a fella he would say no. Once they met they would walk over to Johnny and say "hi how you doing, long time" like they were the best of friends and probably were if the truth be known. He had all the flash clothes and motors and money he wanted or needed. People would help him out just out of respect for who he was and for who he knew. They encouraged him more and more to do the things others would have to think twice about doing. He was now their number one hitman and minder.

He was lent out by them as a mercenary for other firms too, given a wallet with photos of other firms that had to be taken out, talked to or for their own safety needed to join forces with them. Otherwise they would soon find themselves out of business or having a little accident as he would teach those a lesson who had become a liability or nuisance to the main family firm and Mr Nice. People that talk about him or who knew of him said he is one fucking dangerous man indeed. He was someone you definitely didn't fuck about or joke with, unless he had let you get close to him. Even then it was still dangerous and you would have to tread carefully. They said he is heartless and cold to the bone. Not a man to be messed with or to find yourself on the wrong side of. A man like this you must kill before you get killed. She said she'd only found out all this, as once there was talk that upset her.

"I was in a car once and had gone out with all the girls on a night out and had left this club a bit drunk. One of the Firm member's girl let slip, without knowing that I was Johnny's sister, that she liked Johnny. 'Cor he's very sexy.'

'Who is?' the other girl says.

'That Johnny, he can have me any time,' and the other girl said, 'After me first.'

'That fella that came in the club, he can have us all at once if he likes or all together,' they all laughed."

"What about you, Mandy, what do you think?"

"Well he's OK, I guess. OK, he's well fit."

"I think he likes you as he always kisses you first when he sees you."

"I said I really like him too you know. As Johnny had kissed me on the cheek then said hi to the girls by shaking their hands and the girls didn't know he was my brother. Only one of them did but she would never let on, it was best that way. The girls said 'he likes you too by the looks of it as you always get a kiss and he always has his eye on you.'

"Johnny likes to try keeping it quiet that I was his sister as he said it was best, all the men knew but the girls hadn't a clue, well one or two did. One of the girls then says, 'look, Mandy,' to me, 'be careful of him.' She said that allegedly he had been involved in a hit and had shot a gangland member in Liverpool. Her fella had said he had killed 25 people and had got away with it or he had them killed on his say-so. They said he was so cold that even the Devil would be scared of him if he died. He would say to people that owed money, that if you dance with the Devil, then don't forget to play the Devil's music, otherwise you'll end up dead. I was shocked when I heard that.

"The women they loved him, he had a different one every night and sometimes two at the same time no doubt, or so I was told. They loved him and would hang on to his every word. They loved his good looks and chiseled features; they loved the air of confidence that was all around him when he entered the room.

They would all fight to be on his arm, to be his woman or to be seen with him and his pal sitting at the club's tables that cost £2000 a night just to sit at. When he walked in they would all make sure they were looking their best. They wanted to be on his arm and wanted him to notice them. So they too would or could feel what the tremendous power and respect he got.

"He was suave, very sophisticated and very intelligent but very dangerous and mysterious. He never had to queue up in any of the clubs around Liverpool, Manchester or London and a few in Essex. He would know at least one of the doormen that would be working on the door on most clubs or would know their boss. He would walk in with a golden handshake and the manager would be running around after him like a blue arsed fly.

"He didn't love any of the women or girls he had got with but he intrigued them. The ones that had fallen for him wanted to tame the mobster within. They had fallen for him in a big way or fallen for what he was all about, as these sorts of women liked a bit of rough, money and power.

"He said once to me, 'Women could do what a man can't.' That was break your heart. He said he had seen many a strong man battered by a woman and had their heart broken by them. He said, 'It's a pain inside that's hard to brush off. Even the strongest of men can have their heart broken. I have and will only love two women in my life. That would be mum and me,' he said.

"So Johnny would give the women the excitement they wanted or were looking for. He was living the fast life and the women loved the chase. Some women liked the animal within and some the tremendous power and respect he got everywhere he went, in every manor and by every Firm member or person that came in contact with him. Even the other Firm member's girls had a thing for him. Some people would shy away when they knew he had turned up. As they knew if he wasn't here for pleasure, that he was here for business and they knew his business was the killing business. So if he turned up unannounced then someone was about to get it. How he kept it away from me for so long I will never know, maybe I was a bit naive or stupid. He was the Firm's triggerman.

"Mr Nice and Johnny had now built a good relationship with each other and he had come up through the ranks of the underworld. If anyone had disrespected the family firm in London then Johnny would soon be on his way to fuck them up or put them in a hole. With an army of dangerous men to put them in their place, or worse put them in the graveyard without a head stone. Buried somewhere in the woods or floating down the river Lee, anyway he could get rid of the body before the police could find it. Even under the sandpit in a golf course allegedly or dropped out to sea. He and this Irish mob once took this fella into the woods, told him to dig a hole and buried him up to his shoulders then left him there for two days. He had to be dug out by someone that had heard his cries for help. He soon paid the money back he owed.

"If you messed up he would get some of his pals, the Paddies, to lay you in a hole and get the tarmacker to go over you. This gave a new meaning to being stuck on the M25. He was well on top of the payroll from these two firms paying him to kill and get rid of people without saying too much. It put him in a very powerful and dangerous position indeed. So in return for money he would help them out with the things he did best which was getting people out the way, putting other firms out of action or persuading them to join them. As the saying goes 'if you can't beat them join them.' Well they didn't have much choice really when he turned up. He had given loads of them a beating and supposedly killed 25 men. That's why he and they had such a reputation. Johnny would go to work on any firm or anyone giving it the big I am to the Jewellery Thief or Mr Nice. Those that got out their pram a bit; or who were getting too greedy and thought they were better than all the rest. Those who done a lot of talking without thinking and a lot of talking to the Old Bill.

"He would say he had killed loads of people in the army so what was the difference when you're not in there. It's still murder if you're taking care of the wrong 'uns. They're still the enemy. He was a proper nemesis. These two firms had made Johnny into a very dangerous man and given him the power and say-so with the contacts to do what he liked when he liked. He only answered to them, that's why as their reputation got bigger and bigger, they were feared in London and all over parts of England. They had some of the Old Bill in their pockets too, which was common knowledge. Sometimes the police would call on the underworld for a meeting to get someone they knew that would be protected. But once the firms all knew what the person had done, and if it wasn't within the code of effects, then they may or may not have helped the police. For a favour in return of course. That's how he knew many dangerous firms and dangerous friends that would help him out all over the world, at the drop of a hat. These sorts of friends he had could and had been corrupt.

"Money makes people do strange things. He had the highest paid lawyers and barristers in the land. They even had spent time at swinger parties or pool parties at big mansion houses together. Sniffing hard at Columbian's finest with judges, police commissioners and a few MPs. Sometimes even Customs officers, a few big lords and some old pals high up in the Navy and the Army. That's how they were able to move large consignments of drugs, like puff and cocaine over here to England and to America without being caught. As it was all well planned out using the sort of people that were in their pockets with the uppermost social position, you wouldn't think twice that the gear was still going on to the streets if the Navy had taken it off you.

"They had made Johnny one of the untouchables; they even had a firm allegedly dressed up as Hari Krishnas smuggling cocaine and E's over in their drums from Dover to Amsterdam. On the boats they weren't doing no booze cruises they were on the charley runs. Johnny could manipulate people into doing things for him and the firms. He was so good at persuading people he should have been a diplomat, and they knew he had so much respect and money. He also had a lot of powerful people that were backing him and a lot of powerful police after him, well the Serious Crime Squad was. So many people were true and loyal and were now working for him and the two firms. They had around 650 men working for them on the club doors, at one time all over the world a bit like the Sopranos.

"They were all now on their payroll. Johnny had put the fear of the Devil on them all. They knew if Johnny was paid to do something to them then it would be done, not talked about for days. It was planned; the executioner would carry out his evil work, sometimes unseen but heard about later. Which could mean you were dead, maimed, overdosed, set up or taken away and never seen or heard of again. Johnny was number one next to the family firm and that's how he met the Jewellery Thieves, Mr Nice and this Liverpool fella who allegedly had connections with the Columbians too. When the Jewellery Thieves wanted someone under manners then they would call upon Johnny and he would go and arrange it for them. He would turn up unexpectedly with an army of big men to take over the doors and treat people how they deserved to be treated, if you know what I mean.

"Johnny had control of a few doors and clubs so if he didn't do the job himself he would send in the lynch mob. A few doormen to help fly the flag for the Firm. It was done in such a professional manner that they didn't know if Johnny done it or was involved or not. So it was hard for the police to do anything about it. All they knew was it got done, just as Johnny said it would. If Johnny couldn't do it himself, he would oversee that it got done by someone else lower in the ranks of the Firm that owed him a favour or a debt. So they would do the job and then Johnny would take money off their debt and then let the family firm know about his decision and what he had done. If it was done properly the Firm would wipe their mouth with some of the debt for a bit, or the Firm would put a contract on the person themselves, that was in their way. Then you knew it was only a matter of time before someone got paid for doing the terrible deed, which would mean that someone got hurt. Everyone they hurt or killed had deserved it as far as I knew. That's what I heard them saying one night at the club.

"When Johnny was on the phone he would go mad and shout down the phone and say they fucking deserve it. 'So there's no excuse now it's too late. Do they have the money or what? So don't be taking any of their shit. They deserved it, it's too late for being fucking sorry now. So there's no need to cry over spilt milk. Pull yourself together man; there are no worries if the job is done then all good, if not then why not and the excuse wants to be a good one. As if I have to come down there it will be like a ton of bricks coming down on top of you and him. So make sure it happens, do you understand? Have I made myself crystal clear, are we singing from the same hymn sheet choirboy? Then enough said don't phone me on this fucking phone again. How many times do I have to tell you lot use a fucking phone box or come find me and talk to me face to face. You know where I will be at for your eyes only and don't bother me 'til it's done, do you understand? And if it doesn't get done then I'll do it myself and then you'll get done too for wasting my time. Do I make myself clear, Dogshead? If you want to ride on the lion, then don't cry when you fall off and the lion turns round and bites you back. Do you hear me, son? Once you've done it come find me and I'll give you some wages. Until then I'll see you when I see you.'

"They would bring people into the Firm and let them think they were well in with them and put them on a pedestal. Then when they needed a fall guy to take care of the consequences; when something did go wrong; they would bring that person straight back down to earth and put them in their place. Even if it meant putting them in prison for something they didn't do and take the rap for them. After all, he was the main man next to Mr Nice. They were just soldiers in his eyes, as his orders had come from the top Firm and bosses. You couldn't get any higher. No one messed about or took liberties with him or them; he was number one from the top Columbian's firm as far as the firms were concerned. He is very protective of me as you know; he does his best to keep me away from it all."

Mandy looked at the floor and said, "One time when we were young there was a fella in the pub. We had all been in there, Johnny and me and a few close minder friends of his when it went off and I knew then something wasn't right. This fella bumped into me and spilt some drink down my dress. He said sorry and was very apologetic and said can I buy you a drink. The whole pub went quiet as they knew that I was Johnny's sister and they knew Johnny and what he was capable of. He worked with a firm that run the East End at the time, they all knew what was about to come. That's why they all kept quiet.

"Johnny jumped up looked him straight in the eyes and said. 'No drink, mate, you can buy her a fucking new dress, if you know what's good for you. That's £350 quid you now owe me.' The fella laughed. He couldn't believe what he had heard and thought Johnny was joking.

'Listen, mate, I've told you I'm sorry.'

'If you're sorry, then you will buy her a new dress, £350 quids' worth. I drink here all the time. So, son, you best do what's best for yourself, which is to trot on down to Harrods and get a new dress. I'll be here waiting for it tomorrow and, son, it won't take me long to find out where you live, believe me.'

"The fella walked away into the toilets laughing to himself and says to his pal 'Silly cunt. Who the fuck is that mug?'

"Who the fuck is that not knowing what or who Johnny was or what he was all about. Johnny's mate had heard him say that as he had got up and gone in to the toilet cubical. Within a second or two Johnny's right-hand man had walked out the cubical toilets. The man saw Johnny's right-hand man and said, 'Look, I'm sorry, mate,' and went to shake his hand and tried to say sorry again.

'OK, mate, no hard feelings,' as Johnny's right-hand man smiled, grabbed his hand in a firm handshake, pulled him forward, head butted him as hard as he could then twisted him round and banged his head on the urinal.

"Then the doorman came running in and said, 'That's enough mate, you'll kill him, get off him.' Johnny had told him to have a word with him on the quiet but he had gone to town on him and taught him a lesson by banging some sense into him. His other mate stayed in the toilet cubical 'til it was all over. Nice mate!

"Johnny then walked in, looked in the mirror, leaving this fella on the floor bleeding all over his face and said, '£350 and £100 to clean this lot up.' Meaning pay the bouncers and the bar staff. £100, well it was a lot in them days.

'And you won't have to worry about anyone or thing in this manor ever again. Do I make myself clear?' Johnny straightened his shirt up, washed the blood from his shoes, walked out the toilet and said to the girl behind the bar, 'Ring an ambulance, darling, some drunk has just slipped over in the toilets and smashed their head open.' He then said, 'Get your coats,' to his right-hand man and me as now we were leaving. 'Come on, fellas.' Johnny and his right-hand man were dressed in moleskin coats and designer shirts and trousers, he said it looked smart, could conceal their bullet proof jackets underneath their coats, and went well with the Armani suits. He said the moleskin coats were just the job to still look good but hide everything underneath them. We came out the pub and went to get into Johnny's minder's B.M.W and another car, when the police turned up and skidded all around us.

"When they came over to question us, everyone, even the bouncer on the door said the same thing that a man had unfortunately fallen and slipped.

'The man was a bit pissed and as I walked out he slipped and banged his head, ask anyone you like,' Johnny said. Everyone in the pub told them the same thing. They saw nothing but if it weren't for Johnny seeing this man, he would have been left in the pub toilet bleeding all night. The policewoman pulled Johnny to the side as she said she didn't believe him. I could see Johnny pull a few quid out of his pocket and give it to the police officer and she said to him, 'Will I see you tonight?'

'Yes,' he said, and then he kissed her on the side of the cheek as he was only shagging her as well on the sly. But only I see him kiss her, the other police officers were too busy searching the car and Johnny's minder.

"Then the policewoman said to the other officers, 'It's all OK. Nice to see you all again, boys. I'll be down the scrapyard soon so stay out of trouble.' Johnny's friend that we were with that night was the owner of a big scrapyard. His name was George R and he had a son that worked the scrapyard together with him. Then the policewoman turned to her officers.

'It's OK, boys, you can let this lot go and the lady too, everything seems in order now.'

"See, if he could do that, just over a little accident and get away with it, then imagine if someone really hurt me or pissed him off or if he was paid to do something. I know Johnny does still look out for that man to this day. They do a bit of work together as this fella is in the car business. He's a car salesman as well and he sorts out cars for Johnny now and then, on lease or when required.

"People also go to Johnny and the firms if they get in trouble but can't go to the police, he'll sometimes sort it out for them depending on what it was, and at a price of course. He never did nothing for nothing.

"The next day this fella that got hurt had a brand new dress and flowers with a sorry card ready for me. The poor fella, he was quite sweet. They nicknamed him 'Saucy' after that little incident, as he always went red when he saw me. Johnny would joke with him and say that he better not have rude thoughts going on in his head about me when he saw me, otherwise Johnny would kill him.

'You know I can read minds,' he joked. They all laughed but he laughed nervously. Johnny bought the drinks all that night and told the fella he liked him and to have no hard feelings at what had happened, which cheered him up a bit. Even though he had 25 stitches holding his face in place and a big bruise across his forehead. The real reason he was done unbeknown to me, until I met his wife, was he had given her a clump and the girl had asked Johnny to have word with him. So he was going to get it even if he hadn't spilled the drink on me. She was upset with him so this had happened. I guess it was karma on his part, which gave Johnny an even better excuse to sort him out. So he had killed two birds with one stone. Whilst he was with him drinking after their boys' night out, he would whisper in Saucy's ear 'leave the missus alone and start showing her some respect, here take this' as he handed him a few quid 'do something nice together it's on the Firm. She ain't a punch bag, she's your wife, man, she doesn't deserve that I'm sure.'

74

'OK, Johnny. Will do, mate, thanks.' They seemed to be OK after that, him and his missus.

"Well a lot of things Johnny done weren't very nice and some were all kept very secretive but he always had money after he had done a job. That's how I knew he had done something or someone. Then he would go out and buy me some very expensive new dresses, Chanel, Versace, Louis Vuitton you name it. He would spend thousands and thousands on me. He even bought this Cartier watch, which cost two and half grand," as she pointed to it.

"He said it was important to look your best at all times. As people took more notice of you if you look smart and presentable and stick to your word. First impressions last and you never know when you might meet someone for the first time. He always made sure he looked immaculate himself. He was always clean-shaven and every week he had a razor-cut shave from his local barbers.

"They loved it when he came in and they'd have a chat. Once I walked in on him at mum's house and he had this massive body builder with him. They had a few guns on the bed, two balaclavas and a big bag of money. The body builder shouted at me to get out and never come in the room again without knocking first. Pushing me back out the door from coming in to the room to see what was going on before I had a chance to get into the room fully. He really blew his top with me. Then Johnny came out and said. 'I'm just doing business, Mandy.' Things like this women shouldn't see and definitely not his little sister even though I was 20 at the time.

'So please knock before you come in next time, petal OK? Here, go take the girls out for lunch,' as he handed me £500 all in new fifties that had just come from out the bank, but how I never asked. Then he went in to the room again and locked the door. I heard him shout, 'You don't ever fucking talk to my little sister like that again. Let alone put your hands on her, do you hear me?'

'But Johnny.'

'No buts. Just keep counting that lot for the Irish mob. You talk to her with the same respect you talk to me.'

'Johnny…'

'Now, do I make myself clear?'

'Yes, mate.' Then it went quiet and they started mumbling to each other. Planning, scamming and talking about business. I heard Johnny say that he had some steroids on the way and they were all due to make some good money out of them, but then it all went a bit muffled and I couldn't make it out what they were saying. Mum would have gone mad if she had walked in on them and saw what they had.

"I left and took the girls to a nice restaurant in London. I knew the sort of clientele Johnny kept, and some of the women he had in tow would say things to me about him. The people he knew or would meet or be around on our nights out together at the clubs or over lunch. These people always looked very menacing indeed. They didn't stand for any nonsense or rudeness. When Johnny and his friends were around women they would always speak to them respectfully and treated them right, he hated rudeness. They would all get spoilt when they were their company. The women liked his real smooth and very sexy confident ways that he had about him. They all seemed to have an eye for Johnny even if they had fellas themselves, they would still have a secret smile for him.

"I was told one night by the limo driver that any job that was done in the manor had to be taxed by the Jewellery Thief first, otherwise it couldn't go off. How true it was I never found out. If it had gone off in their manor and they didn't receive a percentage then they would use Johnny to find out who had done it and to take their cut out of their takings. It was all around us; the danger, violence, gangsterism, but he just wanted me to see the good in him even though he tried to protect me from it all. It's hard to keep it quiet all the time especially when everyone knows of you or has heard of you and women are throwing themselves at you. He was a gentleman to most women and me but he could turn at the drop of a hat if someone pissed him off, or if the Firm called and phoned him to do something. He said it was just his job to be like that, nothing personal, just business without the pleasure. When needed to be, he was like a loose cannon. Other times he was calm, collective and was very quiet and placid, a very intelligent man."

She thought a lot of her brother from the things she was saying. They were very close and he meant the world to her just as she did him. Her mum was married to a big time gangster that used to own half of a casino in London. His father had won it in a card game that had been set up for him to win by one of the Arifs firm back in the day. Then when he had died it was passed down to his son who then got with her mum.

"That's why I could always hear him say on the phone, around home when they called, 'ah, yes my Cypriot friend and how are you today?' I could just hear them reply with 'ah, English bastard played anymore cards yet.' They would all laugh.

"It was all lighthearted fun to them but to others it was a very serious business and people's lives that they were playing with. He also did a lot of business with the Arabs and the Cypriots and had some offshore accounts, one over in Dubai and another in Russia supposedly. My mum and stepdad were both killed in a revenge killing from a drive-by shooting. That's all I was told, as I was young when it had happened. Maybe the people who lost the casino realized they had been set up and wanted it back. Johnny weren't having any of it and has tried and tried to find the firm or person responsible or even why they had done it in the first place. He wanted the full story not just that it was a revenge killing with no more than that. He wanted all his questions answered. He thinks it was because they had found out about this casino fella's father cheating on them at the card game to win the casino. It was all set up and maybe they wanted it back to pay the Cypriots off a large debt that they now had. They had had a big drugs deal confiscated by the police.

"The police had pulled over one of their trucks and it was all loaded with puff. The only way to pay the debt off was by trying to get back the casino and then selling it on. But the casino fella that was seeing my mum would have said no, so I guess they came and got him out the way. Johnny was in the marines on leave when the shooting had happened. When he came out he went a bit berserk and was a madman at times. He would go round hurting people and demanding answers from different people. Then when mum was buried he calmed down for a bit. He didn't want to see anyone and just trained in the gym and worked at the local nightclub. Then he would go on the quest for answers again. He kept coming to a dead end. Every time he tried to find out the truth behind mum's death, no one wanted to talk about it. When they find out what Johnny is all about and who he now works for they definitely don't want to talk about anything. Nor say too much and don't want to give any names out, even if Johnny starts putting pressure on them and fretting them.

"He hasn't put it to rest yet and never will. Even if he got the fella that did the deed, I'm sure he still won't rest until everyone that was involved with it was dead. A chance to look them in the eye and find out the truth about why they killed our mum and stepdad, and then he could put a bullet in their nut. He's sure our mum had nothing to do with it. Just being with this gangster at the wrong place at the wrong time.

"Me, I miss mum, but it does get better in time. I still talk to her and put flowers on her grave now and then."

Mandy then showed me a photo of her mum from her purse. She looked a bit like Marilyn Monroe. So now I knew why Mandy looked so good. I passed the picture back.

"We were all kept out the way from all the business and what went on back at the house. We were protected from it all and I'm sure mum didn't know half of what was really going on behind the closed doors of the casino or that's what she led me to believe. She was a smart woman and a very strong one at that. He would have different gangsters and faces from all over London coming in our house for meetings. When she asked him why they were all coming to her house he would just say it was out the way of prying eyes from the staff back at the casino and safer for them to be there. He then would pull out a wad of money and say 'why don't you go shopping darling, get yourself a few nice things and get your nails done, have a haircut too, if you like.' 'I'm just worried what the neighbours will think,' she would say, 'with all these flash cars pulling up, look at them I can see them at their curtains.' He would laugh at her and say, 'let them think what they bloody well like, as the people I work with own half of the neighbourhood anyhow.'

"There was a different person hanging around mum's each day, you never knew who was who. Mum would tell me little bits and pieces now and then, but I was too young to understand it all. As I got older it all started to make more sense what was really going on and what my stepdad was all about and involved with. They would come to mum's to have meetings with him whilst I was at school. I would be at school and they would leave before or just as I came home. I'd see them all shaking hands and exchanging money and then say goodbye and drive off in their flashy cars. They were all smartly dressed men and well groomed. You could tell just by looking at them that they had money and were important men.

"I would see them leave and ask questions to mum when I got in the house. She would say it was Uncle Reggie or Uncle Ronnie or Bill or Mr Richardson or Mr MacLean, but I didn't have an Uncle Ronny or Reggie or Frederick or Mr Richardson or Mr MacLean as far as I could remember. The family only really got together at weddings or funerals as far as I knew. I never saw them again once mum was gone and they had said goodbye at mum's and the casino gangster's funeral. Mum said it was best I didn't ask so many questions so I never really did after that. The things he got into would have meant danger for us too, if the other firms knew he had children. Then they would know that he had a weakness and they could get to us if something went wrong.

"Mum would say, 'it's best to hear no evil speak no evil, my little darling,' and she weren't far wrong with that. As I have learned that loose lips can sink ships growing up through the years in this sort of life. So it's always best to hear no evil speak no evil, even if you've seen it happen you definitely say you haven't. And if anyone asks if you know this fella you say no, even if you did.

"When they died the casino gangster's friends moved on. It was said they had links with the IRA. We didn't want for nothing as he provided it all for us. He was a good stepdad when he was there and had time for us. When he wasn't here, there and everywhere dealing with business with different people and other firms. He spent a lot of time at the airport waiting and watching people. Mum said that he was a plane spotter in his spare time, but he wasn't there watching planes he was watching parcels come in and contacting people to get their luggage that was packed full of drugs. I guess we were his best kept secret to those that he had only just met; it was all kept like that for our own safety. Well that's what mum would tell me.

"My real dad was an armed robber who mum was with for 7 years before they split up. She had then got with this casino gangster owner, as dad had got himself nicked and had gone down for 8 years. He had joined a firm of robbers from the West End and got involved with them doing this job and that. They had all done a big bank job for a big time villain that was behind some betting shops. He had told dad if they could pull this job off for him he would only want a small cut, some of the diamonds that he knew were being stored in one of the security boxes within the bank's safe.

"He had heard two diamond merchants talking about it and how safe their diamonds would be now they were tucked safely away in this bank. Which was where his daughter worked behind the till, that's what made him want to know more. As he was walking along he heard a bit of the conversation. Then he decided to walk behind them listening to their conversation much more closely. He then thought of dad and asked to meet him. He said to dad and his crew of robbers that he could have the rest in the bank if he could pull off the robbery. It had no interest to him as long as he got some of the diamonds. Dad had said there were safety deposit boxes of all different kinds with money of all different currency in them, jewellery, expensive watches, paintings and photos. The diamonds were the biggest prize of all. The robbery was all over the news and in the newspapers. That's how mum found out what he did for a living. They had got caught coming out of the bank with bags of gold.

"This fella told him about the job one day when he had gone to put a bet on the Grand National. The fella had told dad that he had a job for him and he said his daughter would help by opening the safe for him, which she did. Once dad had told his friends, they wanted to hit it straight away. The moment they saw the gold bars in the bank, well that was that. The plan for the job went pear-shaped. I think the people that knew about the job guessed they would get the gold bars out for them too but who knows I wasn't there, so I can't say. When dad and his mates had got to the safe they found these gold bars by mistake as she had opened the wrong vault first. So they stuffed the money in the bags ready and the diamonds for this villain and then they found these gold bars, just as they were about to leave which of course slowed the bank job right down, as they were too heavy. They got caught as they were struggling out of the safe with these gold bars that was now in the bags. One of the clerks had nudged the panic button by mistake as she was told to get down and lie on the floor whilst they were all scurrying around frantically filling the bags with money. Dad and his mate hadn't known what she had done. I don't think she even had, as she had just brushed past it on her way down. They had told the betting shop owner's daughter to open the safe as planned.

"They were still in the bank with security boxes open here there and everywhere whilst everyone was lying on the floor and there was dad and his mates with their tights still over their head. The police were on their way as they were loading the gold bars into the bags. They were then trying to slide the bags of gold out of the safe and scraping the bags along the floor to the doors. The police turned up outside, they were finally arrested 'cos as they walked out the police walked in. The police were all undercover waiting for them, and were all over them like a rash. The police gave them a hand into the van, and helped them carry the gold bars back into the bank safely, after the bank was cordoned off and everyone was let out safely.

"Dad had only come in for the money and the diamonds as planned, but when his friends had seen the gold bars their eyes got bigger then their bellies. As the saying goes 'greed got the better of them.' Dad did tell them to leave them but they didn't listen. They probably would have been better off with just a few bars and the rest in money, but no they may have come for the money and diamonds but tried to leave with the lot, bars as well. They would have got away with the money and diamonds seeing as it was just an in-and-out job. They could have been done in minutes like planned. They would have walked in, shown the gun and got everyone to fill the bags whilst one of the bank's staff let them in to the rooms where the security boxes were. It would have been job done, but no, they wanted to see what was in the other safe. They would have been out of there and in the stolen getaway car, dad had told me on a visit to prison once. The gold bars were their downfall and had got them all nicked, this time they were caught bang to rights. As they struggled out the bank they were surprised to see the police, they were everywhere and soon had the gang in the back of a police van.

"Dad had managed to slyly stick three diamonds up his arse before they got him. He had smuggled them out of prison to me on a visit. He told me to give one to mum and to keep one for myself. He said I should tell mum to take the other one to a jewellers in Camden town to get some money for it. He could have some sent in to him to see him through his bird and mum could have a few quid to play around with whilst he was away. With the other two, mum and I had rings made while dad got eight years at the Old Bailey for his part in the robbery." She showed me this big stone on her ring.

"Whilst inside doing his bird he had told mum to move on and not to wait for him as it was a long one. He said it was better for both of them and the kids if she moved on, it was killing her to keep coming to visit. He said that it wasn't fair on her and the kids to keep coming up to see him all the time, even though he loved us all so very much and thought about us all the time. She was heartbroken and hurting for a bit. Then she did move on and that's when she met up with the casino gangster. She had got a job as a cleaner at the casino and when he saw her that was that, from cleaner to gangster's moll all within a week. She was gutted and she loved dad very much, but there was nothing else she could do but just do as he had asked and move on. So she did as she was told, you can't blame her.

"Prison breaks up a lot of lovers, you know. Even though she would have stayed with dad and seen the eight years through with him, if he had let her I'm sure she would have. Mum was very loyal and strong like that, he just wouldn't send out V.O.'s for her or us anymore. She tried to come up to see him but the prison said 'no V.O. then no visiting' it was as simple as that. It must have broken their hearts in two. She would write letters to him nearly every day with photos of us in them and send me off to post them but he never wrote back. He said that it was too emotional to keep coming out on visits in the hall just for half hour and that it was unfair on us all having to be searched all the time. We didn't mind as long as we got to see him. He said that it was useless writing back as nothing really happens in there; it was just the same shit different day.

"Even though Johnny was in the marines and could only go when he was on leave, he still didn't see him. When dad got out, he had seen mum in the local café. He had walked in and saw her sat there, so he sat on her table and that was that, back together again. She was over the moon to see him, a bit angry but upset too. The casino gangster was angry at first, but accepted it without much trouble. He had his own troubles to deal with which was lucky for dad, as the casino gang member's firm could have bumped him off in a moment of jealousy at any time. Dad needed money when he was released from the nick. So he went straight on to robbing a post train on his release with some people he had met in prison.

"They had planned this job while they were let out of their cells on exercise. While everyone thought they were playing chess and socialising, they were planning this robbery. The plans were stuck under the chessboard. Dad looked after this fella in prison, so he would have done anything in return. This fella had nothing not even a stamp, but dad pulled some strings and got him a job in the servery. Dad had got friendly with one of the guards and was now paying him to bring in a little bit of puff here and there. Dad then got his cellmate to sell on to other inmates for triple what he had paid for it and for extra canteen. So dad would halve all the canteen they would get with this fella he shared a cell with. By doing this it helped them both right out.

"The fella said he would help him out when they got out for all his help. He was going to do a big robbery that he and his brother had planed and said he would share it with dad as a thank you for all his help in there.

"Well this was well up dad's street. Before long they were all playing chess, learning about the robbery that this fella had planned. So one night he was down in Kings Cross, they all sneaked onto the tracks and onto the post office train. Armed police caught him leaving the train with two big bags of money and parcels. They told him to stay still and not to move. The phone had gone off in his pocket, he went to answer it. As he did his pal pushed him through the door by accident in the hurry to get out of there. He hadn't realized that my dad had been told to stay still by the police outside. So they shot him as he pulled out the phone. He died in hospital a day later from the wound. His pal was gutted and has never forgiven himself for it. He is now a recluse. He did a five year stretch in Wormwood Scrubs for his involvement.

"The other people that were with him on the train job had heard the shot and jumped off the train. They ran off up the tracks with the police chasing them to the getaway car with all they could carry. They had got away and were now living it large out in Cyprus with the spoils they had got. I never knew who it was. They were sending money over to Johnny and me for a little while, but then it all stopped. The train robber had got nicked when he shot someone in the leg for taking nude photos of his girlfriend from across the street. This robbery had hit the papers in a big way. He was a good robber and had got away with a few jobs before this had happened. Or so Uncle Ronnie said when he sent letters over from Spain to mum. That's how we were able to live close to the fast lane like we did, it was all down to his robberies.

"If it weren't for dad and this casino gangster, then we would of all been in hand-me-downs. Now and again his face was in the papers and sometimes on the police wanted list. The police would still come round every now and then, even if it weren't dad's bit of work. They would just want to ask him questions, I suppose they thought he would have an involvement in it somewhere. If he didn't do what he did, then I guess we would have all been shopping at charity shops like everyone else was back then. Times were hard back in them days. That's why dad done what he did or that's why he said he done it, to us and mum once we had found out more about his antics. I guess there was no denying it at that point, what he was all about. Dad had said that he could give us the best life he could by doing what he did. He said that doing these jobs gave him the freedom to spend time with us, and take us to places and enjoy life better together. Right or wrong, he did have a point. So there was some sort of method to his madness even if he was wearing tights on his head most nights. He would laugh and say it was a bit of a fetish he had to his pals, whilst they were all down the pub celebrating in Kilburn. When robberies went off well they all had a few quid in their pockets and big smiles on their faces.

"After dad finally came out from his eight-year stretch, mum left the casino fella and got back together with dad. Things were good 'til he died. He said that it would be his last job, this train robbery. Mum had heard him talking on the phone from the next room about it all. I had overheard him say to mum whilst I was on the stairs listening at the house late one night. I couldn't sleep as it had been thundering and lightning which had woken me up. So I got up and crept to the top of the stairs to listen to mum's voice, that way I felt a bit safer. If I could hear mum and dad's voices downstairs, I knew I was safe. She was telling dad no more jobs please and that we had enough now and to stop. He said that it would be the last one. Then things would be OK and he could retire. We could all move to Spain as planned with Uncle Ronnie, who was dad's pal he had met from the nick. We could live large and put all this behind us with what was on the train. Well it was his last one, as he had got himself killed doing it. So after, that mum went back to the casino mobster. He had heard the news and had her picked up and brought to the casino. He said that anything she needed he would sort out. He and Johnny paid for the big send off for dad, which was nice of him. Even though there was a little atmosphere from Johnny and me and some of dad's pals for a few years, 'til it all died down a bit. We had the hump with mum too for getting back with the casino owner so quickly after dad's death. Even though he had gone halves with Johnny on the funeral and had paid off the outstanding mortgage for us on the house in Oxford Street. The casino mobster also had lined up Johnny with some work on the doors at a club upon being discharged out the marines.

"He had got caught smoking drugs and selling nicked guns to gangsters. Well mum and the casino mobster had both got killed themselves after that in a revenge killing outside the casino. That's what I was led to believe, or was told back then as Johnny was there and had saw it all happen. He had been on leave from the marines and had gone down to see mum at the casino. He was there in the back of the car when the car had been sprayed with bullets. He just got a glimpse of the fella that did the shooting. As the bike pulled up Johnny looked at the fella that stood there and let the gun off. He then ran over to the car and pulled a revolver out and let off one shot making sure the casino fella was dead. That's when Johnny got a good look at his face. He ran off and Johnny crawled out of the car. Mum wasn't moving, she was dead. The Russian then jumped on the back of the bike as it sped off.

"Still to this day he hasn't seen him since. Johnny was well lucky none of the bullets had hit him. He had acted dead when the gunman had come over to shoot the casino owner, and had lain down as low as possible and watched it all happen. He had shouted 'No get down' but it was too late. The hit had been executed and once the bike had gone he had held mum in his arms. He looked up to see the biker drive off and he got a glimpse of his face again, seeing a teardrop tattooed on the left side of his eye. He had heard his Russian accent as he told the bike rider to drive. Johnny had tears streaming from his eyes, he was helpless and with all his contacts and training he couldn't help her. Loads of people had come running out to try to help but it was too late.

"That day had changed him. From then onwards he was never the same again. Something had clicked in his heart and it had become as cold as ice. Someone told Johnny recently that it was someone at the casino firm who kept fretting about a large overdue debt, and something to do with the Russian mafia taking over parts of London. The person got scared that the casino mobster was putting pressure on him to pay off the casino debts he had acquired. So this person went and hired a gunman from Russia to shoot the boss, the casino gangster before they could get to him. Mum got caught in the firing line and died in Johnny's arms. That's where Johnny's anger comes from; he couldn't do anything to help her, he was powerless. So that's why I only have Johnny left now and it looks like I'm going to lose him too for sometime now, when he gets birded off for these murders. These police aren't on Johnny's or the Firm's payroll. They're from a different force. They are well out of the jurisdiction and some are new to the forces and looking for results to move up in the ranks. They're all connected to the Special Branch. So he was on his own now. He used to be so careful and do everything in stealth mode and to the book. That's why he had got away with killing so many people, or that's what I've heard. Well that's what people tell me about him when they talk about Johnny. They say he is a natural born killer if the price is right, and life is cheap in his mind.

"When I would ask why everyone was so scared of him they would just say he was a very nice man but on the other side of the coin he was a very dangerous one. You didn't want to upset him. He kept all his cards close to his chest at all times and never pulled any ace cards out, even though he had loads of them up his sleeve. Everyone owed him a favour in one way or another, although he kept it all quiet. I'm sure they knew or had heard he was a contract killer; this was just stupid of him. He is the sort of man that he takes only what you owe, no more and no less. If the Firm gave you a day then a day is all you had. He would do what was necessary at the time of the visit each time he came to talk with you. He said he would have to listen to some of the lame excuses about how the money owed couldn't be paid on time and that's when people started to get hurt. He would put another 100 on top of anyone's bill for his time. So people knew where the hiding or killing had come from but they couldn't prove it, well not 'til now. He was a nice fella and now I'm going to lose him too. Since he's been banged up I have learned so much more about him and what he's all about. He's done a good job to keep as much away from me about him as possible, but now it's all out in the open."

She had been through it all with him you could see it in her face, I thought. I looked closely at how beautiful she really was. She had tears welling up in her eyes every now and then as she talked about her mum, dad and brother. We came to a nice restaurant and sat down, ordered our food and wine and waited. She seemed to cheer up a bit more and then said, "So that's my story. What's your story then?" She had opened her heart to me; it felt like I had known her for a lifetime. It made me want her so much more. Mandy then asked, "What about you?"

"Well, Mandy, I got sucked in at an early age by thinking that it was all about making money. I had loads of acquaintances, but not many true pals. I was always trying to be up there with the big boys not caring who I hurt along the way. Having no cares in the world and thinking that you never got caught and that money meant everything. It was all like it was in the movies for a bit, sniffing hard every day, not having to get up until late and earning more than those that had got up early and done a hard bit of graft. Thinking I was charley large bollocks, as we had everyone respecting us for all the wrong reasons.

"It wasn't 'til I started working with a top firm that I found out what it was really all about. It could get very ugly at the top and even uglier at the bottom. I was now well in with the Firm selling a few grams, ounces and the odd nine bar back in my local town. Running money, guns, people and women about, which then led me to be introduced to others in these criminal circles. Then I ended up going in to other manors and doing much bigger things that were best kept quiet about. Like that shooting I never did properly.

"I thought that you could have any woman you want, and say or do anything you want. But looking back, people I knew hadn't made it any better then I probably would have if I had just worked hard or harder.

"Don't get me wrong, some people made a good living out of doing the wrong things but most never do. It's just a quick boost at the time and for the amount of bird you do it for don't seem to weigh up or seem worth it. I'm sure others have paid their price one way or another but it weren't for me. Yes I got to meet loads of nice people, had a few quid here and there which helped out a great deal, but with more money came more risks. It made life that little bit easier, but not simpler, really. With the money came more stresses and a lot of jealousy. It was hard to get rid of the money without someone noticing or grassing you up. Even your friends can turn sour on you when it comes to the crunch and they start to owe you a few quid for gear. I had some great times and some very low times and then I got nicked; done some prison, put my family through it, got myself a cocaine habit and met loads of very strange, dangerous but very interesting people and a few mugs. I had a few laughs, made some good friends and some bad enemies and rubbed shoulders with a few stars and famous people.

"I learnt respect the hard way and learnt that some people were worried or scared of what you knew. The people you would hang around with or now worked for within the Firm, making you now capable of as they were behind you. They didn't respect the person I was; they just looked at you and your reputation that you were now their free meal ticket. Not at you as a person. You now had these contacts that they would only read about or saw in the newspapers.

"I also met some very nice and interesting women along the way and some very ugly ones too. I made some good friends, one called Mr B, a very nice man indeed, a gangster of course. These days everyone thinks they're a gangster and most are just drug dealers. They're on every street corner and they know everyone. It's not like it was before where it was only a select few that could get a few E's or some charley or puff. Now everyone is one or thinks they are one.

"Now Mr B. Some people liked him, some hated him and some were curious and intrigued by his way of life. Also a fella called Old School, now he was proper. Not forgetting Mr P who has now changed from Mr Marge to Speedy Gonzales and is now a retired gangster, found peace with his family and put his old ways to rest. And not forgetting Mark the true Oxford English gentleman and his kind and loving family. Mattie the Mac and his family, they were all gentlemen to Shane and also me in one way or another. They were in different leagues and classes of their own. I got well mixed up in it all and thought I was Scarface for a minute.

"With as much powder thrown at me as I could handle, sniff or sell and as many clubs as I wanted to go to and get in for free. With as much money as I could count and needed to spend, I was pulling in near on 7 grand a week and that was just from the Wood for the big boys. I was being shown round to different faces and villains, as it's all good when the money's coming in but when it don't that's when you're fucked, excuse my French.

"I got myself into loads of debt towards the end but paid every last penny back. Made a few quid and sniffed a few quid; done a few drug runs, stayed in some very nice hotels and landed in some very nasty prisons. I ate in some very fancy restaurants; had some very dangerous people try to kill me and had to become a drugs mule. I had friends steal from me; I had to hurt friends and learnt the only true friends you could have could be your mum and dad but that's only for some of us I guess. I've been stabbed, kidnapped and nearly shot. Done some dangerous things and witnessed some very bad things too that I'm not too proud of.

"I also had protection from the Firm that allowed me to do the things I needed to do when I needed to do them without looking over my shoulder all the time. So you could say I was blinded by the lights and well and truly sucked in. A proper sucker for the pound note, you might say. If I could make a few quid then that was me, whether it be drugs, stolen goods, snide stuff, hurting or collecting. I was there and really not thinking about the consequences.

"And now, darling, that's why I find myself out here in Spain with you, as I have one last thing to clean up. Then I'm done with all this. Being out here with you is the best part of my life so far. And right now I'm trying to sort out the mess that I now find myself in once again. So there you have it. That's me, darling, in a nutshell, I'm no gangster, never have been, never will be. I'm just a gentleman in a league of my own, who if anything is or was a gangster's runner. I'm always trying to pay my debts by borrowing off Peter to pay Paul, and Paul to pay Peter. Or doing this deal and that just to stay above board and make ends meet. As with easy money comes easier spending and a lot of responsibility. Once you're in someone's pocket that's where they like you to stay. Other people call it swings and roundabouts, I call it juggling. It's like I take two steps forward and ten back. I let the big boys play at being the gangsters."

She smiled at me then sighed, "Mmmm." The food came and we ate and drank.

"Would you like to go to a club, Mandy?"

"No thanks."

"OK."

So we headed back to the villa after we wined and dined, entwined in each other's arms. She put her head on my shoulder now and then as we walked and talked. The sun was going down and the cold sea breeze was being blown towards us. It was a very pleasant evening. Now we had got more acquainted, and the wine had kicked in a little. We had both let our guard down a bit and let some home truths come out the bag. I felt a bit closer to her; maybe closer than any man had been before. Johnny would have her stop getting close to certain people. Who knows? I felt a bit less paranoid being around her seeing as she had told me a lot about her personal life. She told loads about Johnny the hit man, and the other people he was involved within the Firm. Which meant a bit of trust had been passed between us now.

Then I said it, "Why is a beautiful woman like you still single?"

She laughed, "How do you know that?"

"Well just a good guess as you never talk about your fella, and I noticed you ain't wearing any ring."

"Well… Johnny scares them all off and they're not man enough to stand up to him. So they leave. I don't want a gangster or villain, and most of them are. Or I just seem to attract them and then they're all full of it. Not all just most. I just want a nice genuine man and there aren't many of them around today. And I don't want someone who would be sniffing hard and banging whores or cocaine sluts left right and centre once my back was turned. Girls in the back of cabs or club toilets after a sniffing session together, or in the back of a limousine on the way home. Some girls seem to do what they do by getting excited by a few quid. I have seen how it changes people. I just want a true and honest gentleman with nothing to hide. Without a worry of him being in and out of prison just a plain old honest fella."

We had got back to the villa quite quickly. It was quite late and we both had a lot to do in the morning. So I leant forward and we kissed each other, slowly on the lips. Mandy then cuddled me and said thanks and goodnight, before going to bed, once again without me. Gutted. I walked over to my bed and set the alarm clock to go off at 4am to give me enough time to get ready for my meeting with the Jewellery Thief at his nightclub in the morning. After all that's why I had come here. I undressed and pulled the cold sheet over me. It was a hot sticky night and the moon was a full one. It shone in through the window so I sat listening to the crickets for a bit before I drifted off to sleep.

The alarm went off and I felt nervous and clammy. This was it, Judgement day. Now I was here out in Spain and would have to face up to it all, just like the note had said back at the Blind Beggars pub. They were right, I had placed all my cards on their table and all my ace cards had now run out. So all I had left was a handful of jokers. I would now know what I had to do or how I was going to pay the 30 grand off for them, and to repay the liberty back to redeem myself. If they would let me that was. Or would they now be getting rid of me there and then? Just like they had done with others who had crossed the line and had followed in my footsteps. I was showered and dressed in no time at all. As

I walked out the door Carlos came up the marble stairs to meet me.

"Hi, señor. Ola, my friend, get in the car. I'll drive you to the nightclub… The Jewellery Thief is ready to see you now."

We jumped into the convertible Audi, Carlos turned to me. "How is Mandy by the way?"

"She's fine. She's still asleep."

"Has she seen Johnny?"

"She's going today."

"OK, my friend, let's go," he started the car.

"Is he OK?" I asked.

"Who?"

"The Jewellery Thief."

"Yes. Why do you ask?"

"Well, I just wanted to know what this was all about."

"My friend, I don't know. He just said that he wanted to see you, and told me to come get you to make sure you're at the club on time. So I have. We never talk about other people's business. You should know that by now."

We arrived just outside the club after a ten-minute drive up the beachfront. It was just getting light. Wow what a club Diamonds was, they weren't wrong. It looked like a castle from the outside, well it sort of was. It had been restored and refurbished into a nightclub; the outside walls were the old remains of the castle. It must have held 1500 people. There were red carpets that ran up the middle of the floor.

To get in you walked up three steps, and in past two glass doors. The floor was all made from marble and had little bits in it that lit up like diamonds set into the floor. There were lights and tables everywhere and nice comfy leather settees. There were stylish pictures of diamonds, jewellery and valuable stones hanging up. Even a V.I.P. bit that said 'gangsters' paradise' on the entrance in big gold letters on a black backing, bordered with gold outlines. It had two big golden palm trees either side of the words 'gangsters' paradise.' There were pictures of gangsters; old and new, a picture of the Jewellery Thief and Mr Nice, and about every gangster that had been to the club or you could read about.

From Dave Courtney to Escobar to Scarface to the Krays and other faces known and unknown.

I walked behind Carlos, looking at the surroundings. There were massive speakers neatly set in to the decor, which were very plush. They were everywhere, in every room with a flat screen TV too playing the movies to the songs that were now playing in the club. This was a proper upmarket club and a bar in every room. Some women were sitting around a table laughing out loud and joking with Big Wheel, the other minder, and two doormen in the main room enjoying a drink and a giggle.

Carlos walked over and said, "Hi, everyone. I take it it was another good night then." As he then introduces me to them all. "This is the Cookster from London; and this is our staff. Big Wheel you all ready know."

"Hi Cookster," everyone said in unison.

Then Big Wheel stood up and shook my hand and cuddled me. "Hi, mate, good to see you again."

One of the girls said, "Hey, Cookster... fancy some champagne?"

"No thanks, darling, but I know what I do fancy." I looked her up and down, me being my cheeky self. I looked her in the eye and she then looked me up and down. She gave me a foxy smile. "Maybe after when I come back out here, if I do that is."

She laughs and winked at me. "OK," she said. "It's here if you want it."

"Is it now?" I said, being a bit up front and witty. They all laughed again. She looked at me again then giggled. They were all quite pissed. I then winked at her and she winked back again. There was something there between us.

"Well your glass is here waiting for you and so am I," as she poured out a fresh glass, then smiled at me again to see my reaction. She was now being very up front, which I liked a lot; I smiled back. She was kind of quiet with very foxy eyes; she was sexy and had some very sexy legs out on show. She had nice dark black hair and looked a bit like Lara Croft.

They continued talking and laughing as I was ushered past them and into the office by Carlos. "Let's go, mate," he said. "We don't want to keep him waiting, do we?"

We walked into the club office. As I went in I looked back and the girl looked over at me again. We both smiled, she turned round and flicked her hair and continued with the conversation that was going on around the table.

I now found myself standing in the office. The Jewellery Thief was sat at a big desk in front of a big screen that monitored every nook and cranny of the club. He was counting the takings for that night; by the looks of it it had been a good one. He was listening to some classical music as we stood and watched him. He picked up the bundles of money, flicked quickly through them and then placed them carefully in the safe. He then picked up his glass of champagne, looked at me then slowly took a sip. He picked up the small gold spoon that was in the small crystal bowl on the desk. "Excuse me for a second" he brought the spoon to his nose and sniffed hard at it. Then as the white powder quickly disappeared off the spoon he placed the spoon back and just sat there and glared at me. For a bit I could see his pupils start to enlarge as he looked at me. He picked up the remote control swivelled on his chair and turned the music off. Told Christine the manger to leave the office, as he wanted to talk some business with his new guest.

She looked at me and then said, "OK" as the door was opened by big Billy the northern henchman that the Jewellery Thief had in the office with him. He then swivelled back and looked at the CCTV. Billy said, "Sit down" as big Carlos leaned against the door.

The silence was a bit eerie at first, as the Jewellery Thief just sat there and glared at me. I was well out of my depth again and I knew it. I was sitting with the crème de la crème of clientele. This was far from small time drug dealers in Borehamwood or London, where you could tell them a few excuses and knock them for a few weeks trying to get their money back. This was the sort of clientele where the police didn't bother kicking the door off with their feet or a battering ram. This was the sort of big time guy where the police needed to use a bulldozer to do their raids, to collect their hundred keys of cocaine and a few guns when they come in. This was the big time and I was now sitting round the Knight's table looking very small indeed, looking more like the jester. I offered my hand to shake his, which he did back as he stood up.

"We have a lot to talk about and you have a lot to think about," he said as he sniffed hard again from the small bowl of cocaine. He paced up and down and said, "Mr Nice has more important things to take care of, if you will excuse him. He sends his apologies but said he hopes you're not wasting his time or ours and that your co-operation is most wanted at this time. If you are he said you will become the most important thing on his list. He will make his way straight over here to personally see you himself and to see that you are in some sort of pain, my son. He will shoot you himself and take you out the equation.

I swallowed hard; he had just let the cat out the bag. I was to be shot, taken out somewhere and have a few bullets put in the back of my nut.

"It takes a lot of bollocks to come here. After what you have done, my friend, and the predicament you now find yourself in." He looked at me hard studying my every move as he paused then said, "Cookster, Cookster."

"Yes?"

"I hear you're a court usher, which may just save your life. Haven't joined the other side, have you son? If you have, you'll find yourself right in the lion's den, and that means you'll be sleeping in a body bag tonight. That's if they find your body after Billy has finished with you." He looked over to Billy then back at me.

The Jewellery Thief wasn't the friendly person I had once met in prison, or the person who had been well happy with me a year ago when he thought I had helped them out by doing this shooting in Kensington.

"No," I said. "It's just a job and keeps me out of trouble, pays the rent and keeps the money coming in."

"So how's it going then?" he said.

"It's OK," I replied.

"This could come in very handy you know, with what I have in mind and what I'm about to put to you. This could be your lucky day, son."

"Why?"

"Well, let me tell you something; Johnny is going to be extradited in two weeks to England. He will appear at the Old Bailey."

"OK… and?"

"Well that's where you come in to it all, son, where I give you another chance to redeem yourself. To put things right, which right now are very, very wrong. I am very unhappy with you, son, right now, and so are other members of this Firm. I want you to find out which courtroom he will be in; find out which prosecutor and find out everything you can about it all. Then once you have everything find out more, like where the prosecutor, lives, sleeps and eats, and who with. Then we can influence him in anyway we can to do things out of the ordinary that he would never think of doing. Like sleep with a friend of yours or with a man when he's drunk. Then threaten to show the photos to his wife or something along those lines. I don't care what you do Cookster or what it takes. I want Johnny out of there. Set him up with loads of drugs. Find something to make him do exactly what you want him to do. I want results Cookster. No bullshit this time, you tried and failed before. There's no room for flyers in this Firm, do you hear me, son?"

He sniffs hard again. "Maybe photos of him taking drugs or accepting money after a case that has gone wrong for him, so it looks like he has taken a back hander to lose the case. Photos of him doing something dodgy or untowards, anything. Find anything he may have done that we can expose on him. Like he has a load of child porn that he downloaded off a copper, if he don't do as he is told, then the allegation will go out to your pals in the press. If you can't find anything then you need to make things happen around him like your life now depends on it. Well it does from where we are all sitting.

"I have already looked into springing Johnny from the courtroom, but he may be arm guarded and it will be too risky. If I thought I could I would. It is quite a high profile case now it's all in the papers over here. Doing it this way will leave fewer questions to be answered. When you do free him for us give the prosecutor the offer of £10,000 that Mandy has. Then we know Johnny will be coming home for sure. Better still get to the police officer heading the case, see if he has something we can get him on. Then he could make the evidence go missing, like the gun or the bullets.

"Maybe you should try to get to the witnesses. I have spoken to most, but there is a few on police protection that no one can get to but you. You're the court usher so you of all people will have no dramas. I have sent the boys round to see as many as we can, or that we know of that were in the club that night to persuade them that their vision was blurred. They were either drunk or on drugs or that they saw nothing. So it's all up to you now, try everything. I don't care how you pull this one off just get it done. You've seen the film *The Runaway Jury*, well if you haven't, get it out and watch it. You might even learn something. It should give you some sort of idea of the things you might need to do.

"Once Johnny has been let off then we will let you off with the little £30,000 you owe me and I'll keep my mouth shut about the liberty you took with us. Mr Nice only thinks you owe the Firm money at this moment in time, not about the liberty you have taken with us, or the embarrassment. He has left me in charge of your future and right now it looks bleak. Very fucking bleak from where I'm sitting. Mr Nice has gone berserk and said of all the people to let me down with money it turns out to be the Cookster, after all we have done for the little git."

The Jewellery Thief then shouts, "I could be a fucking fortuneteller. If you fuck this up for me then you are a dead man. That's your future, son. I don't need any crystal fucking ball to see that. You will do this Cookster and not just *let us* believe you have this time round. Do you hear me? Am I talking good plain fucking Queen's English? Do you understand the alphabet, son?"

I kept nodding.

He was blowing a blood vessel as each sentence came out, "Son, the Firm's the one Y.D.A.Y.A.T. Do you understand?" he sat down again, shouting at me and leaning over the desk so he was right in my face.

"What's the Y.D.A.Y.A.T?"

He loses the plot again. I should have just sat there all quiet and carried on nodding but no I had to open my big mouth once again.

"So you didn't fucking understand did ya? So why are you sitting there nodding your head like fucking Churchill the dog as if you do know, son. Well let me explain it once more, loud and fucking clear, as you seem to be a bit Mutton Jeff. Either that or you are a completely stupid cunt. Y.D.A.Y.A.T. stands for YOU DO AS YOU ARE TOLD from now on!"

"Yes I'll do it."

"Well, son," he said raising his voice that bit louder. "You don't have any fucking choice, now do you?" As he pulled open a drawer in the desk, leaned forward and took out a bullet, rolling it in his fingers and from side to side; looking at me. Then he throws it at me. It hits me on the chest then falls onto the desktop; spins round a bit then come to a rest pointing at me with the tip under my chest. Of all the places to stop it had stopped there, just like that.

"Look close at that bullet, son, as it's got your name all over it." He looks over to Billy the big northern henchman, who then grabs my head and pushes my head onto the table right next to the bullet.

"Go on look at it, as this will be the last thing you see once this enters your brain," the Jewellery Thief shouts, "once Billy pulls the trigger, son." I looked down and looked more closely at the bullet my head was pushed on to the table all scrunched up. It was a 9mm and fuck me it felt cold on my face let alone having it fired in my nut. He had had it engraved with my name on it.

"See we ain't playing games, son." My arse was now twitching like a rabbit's nose. "So get it done… Or I'll get you done…" He was getting very angry now. "Whilst you're down there pass us that bullet back here, we might need it very soon." I was let up and Billy the northern Henchman let go of me.

I then handed it back. "I'll get the next available flight back and get on it right away."

"I know you will, son." He stared.

I was getting a bit uncomfortable now that had happened. He had got his message across and I understood completely. So now I wanted to be out of there fast before he lost the plot again.

"Enough said then between us, 'til this little matter has all been cleaned up... and Cookster?"

"Yes?"

"We ain't walking round the prison fucking playground now. So there are no prison guards to save your arse if it kicks off and gets too out of hand for you. Do you hear me? So don't fuck this one up, son, will you? Or the only place for you will be with the worms when they bury you. Hope you had a nice stay in my villa and make sure you clean up your fucking mess before you leave. I'll tell Mr Nice that you have seen the light and that you asked how he was. That you thanked him for giving you another chance to pay the money back you owe the Firm. He thinks I have gone to all this trouble to get you over here for an outstanding debt, and that's the way I would like to keep it. Otherwise I'll be the laughing stock if he knew the truth, and you would already be dead. When he gets back from Colombia I'll let him know how the law of the land lies with us but if it goes wrong, he will know the disrespect you have shown us all."

"Yes," I said.

"Now fuck off and do one. I don't want to see you again 'til it is all done, and if it ain't then I won't see you again will I, son. You'll be buried somewhere and a thing of the past. The only thing you'll get from me is a wreath, and you'll be just a distant memory."

"Thanks. It was nice to see you again and pleasant to be out in Spain." I said licking his arse for some Brownie points; after all he had just bitten my head off and given me another chance to redeem myself.

"It's nice to get away even if it's just for a short break," I said trying to pull my tongue out of his arse. My arse kissing had worked.

As he calmed down a little, he said, "Well once this mess is over, son, and Johnny is a free man, you'll be welcome over here as often as you like. I'll even get you a job on the door at my club if you want it, but until then you just get your nut down. Get on with this little job and get this mess sorted out and this money paid back. Then we'll talk again. Otherwise in time, I will have forgotten all about your miserable existence and you'll be pushing up the daisies. Fuck this up and I'll be on the ginger hunt. Now Billy, get this piece of shit out of here."

Billy grabbed me once more, pulling me to my feet and telling me to move. The Jewellery Thief then said, "Tell the manger to come back in," as Billy threw me out the door I heard Carlos say, "Yes, boss," as it shut again. "I'll take him back to the villa."

I stumbled out the office, a bit shaken and a bit worse for wear after hearing all that. Carlos then came out shaking his head as he looked at me and whistled a sort of 'sounds like you're in trouble mate'. Then he told the manageress to go back in. We got just outside the office door and I looked up, smiled and said "You could say that; trouble you don't know the half of it, Carlos." I then said to Carlos. "I didn't know he did coke."

"Well, mate, it gets a grip on us all sooner or later. If you're round it 24/7 like this lot is. It's like sitting around a table of women with their tits out, if they keep sticking them in your face for too long you'll end up sucking on one of them, won't you."

"Well, I guess you're right." We laughed, which made me feel better again. Then we walked up to the table where everyone was still sitting. The cute, sultry looking girl handed me the glass of champagne. Our fingers touch as she passes the glass to me. She was flirting with me the little minx. We looked at each other with that sort of look of 'you know you wanted it and you want it now'. I could tell she liked me and very much, flirting hard with me but I had to get a grip of things to get this job done. My life depended on it. Even if she was hot and wanted me to take her over to the gangsters' paradise part of the club and start kissing and caressing her passionately. Then whilst the going was good she would gently ease herself up on to the first table we come to. I'd gently pull up her dress as she would be pulling eagerly at my trousers. I would then lift and pull her g-string to the side after a couple of rubs, she would be inviting me to come in with her other hand frantically pulling at my pants to unleash the beast within them. So I'd give her a good hard seeing to while she was laying there, legs apart; sunny-side up on one of the tables. All this would have happened faster than I could have drunk my whole glass of champagne down in one gulp. I drank the champagne straight down in two gulps.

"Still alive then," Big Wheel said jokingly, bringing me out my daydream. He had heard the Jewellery Thief shouting at me from sitting where he was. My attention came back from her eyes to what was really going on in front of me, and what Big Wheel had just said.

"Yes," I said back to Big Wheel. "But for how long who knows." He laughed, and then they all laughed. They thought it was all a big joke but for me it was my life on the line. I placed the glass on the table. Carlos pulled out a glass box from behind the D.J.'s boxes. He walked back to the table, opened it up and did the honours by putting some lines out onto the table in front of us all. Now we're talking. We all hoovered the powder up. Passing the fifty-pound note round that Big Wheel had kindly rolled up for us to use. We were now passing it around like we were playing pass the parcel. After my line, I said bye to all of them. Then the quiet looking girl stood up and said, "It was nice to meet you."

"You too, darling," I replied.

Then she cuddled me, pulling me close and pressing herself on me, she then whispered into my ear, "I want you" which made me blush a bit. She moved away and said, "Come back soon."

"I sure will, honey." She was thinking the same thing I was. I passed her the note, and then kissed her lips full on. "Don't worry, darling, keep it wet and well groomed for me won't you?" I whispered back in her ear, pulling her near to me again. She smiled back like she had won the lottery and giggled. I winked. I then asked Big Wheel for a 100-euro note and wrote my number down on it and gave it to the girl.

"Here, darling, get yourself something nice and give me a call soon," then I walked out the club with Carlos just after I gave Big Wheel a firm handshake. He said, "Take care, mate, and give my best to London."

You could tell he was missing it, but for his own good he had to make a life out here now and the Firm was now his new family. Whether he liked it or not, I suppose he was under the same manors as I was. The (Y.D.A.Y.A.T), you do as you are told. I left and walked out with Carlos to the car and before long I was back at the villa saying bye to Carlos.

When I got back Mandy was ready and looked a bit worried about the visit to Johnny.

"Hope they let me see him."

"I'm sure they will, darling. You look fantastic. Do you have your I.D.?" I said. "Otherwise you might not get in."

"Come here." I cuddled her and told her everything that had just happened and that it would all be OK. I'm sure of it. She smiled nervously and had a tear running down her face that I wiped away with my thumb as I held her face. I told her about the plan that the Jewellery Thief had come up with. She was sobbing and said that the money meant nothing to her; just having Johnny back would be better then having it. I said, "Look don't worry about it now." I kissed her on the forehead.

"I could use it to help free him if I need to." Just like the Jewellery Thief had anticipated, or had they clued her up already without me knowing?

"We need to go in the next day or two," I said. "Let's book a flight back to London so I can get working on this plan to get Johnny home and dry."

"OK, I'll go pack. You get down the airport and get our flights back to London sorted out OK? I'll see Johnny and then we can go back to England as soon as possible. If I can help with this plan let me know," she said. "I'd like to help as much as possible."

"OK, I'll keep you in mind, Mandy, we'll talk more later. Go see Johnny now and I'll meet you back here."

"OK."

The cab came and she left to see Johnny. I had told her not to tell Johnny anything, just to plead not guilty. As Mandy was about to leave I wiped away the rest of her tears from her face. Mandy left and I lay back on the bed and just started buzzing from the Champagne and the lines that I had just had back at the club. Then I slowly looked out the window to see the sun, I felt the heat on my face. I closed my eyes and thought I could get used to living out here, away from the rat race back in London. Away from the phones all going off and everyone calling you morning noon and night for their drugs. Once again, I was a lucky man. I had been given one more chance, but luck had to run out soon. I thought.

Mr Nice and the Jewellery Thief were rightly pissed off with me after all they had done for me when I had come out of prison, and this is how I repaid them. Well I did try to do it for them. So I guess I did owe them the thirty grand still, seeing as I hadn't done the job completely. But I did take their money even if Mr Nice was pretending he didn't know for reasons unknown to me at this time. Or did he?

Finding the Prosecutor and the Police Officer and Making Them Work for Their Money at the Old Bailey

Soon we were back in London. Mandy had thanked me for coming out there with her; being able to see her brother meant the world to her. So I had scored some Brownie points in her eyes. I had to get to court to find out all the info I could on Johnny's case, which shouldn't have been too hard I thought. After all I worked at the court now so I had access to most things. I kissed Mandy on both sides of her cheeks and gave her a cuddle and said my goodbyes. I then went home ready for work the next day.

I went into work and went straight onto the computer to look up Johnny's name and there it was. The date he would arrive in England and the date he would start the trial at the Old Bailey. I phoned the C.P.S. unit to see who had been allocated to the trial, and who the caseworker was or which C.P.S. lawyer would be taking on the case. Within ten minutes all was revealed to me on screen and sent over by fax. It was a C.P.S. lawyer called Craig Douglas who was dealing with Johnny's case. Bingo! That was our man, Craig Douglas. Now all I had to do was find out who the copper was on the case; the one that would be dealing with the evidence. Then get to the Old Bailey and find more on this Craig Douglas fella; see what he looked like and try to get some photos of him if I could.

I left work and headed to the Old Bailey; the place was massive. I thought I was lucky being able to come in the front way, not having to be forced to come in round the back handcuffed off the sweat box (security van). Being escorted to a dark damp dingy 2 x 4 cell; to smell the musty smell from years of abuse that had gone on and to read all the writing on the walls.

Many unfortunate people had done and Johnny was about to embrace, well most had deserved this type of treatment. As luck would have it I just walked into the courthouse past the security guards and the metal detector and into the foyer. An announcement came over the speaker: "Craig Douglas, court four please, court four, Craig Douglas. All in the case of Stevens, court four." So there we have it court four it was.

I headed straight there and into the public gallery to see how good this man was. I walked into the court and sat down behind the glass in the gallery. I looked down to see the prosecutor Craig Douglas, a well dressed true Englishman in his late 40s. He had black hair that was neatly combed to one side in a parting. He was quite a small man but was very well spoken with precise English. He took his time before he spoke to say every word and explain everything in great detail, slowly and precisely. He wore a gold bracelet on his right wrist and had a ring on his finger, like the one from *Lord of the Rings*, with what looked like the same sort of writing or engraving on it. He had definitely been an Oxford university graduate at one stage. That's how close I was studying the man. He was very good at his job and very clever at getting his story across. I sat there listening attentively to him putting his case across to the judge and jury. Wow, this fella was well on the ball, and made no mistake of adding everything; putting in every last detail he could get away with to try and get the wrong answer. To get the result he wanted to prove the fella's guilt. He was asking the same questions but in a different way without being over-ruled by the defence's lawyer or the judge.

Johnny would have no chance of getting off. A man like this would have no involvement in the things that we would try and put on him. He knew the law with his eyes shut and would be able to make sure Johnny went down. I sat there and thought about how we can't persuade this prosecutor; he was mustard at his job. We stood no chance with trying to make him look bad. What I did notice was how the police officer was struggling a bit once he was called to the witness box. He kept asking if he could refer to his notes. Maybe we could find out who the officer was in charge of Johnny's case and who would be exhibiting the evidence. That might be the way forward and a little easier. Maybe that could be our weakest link or at least give me something positive to start with, I thought.

So I left the courtroom, went back to Barnet court and found out all the info I needed on the court computer. Once again the computer came back revealing all. It was Sergeant Tony Daniels dealing with this case. He was our man. He was the one we needed to get to. Not the prosecutor, this was the weakest link. This sergeant was heading the case with the ballistics expert, with evidence of the guns that Johnny had used in this case. So this was it. It had to be him and no one else I would concentrate on. We would work on him, the copper or should I say sergeant. I wrote his name down in my diary and left Barnet court sharpish as if my life depended on it. Well, looking back it did.

While I had been in Spain, Tom the Moose had been taking care of the business back in B/wood along with the Hairy Fella. In between shagging birds, banging out geezers left right and centre for the debts that they had run up, getting off his nut in the Woodcock pub and hiding from the Old Bill, he had also had been doing a few errands in London for the bigger firms. While making us all enough money so we could all put 500 quid in our pockets and a few lines up our noses whenever we felt the need. It was time to get the Moss ready to do some surveillance work on this sergeant, instead of it being done on him for once by the Old Bill.

So I had met up with the Moss at the Directors Arms pub in Manor Way, Borehamwood. He was sitting there with some other unsavoury characters who wished not to be identified and Phil the chef. He served up top nosh with top gear, as everyone else's cocaine was cut and at £40 a gram. For us it was all free and straight off the lump. To them it was more like disco dust than cocaine. So I walked in the boozer and sat down, even though I was on pub watch. I clued the Moss up with what we wanted from him and he agreed he would do it and put his ideas across to me. Soon he was up and ready to do this bit of work with us, which was to find out as much as we could on this copper. So we could corrupt or persuade him into losing the evidence on Johnny's big day in court.

Tom the Moose got right on the case and started to find out as much as he could within days. Following the copper back and forth to the local police station in Kentish town, to his house and to all the locations he would regularly go. He had logged down all his movements and found out what we needed to know about him. Where he lived, his car, the family, the kids' schools, the place he drank and the people he would meet. Also these odd massage parlours he went to on Thursdays over in Barnet. Yes everything, even the fact that the copper had turned a blind eye to having two girls working in a flat, just so he could get his own kicks. And surprisingly or not to an old villain's gambling den at the back of a pub that only opened after hours, backed onto a strip club just off the Finchley Road.

Now what we needed to do was set him up with something; or tell the villains he was playing cards with that he was a copper and then offer them the cash to get rid of him for us; or offer the copper the cash to lose the evidence somehow or some way. If there's no evidence then there's no proof of Johnny being there, or being connected to the killings. All they had on him were the prints on the gun; once it was gone it was gone. Now Mr Nice had seen to it that all the witnesses had been spoken to by members of his Firm and did not now want to attend court for reason unbeknown to the police. We had found out that this copper had loads of gambling debts to a big time crook that was well connected to a big Irish firm in Islington. He was meeting up with him to gamble most Fridays.

The copper was in the process of getting divorced as his missus thought he was having an affair with another copper, due to him being out late most nights and working so much. She had had enough. The Moss said he had been outside their house watching them argue.

"Work, work, work that's all you ever do, coming in at four and three in the morning expecting things to be OK. I bet you've been with her again," she shouted.

"I have been working late. I'm on this big case."

"Saying you're working late, leaving me to take care of the kids morning noon and night, and there's never enough time for them or me. That's it; I've had it with you and your drunkenness. We're getting a divorce."

Tom said that she was really going to town on him and started throwing his belongs out the window. Poor man Tom thought. Well he was going to loads of massage parlours. So in a way she was right, things were going from bad to worse for him all within a couple of days. Now the missus was taking him for all the money he had, for her and the kids by the sounds of it. That would now mean she would also be taking the family house away from him. He managed to get back in the house and calm her down a bit and he started bringing his stuff back in. She couldn't put up with his ways for no longer as she kept shouting her mouth off. Everyone outside their house could hear whilst she had a go at him. He was under a lot of pressure and she was adding to it, by the looks of it all.

"Some women, they just don't understand," Tom said. "A man has to do what a man has to do, you know the apple."

The copper was also in trouble with loans that the missus had run up on his card and they now had money problems and to top it all off he had now developed a drink problem. With all the stress he was getting who could blame him? He was under tremendous pressure from his job, and now the missus had cracked, to add salt to his injury this crook he was playing cards with kept telling him after their card matches that he needed to get his money sorted out soon. The crook was a snout, but as they got to know each other more he had run up a big gambling debt with him and it wouldn't be too long before he wanted it all in, copper or no copper. His patience was running out and other people he knew now wanted their money from him. He was on a downward spiral and now things had just got worse.

We were now on his tail looking for ways to make him slip up even more, in order to get Johnny out. But to our own advantage he seemed to be doing just fine, without us putting the pressure on him, just yet. He was no doubt our weakest link and not the Crown Prosecutor in Johnny's case. He was working rackets undercover with C.I.D. and dealers getting them to grass on each other for backhanders, which was a dangerous game to play. Well he did have the law on his side and he was working for the law so he was safe for now. We might have blown his cover that he was in fact a police sergeant, or showed his photo about to other villains that he was on the tail of. So really us coming along when we did must have been the answer to his prayers. Once we had turned up we had the money and he had the problems, which we could solve, only if he cooperated with our demands.

The money Mandy had would sort him right out, or at least put his life back on some sort of track for a bit. He liked going to a poker club on Fridays, behind the strip bar, the Golden Buck pub just on the outskirts of his manor, which Tom had found out all about. So he was rubbing shoulders with villains and crooks and hookers by night and with the law by day. If they all knew he was a copper then he was a dead man.

So it was time to get the lovely Mandy to do her stuff, get her in there somehow and start gambling, or to take a gamble on him falling for her. Well she was proper gorgeous and you would have to be a bit gay to say no to her sexy advances. We would have to look at a different angle to get Johnny out of all this mess if it all went wrong. We would have to ambush the court, but I'm sure armed police would be protecting it just as the Jewellery Thief had said. This was quite a high profile case and it would be too risky too do that as we would then all get nicked and be sharing a cell with Johnny, which would have been no good. Mr Nice and the Jewellery Thief would have tried to pull it off if they thought they could of got away with it that way, or if they thought it was the best way forward. They were the ones if anyone who could pull something that big off. So maybe it would be nigh impossible to do it. That's why they had got me involved I guess and not killed me. They knew I was now a court usher and I owed them a few quid so my hands were tied. If they got caught trying to ambush the court for Johnny and it went wrong then we would all be banged up. So I had to do it this way. It was the only way.

So this was the plan. It was too hot to try and get Mandy into the card game all unannounced and would have been a bit dodgy.

If they knew an outsider had just walked in and was now sniffing around they may have got a bit suspicious. So on Friday night after the sergeant had been gambling and drinking we had Mandy lie on the floor near to where his car was and start crying. We had some fella over her shouting at her and making out something untowards had just happened or was happening. When the sergeant came out a bit tipsy he saw Mandy, heard the commotion and ran over to her.

"Oi! Stop that. Leave her alone." Every one loves a hero and most men would have done the same. So the fella we had planted there ran off once he saw this copper come over towards him. He ran round the corner to our car and collected his £100 from us for doing what we had asked of him. He told us that she was now with the copper.

"What's up, love?"

"Nothing, leave me alone."

"Look it's OK. I'm a police officer," he said quietly so as not to be heard by anyone.

"Thank you," she said, "you must have scared him off."

"Who was it?"

"He was going to hurt me. He always does that after a drink. He's my ex partner, he won't leave me alone. He's infatuated with me, and keeps stalking me everywhere I go. I ran down here from the main street just to get away from him but I fell and he came after me and grabbed me. If you hadn't have stopped him he probably would have hit me again." The sergeant helped the gorgeous Mandy to her feet.

"I can see why he is infatuated with you. You're very attractive," he could now see her in her full glory. She giggled and pretended she was a bit tipsy as she fell against him on purpose; brushing herself up against him. She pulled her heels on properly and adjusted her low cut top. Once she sorted herself out and was properly on her feet she said, "If you're a police officer, what are you doing in there then? I heard it's a right old pirates' den. Full of crooks and villains. You have to go though the massage parlour and past the strip bar to get to the pub bit."

"No. I play cards in the back room here."

"What sort of a police officer are you, gambling in there late at night then, with all those villains and pimps and women showing of their bodies dancing naked? You don't have to impress me, mate. I've heard it all before. Some fella once told me he was a rocket scientist and another told me he was the owner of Walkers crisps. Look thanks for your help."

"No, I am a police officer."

"You're pulling my leg… Copper. Ha, Ha… like it. Nice try, I know women fall for a man in uniform but you're wasting your time here. Thanks for your help but you'll have to do better then that to get into my pants, darling. I'm not your average blonde you know. Of all the things and chat up lines I've heard tonight, now I'm here listening to a man, coming out of a strip bar that plays cards at the back of some seedy little place trying to convince me he's a copper… Ha." Some people were coming out the door just as she was talking a bit loudly.

"Ssh Ssh you'll get me shot. I am a police officer, well sergeant in fact." As he pulled his badge out slyly but quickly and flashed it for Mandy to see then put it away. Just out of sight of the people leaving the place he had just came from.

"Shit," she said, "you really are a copper. So let me think, you're in there doing some undercover work then and I've just blown it for you."

"Something along them lines."

Well, if the truth was known he was in there on undercover business, even though he was getting to like the cards and the girls and the drink. The men he was meeting up with to play cards on a Friday night at this den were an Albanian women trafficker and a Romanian forger who was forging papers and passports for illegal immigrants to come over to London. With these forged passports and papers they would pay about £2000 to be able to stay over here. Once they had arranged to bring them over they would be working for them until the money was paid back. The trafficker was bringing women over to work in the brothels for three months at a time. Then he would send them home again once they had made them all a few quid.

The sergeant was posing as a wealthy businessman that would fund such things for a good return on his money. He had been tipped off by the barman at what was going on in there. He had overheard them talking about the women and their business saying that they needed to get some money together. The barman had said he knew someone that would be able to help the fellas out. So the bartender had gone to the police. And alas, the sergeant, no questions asked.

The sergeant had been placed in there, and once they had all played a few cards and got to know each other, that's when they all started planning deals and plotting to bring more women over here. So while they were all meeting the sergeant was also gathering evidence and info for his team, to infiltrate their rackets and have them all nicked and not just the ring leaders. But whilst he was doing his job he had got a bit too involved in it, drinking and getting hold of the girls after he was off.

So all I had to do now was blow the sergeant's cover to these two villains and sit back whilst they killed him, job done easy as that. I was just about to ring Tom once I had found out how to go in there and spill the beans on this sergeant. Then it dawned on me. If they killed him then the evidence would still be at large or he would just have these people all nicked before they could react to me blowing his cover. It was the evidence that needed to be got rid of not the sergeant. We had to do this all a different way so he would have to do as we told him to, if we were to do this properly.

"Come over here so we can't be heard if someone comes out the club," the sergeant said to Mandy. "I'll talk to you nearer my car."

As they walked over to near the copper's car Mandy said, "Look, thanks for your help and all that, but I must go it's late." She turned and took a couple of steps off from where they were standing.

"Look do you need a lift?" the police sergeant said, "it's getting late and a good looking girl like you out here late at night. Well you never know…"

"Yes please," she interrupted. "That would be nice. Thank you. That's really sweet of you."

We were now in business. The first hurdle had been jumped.

"It's quite late and there aren't many taxis about round here." He then walked round to his car and pushed the button to open the doors. They both got into the car.

"OK, tell me a bit more about yourself then," Mandy said. As she sat down on the car seat her dress rose up, flashing off some very nice legs.

"Well," he said while glancing down at them, then at her. "It's like this. I'm here most nights working undercover, as well as having a little drink and showing my face every now and then. I go in there to have a bit of fun and then on some days I stay straight and watch what goes on in there and report it all back. Ready for when we can bust the joint. I work hard so I figure, why shouldn't I have some fun every now and then? Even if I am on the job sometimes I'm on my own with just a bug and a team listening in. They can't see what I am doing but they can hear it. I don't always wear it, it's too risky. Only when there's talk of business the next day will it go on. So then I can bend the rules sometimes, we're all human. This is the only place I can come where people don't really know me or know that I'm a police sergeant. Once people know that, they don't want to talk and think a little bit differently about you. They watch what they say around you all the time; it's difficult sometimes, but here I can be myself, have fun and try to get a bust at the same time. There's nothing wrong with bending the law now and then if you get the results you want."

"Oh it's very exciting, so it's our little secret now, then." He laughed as he kept looking down at her sexy legs.

"Well it's safe with me," she said. "You're a good looking police officer."

"I'm a sergeant," he boasts again.

"Even better," Mandy says. "My luck must be in tonight then." He smiled, as the car pulled away.

"Sergeant. And by the sound of it, you're a bit of a risk taker too." He smiled at her. She was now flirting hard with him. She knew it wouldn't be long 'til he was putty in her hands and do exactly as he was told.

"I like a man that takes risks." Men are sometimes weak. When it comes to a bit of pussy they seem to go all silly around very good looking women.

"So you drink and drive too then."

"You sure you ain't a police officer yourself with all these questions?" He joked. "Anyhow I've only had four."

"That's four too many. I wouldn't want you to be giving my evidence."

"Would you like me to take you home or not?"

"OK, I'll direct you."

Within ten minutes they pass Tom the Moose and me in the car as we had pulled up outside Mandy's place. They then get out four doors down from Mandy's.

"This is me," Mandy then leans over and kisses his cheek, puts her hand on his thigh near his crotch, and thanked him once more. "Here's my number, ring me sometime when you're free and you're not trying to save the world from the darkside of life and if you want, let's go out."

He looked at her and then said. "OK. I'll call you tomorrow." I bet he thought his Christmas had come early.

"I know you will. It'll be nice to get to know you on a personal level. As it's not every day you meet a police hero. By the way, I hope you're not married."

She winked at him then walked away from the car.

Tom had clued her up with everything before all this happened, so she knew full well. She had left her bag in his car with a pair of frilly knickers inside, her photo, some make-up, a brush, tooth brush and a box of Durex, in the hope he would look in it or better still his missus would find it. He then waved at her and drove off, watching back at her in his mirror as she walked on. Tom and I slid down in our seats as he passed us. The plan was working and better then we thought. All we had to do was wait for the call. If he didn't ring then we would need to try something else.

Within two days Mandy told me he had rung her. Result. He rang and said he had her bag, and that it had caused a problem with his missus. She was the one who had found the bag and looked in it to see whose it was, only to be confronted with a pair of Mandy's frilly knickers and box of Durex and other girly things. She had gone berserk and although it was all innocent, it had just confirmed her doubt that he was seeing other women, even though he wasn't. Even though nothing was going on between Mandy and him yet it was all above board for now. But it did have the effect that Mandy wanted. "Can we meet?" he said.

"You're married," Mandy said.

"I just want to give you your bag back."

"Is that all?"

"Yes."

"Let's meet at a local restaurant."

There he was trying his luck, trying to get her on his arm, which didn't take much effort. Now things were really bad at home with his missus and her suspicions had been confirmed in her own mind now, even if he wasn't doing anything untowards just yet.

Mandy laughed and said "Women, they can be so temperamental sometimes," pretending that she was well on his side. Mandy was playing him well. He started to open up about this big case he was in involved with, trying to impress her a bit.

"Tell me about it then," she said.

"There's this big gangster fella, who is well connected to the underworld in London. The serious crime squad have been after him for years, you may have seen it in the paper. He had shot two fellas, they also were gangland members; one had turned grass and one was just shot, we haven't worked out the motive yet. The other killing was done in Spain and that one in Kensington, London. I'll soon be at the Old Bailey overseeing the trial."

If it went well then chances are he would be promoted for his hard work seeing as they had been after this fella and the firm for a long time. Now all she had to do was find a way to get him to accept the money. Within no time from meeting at the card games, he was falling for her in a big way. In fact he was infatuated with her now. The missus had thrown him out and he was now staying at an old friend's house. He had even started sending her flowers and texting her. Just like most men would, if she had put on the charm with them and they thought their luck was in. He was well into her, and wanted to see her more and more. He was trying his hardest to get her in to bed with his flirty texts. She was playing hot and cold to make him more eager.

So the plan was working. At this rate, we wouldn't need to corrupt anyone else in Johnny's case, it would collapse and the case would be as good as over. Johnny would be a free man once again. Mandy was playing the copper more and more, he started to get closer and closer to her and before long he was opening up about his personal life. He took risks, even though he was going to get a promotion for Johnny's arrest and the bust with the Romanians and the Albanians. He also said with all the pressure he started to have a bit of a drink problem and would soon be looking for a new job if he didn't get this promotion. He had been in the job for twenty-five years now and it was just routine and had changed a lot since he had first joined. Now there was so much paperwork and pressure to hit the targets that needed to be met by the government. He said policing wasn't the same any more. He was telling her his problems and work, about the cases that he was working on and the pressures that went with them. Also the hard work he had put into them, just to get the bust they were all waiting on with these fellas he was playing cards with. He was also talking more and more about Johnny's case. Not having a clue, he was with Johnny's sister and all the info he was giving off was fed straight back to us.

One night they had met up as Mandy had said she wanted to see him. "I really need to talk to you." It was important and getting nearer to Johnny's case. "I need to meet you now." Knowing full well he should have been on duty in a marked car. Tom had been watching his moves.

He refused at first. "I can't come yet, I'm working, it will have to wait."

"Come on, big boy, I'll let you put your cuffs on me and I'll show you what I can do with your truncheon."

"What's so important?" he said.

"It can't wait. Come now. We can have dinner at my mate's place then I'll tell you.

He said he couldn't, as he was on the job and needed to be ready as soon as the radio went off.

"Come see me now. Please I'll make it worth your while as I may have to leave the country tomorrow."

He fell for it and he soon arrived once he had done what he needed to do there. He was still in the marked police car. She kissed him and put her hand on his crotch. "Let's eat first and have dessert after."

He said they had to be very quick. He had left the radio in the car and put on a casual jumper so he would be served, looking like he was off duty even though he was at Mandy's friend's restaurant.

It was 11.30 at night, her mate's restaurant was empty. They had a few glasses of wine, he knew he shouldn't be drinking but she kept them coming knowing he liked a drink. Mandy was coming on strong to him; she was wearing a very nice, short elegant dress. He kept saying he needed to get back to the station but she looked so good he couldn't pull himself away. They should go back to the car so he could at least radio in. He was due to radio in soon, as it had been quite some time since he had.

"Don't worry," she said, as she led him to the police car. She then started kissing him passionately and telling him that she loved a man in uniform, it was very sexy. He was well pushing the boat out for her, he took of his jumper and she made him put on his hat and started wearing it herself. She then got him into the police car and they started kissing and caressing each other all over. Then Mandy pushed him off.

"What's up?" the Sergeant said. "I know you want it."

"Yes but let's do a few lines of cocaine first."

"What, I can't," he replied.

"Can't or won't?"

"I have to go back to work."

"And I have to leave tomorrow."

"Leave? Why, and go where?"

She lied and said she had to see her Nan and would be gone for a week so they had to make the most of it now.

"Don't worry about work," as she pulled a wrap from her bag.

"I should arrest you for that you know."

"Kinky. Come on then arrested me. I did tell you I like being cuffed. It's very saucy, big boy, where's your truncheon?"

"Mandy, I'm a police sergeant." He came to his senses a bit and evaluated the situation he now found himself in. "We can't do this. Not here. Not now."

"Keep talking, you're making me wet," Mandy says.

"Stop it. Stop right now."

"What? OK, so let's get this right," Mandy then says a bit angrily. "You're a police sergeant that drinks heavy, and gambles his money away whilst undercover or not, and one that don't care for his family much. Otherwise he would have tried to make it work. Instead of going to see hookers and working all the hours that have been sent just for a promotion at the risk of losing his wife. Walking away from her when the going gets tough."

"How do you know about that?" he said. She knew because Tom had told us when he was finding out the low-down on him. We had clued her up with it all before she had met up with him. She had nearly let the cat out the bag by saying it all, he had only told her little bits.

She came back quickly with, "You men are all the same and all up to that sort of thing. So just 'cos you're a copper don't make you any different. Copper or no copper. We all have needs." She winked at him and pouted her lips a little. "So whilst you're with me, you should start letting your hair down and loosen up a bit and stop being so serious about things all the time." She put his hat on her head again and smiled seductively. "I'm sure you'll be wanting me to slide my pants down in the back of the police car and climb into the back seat, would lose your job for that one too. So chill out a bit." She then pulls her dress up a bit flashing her stocking tops and a glimpse of the thong she was wearing. She slipped down a little resting her heels on the dashboard. "So what's the difference now eh? While you're with me, relax." He laughs in disbelief at how full on she was being. It was working.

He was getting more and more sucked in by the minute, or turned on, one of the two. She let her hair fall down to one side, unbuttoning some of her blouse revealing just enough of her nice firm pert breasts. He smiled at her and Mandy smiled back and winked. She then opened the wrap and dusted the powder on to the top of her breasts. Like, a proper little minx.

"Surely you can't refuse an offer like this, Mr Policeman. It ain't going to stay there for long. So are you going to nick me, or are you going to be a real man and sniff and lick this lot off my tits?" He just sat there in silence staring at her tits in disbelief. He couldn't believe what was happening to him or the sort of predicament he now found himself in. Mandy then said, "Look, you can't have been straight all your life and I already know you're a little crooked, you said so yourself. So come on, big boy, let's get naughty. I know you like a drink so what's the difference here then?"

"OK, let's do it." He leans round in the seat, "it can't hurt, eh." He leans over towards her breasts and kissed her on the lips again.

"Don't worry we'll be OK, you'll see. Just sniff that lot off my tits first," as she pulled back from the kiss. "No one's around, look."

As they look round in the underground car park the only vehicle there was a white van which Tom had been parked up in opposite the police sergeant's car. Tom had been following him and Mandy around all the time like he was working for the paparazzi. Tom had got into the back of the van which was now facing the police car in the underground car park. The windows on the back of the van had been blacked out but he could see everything as clear as day. Tom raised the camera and said. "Go on, go on, sniff it off those tits," under his breath. He started taking snaps and whispering to himself, "go on; go on; do it; do it." He couldn't get the photos he needed, the angle was wrong from inside the van. The shot he could get was just of the back of police sergeant's head in his uniform, kissing some blonde girl and that wasn't enough. He needed a face shot. So he climbed into the front of the van, slowly opened the front left door and carefully slid down onto the floor, closing the door. Then all hunched up he ran over to the sergeant's car, just at the moment the sergeant was bending down to sniff his line off Mandy's tits. Mandy held his head down as Tom ran over and got closer so he wouldn't see him straight away. Snap, snap went Tom's camera as he gave a new meaning to David Bailey.

We had him bang to rights now with these photos. Any hope of ever getting his marriage back on track was definitely over, and his career was down the pan. He would have to do as he was told from now on. Sniffing drugs off women's tits is for villains, gangsters and bankers with more money then sense and no cares in the world with nothing to lose. Not for police sergeants that are on the job and should be looking for criminals. With no option but to take the money when we offered it and do what we asked of him. All he had to do was lose the evidence that could convict Johnny. The gun.

There were no witnesses now as the Jewellery Thief had spoken to them all, those that had been to the club that night and the others that were going to give evidence would now be telling a different story. They weren't credible as they were all on one thing or another. So with evidence out the way it meant Johnny would have a good chance of getting off and would now have a secure alibi for that day. He would be a free man once again and would walk out of court to everyone else's amazement.

As the sergeant looked up from Mandy's tits Tom took some more snaps. The officer looked straight at the camera and Tom said, "smile." The sergeant looked up with whitened nostrils, loose bits of cocaine all around his nose, bits falling out where he hadn't sniffed it hard enough. Shit, he had realised what was happening.

"You've set me up; you fucking bitch!" and slaps Mandy in a rage of anger, wiping the cocaine off his face. Tom got that photo as well, of him hitting Mandy.

"Who's that?" the sergeant said as he raced to get out of the car to catch Tom and get the camera out of his hands.

"Stop you're under arrest, this is the police!" As if he didn't know. But Tom had what he came for and was now out of there like a rabbit running towards its hole, heading full speed back to the van. Tom got back into the van as fast as his feet would move, with the sergeant like a greyhound, hot on his tail.

"Stop, it's the police." Tom managed to jump into the van's driving seat; he then threw the camera on to the passenger seat. Then he quickly turned the key and started the engine up. As he reversed back he knocked the sergeant to the ground. The sergeant got up and limped back to the car. Tom had left the underground car park with a screech of tyres.

He was out of there and heading to a flat in London ready to download the snaps he had taken for me onto the computer. The sergeant got into his car to face the now very worried Mandy. He picked up the radio and then said, "All units." They responded with "yes?"

"Sorry, false alarm."

"Where are you, Sarge?" the voice on the radio comes back.

Mandy says, "Look, calm down and listen to me," she pulls herself together and wipes the powder off her tits and does up her top.

"It is a set-up but we can talk it through."

"OK, I'm listening. It best be good." He placed the radio down. Shit he was mad and very confused.

"The case and guy you have been on about; the high profile one; the one in Spain that's due to come over here to be tried for murder."

"Yes?"

"Well that's my brother, and yes he does work for a very well connected firm, you lot call it the underworld."

"Shit, you fucking bitch, you have set me up, right up. I trusted you. As if I ain't got enough problems without you pulling a little stunt like this out the bag. You little whore." He grabbed Mandy and went to push her out the car. "Get out, and go, get out." They struggled and Mandy shouted. "Calm down, stop and listen to me. Listen to me." Mandy holds her eyes to his. "Look although this is a set-up, just listen to me. Will you do it for me?"

"Do what?"

"Look, even though at first it was a set-up I've grown to like you too, you know. So this isn't easy for me. This is what I want you to do for me, and how it will work. I'm going to the police to report you for hitting me."

"Well that's just great isn't it?"

"So listen. You have no choice. OK?"

"Get out," he said.

"No listen," Mandy shouted again. "All this little mess can be cleaned up and so can all your other little problems. If you just listen and do as I tell you. I have a hundred grand and it could be all yours and the photos of you sniffing cocaine and hitting me are safe for now. All we want is my brother out of there. My allegation of you hitting me will be safe unless you don't do as I ask of you. So if you take the hundred and the photos the allegations will stop once we put things in motion."

"Just like that?"

"Yes just like that. All I ask in return is for you to lose some evidence; the gun on the day of the trial."

"Lose it?"

"Yes. So it never shows up again. It's as simple as that." It went silent as the copper contemplates his options; he looked down and assesses his thoughts as he now found himself in a bit of a checkmate position.

"I can't do it," he says.

"Can't or won't?"

"I'll be finished if I do that; I'll lose my job and everything I have worked for if I get found out, the promotions, the lot."

"Well you ain't far off it now with what we have on you," Mandy said, "you said to me the missus has fucked you well and truly over by wanting the house, and if she does get the divorce you'll be paying her childminder. So you have to work the extra hours to pay her and it won't be long before the gamblers will want paying their debts and we could blow your cover to them too. Once they hear you're a copper, well who knows what will happen to you." Then she continued with, "If you don't you will lose me too," pushing her luck and making out she thought a lot of him. It goes silent again. You could almost hear him thinking aloud at his options. He was well and truly caught in the net. He didn't have many options right now but to do as Mandy had asked of him. The cards had dealt him a rough hand, but we had thrown him an ace card.

"Like I said, if you do it then the £100,000 is yours and so am I."

Then he buckles and says, "OK, I'll do it. You're right I haven't got much to lose now have I as you have made sure of that." Bingo. We had him. "I'll do it for you, Mandy."

"OK." She kisses him on the lips. "Thank you. This is what I want you to do for me. You'll be fine," as she wipes off the rest of cocaine from her tits and pulls her clothes together again.

"The day before the trial I will transfer, via my solicitor, the money to your account. It will be through an estate agent for a false sale of a property, which you had an equal share in just as the papers will say once they are drawn up on false deeds to a flat in Windsor. My solicitor and the estate agents can make up some moody papers for me, for the sale that doesn't even exists just as they did to get the money in my account in the first place. The papers will be drawn up ready for the money as it is now, waiting to go into your account. Once I finish here with you, they will be all drawn up and the bank will be notified that the transaction has been made between me and you. The solicitor's ready for the money to go straight in to your account on the morning of Johnny's trial, so I will need you to give me your bank details. Do we have a deal then?"

"I don't have any choice do I?"

"No not now. Look no one has to know, just us that are involved."

"Once it's all done, Mandy…"

"Yes?"

"Will I see you again, after I've done this for you?"

"Yes of course you will," bluffing and leading him into a false sense of security a bit more, "once you have done this we can do whatever we want," Mandy said. "I have no choice but to see you again. You're a nice guy and you're going to help me. So why not? After all, you're doing this big favour for me, which is a massive thing to do I know. So why wouldn't I want to see you again, you're helping me by getting my brother off the hook. It's a very big thing to do for someone you love and have only just met. So why not see you again? I guess I too have no choice, but too see you."

"OK, I'll lose the evidence."

Mandy smiled with joy, "So you'll do it then?"

"Yes." He kissed her and she kissed him back; she was over the moon.

Then he said, "No hard feelings."

"None taken," said Mandy although her cheek was still throbbing from where he had slapped her.

"With the money you and me can disappear and sort out all your problems or it's a little start for a new life for us both somewhere hot." She had melted his heart and he was now putty in her hands.

"You're right; I haven't got much left here now. OK, Mandy, leave it to me, I won't let you down."

"OK, take me home now please."

They arrived at Mandy's and the sergeant apologised for hitting her. She said, "It's all OK if you do as you're told. I need your account details so I can make sure this transaction takes place."

"OK, give me a pen and I'll write them down," he signed his name on to a piece of paper so it could be traced onto the deeds of the bogus sale of the house later.

Mandy kissed him and said, "I'll be waiting at Heathrow airport for you after Johnny's release."

"OK. So I'll see you in court and then at the airport." Then he left her house and went back to work like nothing had happened between them. Which was good for us.

Mandy rang me to tell me to meet her at her place after the sergeant had gone. I went to Mandy's and she explained what had happened. The plan was progressing and had all come on top. We had more on him now and things were going better than we thought. I told her to phone the police and start the allegations of assault. So he would know we meant what she had said and that she could always drop them whenever she wanted to.

It weren't long before the police were round at Mandy's taking a statement and telling her that they would look into matters for her. By then I was long gone. Knowing the police would soon show up at Mandy's that was the last thing I wanted, them seeing me there, asking me all sorts of questions. Or them seeing my face at Mandy's and getting suspicious and start asking her questions, like how she knew me. Or what our connection was. They might have twigged what was going on. I was way out of there, the less they knew about me nowadays the better.

It was time to meet up with Tom the Moose, back in the Wood to check out the photos he had taken. There were a few but only two that were good enough to put the officer right in the picture to do the trick. We had the sergeant bang to rights but without these photos we would struggle to prove anything. One of him smacking Mandy's face and one close up of him sniffing cocaine, it was all over his face. I could feel the same sort of excitement the police would feel when they had the photos they might need and the evidence backed up in place to make an arrest or do a bust. The plan was in place, we were ready.

Photo evidence for the police meant a sealed bust. But for us it meant a sealed deal, the sergeant would now do as he was told. Otherwise he would end up in a lot of trouble. I would blow his cover on the lot, the card games, him hitting Mandy and sniffing cocaine with Mandy in a marked police car. Tom the Moose placed the photos into a brown envelope and then placed them in the drawer for safekeeping. Ready to take them to the courtroom to hand to Johnny's lawyer on the day of the trial so he could put them forward to the C.P. barrister if it all went pear-shaped and didn't look to good for Johnny. I pulled out £1000 that I had got from the firm's money and gave it to Tom for his handiwork. Then I left knowing the photos were safe and ready to be used if need be. One false move and I would get Johnny's barrister to place them on the prosecutor's table to discredit the police sergeant as to the evidence they had just heard.

The Night Before Johnny's Trial
and the Trial at The Old Bailey

Two days before Johnny's trial a warrant had been granted by the local magistrates in London for the sergeant to oversee and do a big drugs raid on a crack den in Hackney. They had had it under observation and gathering intelligence on it for a year now. The 15 police officers involved were all told to be at the police station the day before so Sergeant Holmes could brief them all on what was what before the morning's raid.

Mandy had sent him a text saying I love you and thanks, he sent one back saying it's OK and I can't wait to be together. We had him; he was doing it for us. The next day early in the morning before Johnny's trial, 15 police officers were all kitted out ready and waiting in the vans, ready for Sergeant Holmes to come in. Waiting for the signal so they could set off and go and execute this warrant. The info they had received from a snout said today was the pick-up day for the crack den and this was the best time to raid as everyone in the drug chain for this bust or involved in it would be there early in the morning ready to sort out business.

They had now put more observation on the address and knew today was the day for the warrant to be used. Sergeant Holmes arrived at the police station; got out his car, walked into the custody suite and past the police stores. He stopped and looked around to see if anyone had seen him arrive, no one had. So he then walked into the police stores as quickly as possible, shutting the door behind him.

There were aisles and aisles, rows and rows of exhibits that had been bagged ready for their court appearances. The sergeant started to walk around looking down at each row of exhibit, when he finds a knife in a bag with a court's destruction order all ready on it. So he quickly acts by picking the bag up. This is it, he thought, as he picked up the bag he then walked along looking at drugs, money, baseball bats, phones and other bits and bobs ranging from clothes to keys, to credit cards, Samurai swords, Tanita scales. You name it; it was here in the police stores. Whether it had been used in a crime or had been caught and was awaiting the owners to collect it.

He then found what he had come here for, after looking at other guns in bags, he saw the guns that Johnny had used. He picked them up slowly and then looked to make sure that it was the right ones he needed. They were. Then he walked to the entrance of the stores and walked into his office with all the bags and closed the door behind him.

He then sat down at his desk and placed the three bags onto the desk top in front of him and turned on the lamp. Then he sat back and thought to himself; if he placed the gun in the destruction bag then there would be no evidence if the guns got destroyed by mistake. It would have been a genuine human error and no one would know about it or suspect anything else. Or would they twig that the bags had been tampered with? Not if he places them into a new bag and places a new plastic code tag on to the bag and seal it up and just changed the numbers on the paper work and computer. It would then all look above board and the numbers ran in sequence once again. So if it were looked at then it would all look cushy for now.

Then he walks to the filing cabinet and pulls the records and papers out for Johnny's trial. He picks up the bag with the gun in it, opens it up and places a new bag on to the table that he has got out of his drawer. He thought if he placed them all into the bag with the knife then they would all be destroyed together once he placed them back into the stores. The court destruction order would be collected for destruction and the person would just pick up the bag and then within a few minutes it would be gone and too late to get back. It would all be put down to human error and the case would collapse. Then he would have done our little job and Johnny would be free and he would be off with Mandy and the money. Or so he thought. I'm sure Johnny will put a stop to it once he was free.

He then places the bags back onto his table, pulls open the new bag and starts to open both the bags; the one with the knife and the other with the gun. Then he changes the numbers around on them so it would be the guns destroyed with the knife.

A police officer appears at his door. "Come'n Sarge, everyone's ready and waiting and getting impatient; everyone's raring to go. Time's moving on, if we want to pull this off we best leave now."

"OK," Sergeant Holmes replies, "let's go." He gets up leaving the new bag there on his table with the bags behind on his table, untouched ready for his return. He could change the bags over or place them in the same bags ready to be destroyed in a few hours or so when he got back. He picked up his hat switched off the lamp and they walk out the office, out into the yard to the vans and they both get in.

He could feel the excitement, the nervousness and the anxiety from the silence of all the officers on board. They never really knew what would happen when they arrive at the scene. Yes, they had been briefed about the raid but when it happens it can be a different ball game altogether. You never know what to expect when you kick someone's door off. There can be all sorts of different reactions from the people inside. I know and I'm not even a police officer. The vans and two cars pull out of the station and speed off to the address in Hackney.

The police vans speed through London, then creep up to where the address is. By now it's about 4.40am in the morning. Not much is happening as the police arrive and look on at the flats. It was winter so it was still quite dark, just starting to get a bit lighter and the wind had started to pick up a little. The birds had just started to sing. The lights were off in the flats as the police looked at them. The two police vans pull up out of sight, down the side of the road not too far from the address but a little out of sight. One or two flats started to switch on their lights. The police vans had parked up with Sergeant Holmes in; there was silence as they waited.

All of a sudden the radio goes and tells the sergeant to bring his attention to the flat. He looks at the place with his binoculars.

He sees two girls leave the property they had come to bust. They were hookers that had just come for an early quick fix after a night on the streets. He watched on as the door shut behind them and the girls started to walk away. That was the cue he needed as the van door slides open on the police vans, to the sound of the sergeant and the radio saying "Go, go, go, go."

20 police officers, in riot gear and baseball caps with vests on, jump out and start running across the grass to the flat door before anyone in the flat could move. They were now all in position ready for action. The two hookers were caught as they tried to run off when they saw the officers running over to them with badges out, "It's the police, stay there, don't do anything silly, ladies." They were then led away and searched. The police found they had in their possession, 4 rocks, a rap of heroin and 500 quid; they were nicked on the spot and driven off to the local police station. They confessed what had been going on in the house and why they had gone there in the first place, which all added to the police's evidence.

The police reached the bottom of the stairs and turned to the door. They placed the enforcer in place on the door, as quietly as possible and with 2 big bangs the door was taken clean off its hinges. With an almighty bang, the doorframe splintered and buckled and the door flew open to one side, all in slow motion. It came to a smashing crash as it rested on the side of the wall in front of them. Ten police officers came rushing into the premises, like a pack of hungry wolves, shouting and screaming as they enter the building like they were Roman Gladiators with batons held high and shields at their sides.

"Nobody move; stay where you are; hands on your head; this is the police." They were like growling Rottweilers as they entered. "It's the police, stay where you are, nobody move." They quickly moved from room to room, arresting different people pushing open doors and making sure rooms were clear of people as they moved in, and the front door falls fully open. One of the fellas runs into the bedroom and kicked the door shut.

"Get on your knees. Lay on the floor, hands on your head." The police handcuffed one of the people in the crack den and three other hookers that were in the front room off their nuts not knowing what was really going on. They had clearly been smoking and didn't know what was going on around them let alone in front of them. The police enter another room, which was the first bedroom; a man in his late forties is in the room with a blonde lady. As he sees it's the police he throws a big bag of cocaine into the air just as the police enter the bedroom and say "stay where you are." It goes all cloudy in the room and the police have trouble seeing the man. He pushes the woman in front of them to slow them down coming in to the room. Then he grabs a handful of money and jumps out the window. As they grab the girl and arrest her, the fella is off as fast as his feet will carry him. Two officers wrestle him to the ground and arrest him as he still struggles to try and get away.

Then the other man that had run in to the second bedroom leans forward and pulls a gun from the drawer in front of him and tries to run out the door, but sergeant Holmes is in his way and is just entering at the same time as this fella is trying to leave. As he runs into the police sergeant the gun goes off accidentally, letting the sergeant have it at point blank range, just under his bullet proof jacket. The police officer falls back out the doorway as the door closes. He gets the bullet right under his bulletproof vest, straight into his abdomen knocking him to the floor. As the sergeant hits the floor the other coppers leave the area and the house, shutting the damaged door behind them.

The police all move out the house faster then they had just come in. Now there was a gunman on the loose. Two other police officers find stolen credit cards stashed in a bag in the toilet cistern and leave. Once they are told and hear the gun go off they now know for sure, that someone was armed in the house which made it even more dangerous than it originally was. As they leave, they see the gunman on the loose, but get out while they still can. Then the gunman leans by the front door that had been smashed open. He looks out the keyhole and can now see all the police cars outside. He slides down the door in a desperate state. He then looks at the sergeant. They are now at the same level, as the sergeant had slid down the wall from the bullet wound. Then the gunman looks into the room he had just come out off.

The sergeant says, "It's not worth it, son, they'll get you."

"Shut it," he replies. Then the gunman looks at the bed, stands up, runs into the room pulls back the sheets from the bed; opens the wardrobe, gets a rucksack and a bag out, places them onto the bed. Then he gets a pair of scissors out the drawer and tears a hole in the bed and reaches down into the base of the bed and pulls the bag of cocaine and the money out and starts putting them in to bags.

Once the police are outside they evacuate the area and people nearby. Then they radio for back-up, get the police tape out and block the area off. Ready for the armed response to come in. Within 10 minutes a plain blue car with a blue light flashing on it skids to the scene and all five SO19 police officers jump out, go to the boot, grab their guns and position themselves around the building in place ready to move in on the ground floor flat for the gunman. The negotiator comes into action with the megaphone held up and starts to talk.

"Come out with your hands up; place the gun on the floor." The man inside hears the megaphone, leans forward, puts his face in the bag of cocaine and sniffs hard. Then he looks to see how many bullets are left in the gun and replaces the clip back. He looks at the sergeant, bleeding on the floor. He goes to walk out, then sits down on the bed, picks up the pipe and has a quick blast before walking out.

The sergeant says, "Help me, please help me." The guy looks away and then a look back again at the sergeant and says, "Look, I'm sorry." He returns back into the room, puts the money and drugs in two bags and tries to do the zip up on one of the bags. He's buzzing and starts to get panicky as he struggles. But in his panic the zip breaks on one of the bags. He has tears of frustration in his eyes now. He knew he was going away for a long, long time.

"Shit," he says as he looks around, then at the sergeant and kicks the cupboard. He sits on the bed and starts to cry a bit "Fuck, fuck, fuck, please help me," as he looks up at the ceiling, then brings the bag of cocaine to his lap, leans down and sniffs hard at the powder once again. He then pulls himself together puts the bag with the powder in over his shoulder. The other bag with the money in he picks up and keeps in his left hand. Then he walks past the sergeant, kicks opens the door and walks out of the house. With the gun at his side he walks towards the police cars slowly, as all the lights go on around him. The man walks out with cocaine all over his face and two sports bags open; one full of money and the other had about 3 keys of cocaine all crushed up loosely in it ready to be washed in to crack if need. As soon as he is in the doorway he starts to swing the gun about and demand to have a car out of there. He then puts the gun down to his side and walks towards them more and more. He has the bag with the cocaine slung over his shoulder and the other in his hand. He was well out of his nut on the cocaine. He must have sniffed and smoked back inside to get the courage to come out. The way he looked it was like he had no cares in the world.

The officer with the megaphone said, "Stop walking and get down on your knees. Don't come no further and throw the gun in front of you. On your knees, drop the bags and place the gun on the floor with your hands on your head, otherwise we'll have to shoot." He just ignored him and carried on walking. He looked in a right state. He had a blank expression on his face.

He starts waving the gun around franticly shouting, "Get out the way, I want a car."

The negotiator man shouts through the megaphone, "Put the gun down or we will shoot. Get on your knees and lay down with your hands above your head. Place the bags on the floor, walk forward and drop the gun. On your knees, then lie on the floor, with your hands stretched out in front of you." He then gets on his knees turns to the megaphone and lets off a shot and shouts, "Fuck you." The police marksmen takes a deep breath and puts his finger on the trigger and slowly squeezes. All this is done in slow motion as he lets out a breath that you could hear. The bang after rings through the air. The marksman looks out from behind his balaclava and through the marksman's sights, to see the man with the bullet wound in his chest drop the gun to the floor. Then he stands up, walks shakily forward a little, stops, then suddenly stumbles over, as he drops the bag of cash on to the floor and falls face down on to the ground. The bag on his back opens up spilling a large quantity of cocaine out everywhere. The marksman then looks up from the gun and puts his thumbs up to the police below. The wind catches the bag of money and the money starts to fly out of it in all different directions, followed by the white powder being blown up and around by the wind. Another officer sees the marksman's thumb go up and quickly runs over to the man who had hit the floor. He kicks the gun a bit more out the way from the man and kicks the bags to the side.

The man lies there almost dead on the floor whilst the police cuff him up and shout for a medic. Other officers then rush back into the house to get the sergeant and also one of the others that they had cuffed and left behind in the house. They needed to get help to the sergeant and get him out of there fast. They got him some help as the paramedics rushed in with the police but with great caution. Just in case someone else was in there armed. They got into the house again and ran to Sergeant Holmes' aid, but he was in a bad way and slipped away there right in front of them. They were too late. He had lost a load of blood while all this was going on.

"Quickly get him to the ambulance," the first police officer said. "Don't go Sarge, stay with us, mate."

He opened his eyes wide and said, "The gun in…"

"In what, Sarge?"

"The gun in my office…"

"Yes?" Then his eyes came to a rest and stopped moving from left to right as he took his last breath in front of them. The paramedic tried to give him first aid but it was too late. He was a gonner and there was nothing he could do to save him. The other ambulance crew came over and took the police officer away in a body bag and another arrived for the man that the police marksman had shot. The forensic team turned up on the scene once they had taken the man away and the coast was all made clear with all the other arrests that they had made, before all this mess had happened. They start to go over the crime scene like a load of ants that had just been disturbed from their nest. Out came the white tape with the blue police writing all over it and up went the white tent as the area was guarded off as the TV reporters stood outside and started to report what had just happened.

The money from Mandy's account had been transferred into the sergeant's account but now he was dead. Mandy and I were unaware as to what had just gone on, things seemed to be going well for us. The money went automatically in to Sergeant Holmes' account from Mandy's estate agents account with ease, through the help of the solicitor around about seven hours after he had got shot. We were still over the moon that our plan had worked and were confident about our day in court now everything was in our favour. We were still under the impression that Johnny would soon be a free man and all our hard work would all fall in to place. Now it was just a matter of time before we watch Johnny walk free from the dock and get away with murder. Whilst everyone else sat back shocked and gobsmacked on how the case had crumbled and had been thrown out through lack of evidence. They would all be a bit confused as to how we had managed to pull it off. After all Johnny was bang in trouble, but that was for us to know, and for them to maybe find out later how we done it. Or once they had read this book.

A Day at The Old Bailey for Johnny's Trial and to See How Our Plan Had Gone

This would be our day, Mandy's and mine. It's amazing how confident you can feel when the odds are in your favour and you're now holding all the aces in your hand. We knew Johnny would get off, after all we had done a lot of work to make sure he would. The police sergeant had done his job, or we were led to believe he did. Just like he had promised Mandy that night when they were in the car.

I'd arranged with Mandy that I would pick her up and drive her to the Old Bailey that morning ready for Johnny's trial. She was excited just as much as I was, to see the look on the police's faces when Johnny walked out of the dock a free man. He would have got away with two more murders. The Jewellery Thief would be well happy with me now. Everything would be hunky dory for me once Johnny was off, I would have done as they had asked and would have paid the 30 large back and redeemed myself. I'd be back out in Spain living it large in no time at all without a care in the world. Welcomed once more into the Firm with open arms just like the night back at the History nightclub. Once Johnny was free and he knew it was my work that got him off, he would also have to treat me with some respect from now on.

I arrived at Mandy's. We both began to get very nervous and excited all at the same time. We knew Johnny would be getting off, or we hoped he would. Tom the Moose was waiting back in the Wood at the Hairy Fella's in Lemming Road on the other end of a phone. He was ready to burn all the photos taken or to bring them to court as soon as I made the call to him. So if it did go pear-shaped, I could put the photos on the Crown Prosecution table just as Mandy had said to the sergeant I would. Once things were okay and Johnny was free, then they would have to get the cocaine ready and the champagne out to celebrate our result. Mandy had a letter ready to give to the police, dropping the charges and allegations that she had made against Sergeant Holmes for assaulting her.

So everything was in place and ready to go. I even had tickets booked ready to take Johnny back to Spain after our little champagne and charley party back at the Hairy Fella's on his release. Well if he didn't want to go with me then at least he could go with Mandy. No drama and I would just stay back at the Wood with a few friends of mine called Wez and Stewart and get nutted off the cocaine. Sitting there playing the X box all night talking loads of charley bollocks to each other on how we helped build Heathrow's Terminal 5.

As long as the Jewellery Thief saw Johnny and knew he was free, I could relax again. My debt would be paid to them, the liberty would be forgotten and everything would now be hunky-dory. I then could walk away like I never existed, and get on with my life without worrying what might pop up next or who might turn up and try and kill me unexpectedly. The skeletons would be put back in the cupboard and all the favours I owe would all be done and dusted. I wouldn't owe anyone anything; a clean sheet; a fresh start; a new way of life with new friends. I would be my own man and wouldn't be in anyone else's pocket for once in my life. I knew now I would be welcome in Spain any time I wanted and on my terms this time, not on their say-so.

Mandy and I entered the Old Bailey both taking deep breaths as we went in. There was no sign of the sergeant, but other police officers were there waiting hanging around for their cases. There were solicitors and barristers all around us moving to and fro to their courtrooms just looking at us as we came in. There were two other faces outside our courtroom that knew Johnny. They said Hi to Mandy, then she introduced them to me. "This is the Cookster a dear friend of mine." They were Johnny's pals from old and looked very menacing. The other villains and faces that were in the Firm had stayed away from court. It was too risky for them to show their faces here and definitely not to be seen by the police.

They were all dressed very smartly and one of them had a haircut like action man and did look like the figure a bit. The other one had black cropped hair and had a scar down his face. They were very clean cut; their shoes were very well polished like they had spent hours going over them. They were very disciplined men, men of order by the looks of them with nothing out of place. They were marine boys and were on leave just so they could see Johnny. They had been good friends in there and wanted to see if they could help in any way, with character references even though he wasn't in there any more. They had all remained good pals. I thought they were the Flying Squad at first, but the Flying Squad had arrived at court later dressed just like the marine boys. They were here to sit in on the case, to see their hard work unfold and to see Johnny off to "nick". We shook hands and got a bit more acquainted with small talk.

Johnny's barrister arrived all jolly and reassuringly… he said to us, "I'll be straight to the point. No amount of money is going to get him off this time, I have gone over and over this case for weeks and weeks with a fine toothcomb and I can't find any loop hole to get him off. Not even if I went for self-defence. He would still have to explain the other shooting in London. Not even if the Firm pay me another 20 grand could I get him out of this one." It didn't look too good but we were still confident, because we knew something he didn't. Who needs a barrister? We had made sure Johnny would walk. So who cared what the jumped-up barrister had to say. He was just there for the money and everyone knew it. The Spanish evidence was overwhelming and Johnny had no choice but to go guilty on these charges to get a third off even if he didn't want to. The usher arrived and said we had 10 more minutes before the case would be called. We all started to get a bit restless; in time the usher came back. The barrister and the other two faces that had come to support Johnny went into the courtroom.

I waited outside with the witnesses, some police officers and Customs officers that had come to give evidence against Johnny. I didn't want Johnny to know I was here, he didn't want me near his sister. That's what he had said the last time we had spoken that night when he had got me outside Mandy's. To see me now with her, he would have gone mad. Especially in there where he couldn't do anything about it, unless he could get a call to his pals on the out to mess me up real bad. I waited outside and gave him a bit of respect by doing so.

Mandy and the two marine fellas made themselves comfortable in the gallery at the back of the court.

"All rise," the usher says as everyone stood up and then sat down again once the judge had come into the room. Then the barrister sat down and opens up his case papers. The jury came in and all sat down. Then with a turn of keys, Johnny was ushered through the door of the secure dock by two security guards. The security guards stood either side of him.

"Remain standing," said the clerk of the court to Johnny as everyone else sat down in unison. "Is your name Johnny Mansion?" the clerk asked.

"Yes."

"And you live…" he continued. Mandy looked at her watch and thought the money should or would have been in the sergeant's account a long time ago by now. So there shouldn't be any worries, but where was he? Johnny would be free very soon. All he would have to do was go through the formalities of the court and then we could all go home. I could sleep at night again with out any worries. We would all be sniffing hard at Colombian's finest.

Mandy's mind returned back to what was happening, as she scanned the court for the sergeant but there was no sign of him. She knew if he was giving evidence then he wasn't allowed to be in the courtroom until he was called.

"You face two charges of murder. One here and one in Spain," the clerk said to Johnny. "How do you plead?" Johnny looked up at Mandy. She looked back and smiled.

"Plead not guilty, your Honour." The barrister looked up and pushed his glasses on his nose a bit more, then looked at Johnny a bit confused as he said it again. The police that were there looked up at Mandy as Johnny said it a bit louder.

"Not guilty," but a bit louder and more confident this time. The barrister had to swallow and stood up.

"Sorry, your Honour. Can I just have a second with my client?"

"Very well," the judge said. The barrister then walked over to Johnny. They whispered then he sat back down. That's not what the barrister wanted him to do. He had advised Johnny to go guilty when he had seen him down in the cells, but here he was saying not guilty. He hadn't listened to the advice and the barrister was a bit unsure.

"My client wants to plead not guilty, your Honour," as he looked over to the C.P.S then back to the judge.

"Yes not guilty," Johnny says again.

He had changed his mind at the last minute. Mandy had told him to go not guilty when she had seen him in the Spanish nick whilst we were out there. So now the barrister would have to do his best to fight his corner, or the best he could, considering the circumstances he now found himself in. He would now have to work hard for his money with Johnny's not guilty plea.

"OK. Take a seat," the clerk says.

The prosecutor stands up and says, "Before we start I would like to make an application, your Honour."

"OK, go ahead then."

"Well bad news I'm afraid, your Honour. Sergeant Holmes was killed in the early hours of this morning in his line of duty. He was the man in charge of this case and he is the one that would have exhibited the evidence." Mandy's head went numb. Dead? How? What? She thought. Did Mr Nice order his killing without telling anyone once he found out about all this mess? She listened on in disbelief.

"Sergeant Fryer will exhibit the gun in this case now."

"So be it," the judge said. What gun? Mandy thought. The gun should have disappeared like the police sergeant said it would.

"Are there any objections, from my learned friend?"

"No, your Honour." As Johnny's barrister stands up and sits back down again. Mandy then looks at Johnny in disbelief.

"OK, I shall proceed to open this case."

"Very well," the judge says.

"This is a case of two murders, your Honour and members of the jury."

"I'm very aware of that," the Judge says, "let's get on with it. Continue." As Mr Douglas opens the case, "On the day in question…"

The trial was now in full swing. Well it seemed like a blur to Mandy now. She knew the gun was still ready to be put forward to the court, and that she had now had lost £100,000. She had handed it over, it was well gone and there was no way of getting it back even if she wanted it back. She listens in again. "So you see, your Honour, the same gun had been bored out and was used in both shootings. One here and one in Spain, with that I produce exhibit pt5761 and pt5762. Can the gun be exhibited now? The other officer pulls up a bag with the gun in it. The usher hands it to the judge then shows it to the jury as they look on at it.

"That's it for this officer, your Honour."

"OK, you may leave the dock."

"OK. Now I will call the forensic officer and the ballistics officer, your Honour; first the forensic to explain more about the gun," the C.P.S lawyer says. Mandy's eyes welled up with water. She was gutted, as little drops started to leak from the corner of her eyes. Not only had she just lost the money, but also she was just about to lose her brother too, for a very, very long time. She then focused her attention onto the case once more.

"So the gun links the suspect to the crime scene and has one fingerprint that matches his prints." Then the ballistics officer comes to the stand and does his bit to add salt to the wound. "The same bullets were fired from this gun, killing the person in question in Kensington, the very same as the one seized in Spain. Both bullets were fired from this gun that had killed both men." He held up the bag with the gun in it that had been used.

"Thanks," the C.P.S. barrister says, "that's all, you may leave the court. Unless of course anyone else has any questions for you." He looked around and no one responded. "You may leave the stand," he said. Then another officer was called to give his evidence. Mandy looked at her watch then back to what was going on.

"We also identified a footprint that was left behind at both crime scenes by the suspect in question. After looking at them in great detail they gave a perfect match of the shoes that belonged to the person who must have been wearing them when both killings were done. These also turned out to be the same ones that were found to be worn by the suspect on the day of his arrest. The day he was arrested on the plane to Marco with his lady friend trying to smuggle 50,000 E's over found on her person and has already pleaded guilty to smuggling them."

Johnny's barrister stood up. "Your honour, that's irrelevant to this case."

"OK, no more questions, your Honour," as he turns away from Johnny's barrister, "that is the Crown's case sir," as he sat down. The C.P.S. lawyer had come to the end of the opening and had put his case across.

"Thank you, Mr Douglas." Johnny's barrister stood up. Mandy had to leave the court, she was in bits. She looked at Johnny then left as more tears rolled down her face. She was in a right state. She ran straight into my arms.

"He's OK then; they've let him off?" I was excited and wanted to jump with joy. Our plan had worked.

"No, no, much worse," she started to sob, "the police sergeant is dead."

"What?"

"The gun was brought into court, the £100,000 will be in the sergeant's account and we can't get to it or get it back as the police would now be all over the sergeant's stuff. He was shot last night or early this morning in some drugs raid over in London. The money would have gone through early this morning, the estate agent done the transfer last night with my solicitor."

All this had happened while I had sat outside on my own, just thinking. I had thought that Johnny would now treat me as a brother. If he knew the trouble I had gone to to get him off these charges, he might have looked at me in a different light, even though it was a favour for the Jewellery Thief to pay back the 30 grand I owed. He wouldn't have to know about that bit. I had sat outside out of respect thinking everything was cool so that he would have not got the hump with me being there with his little sister. After all he had enough to deal with right now, sitting there in the dock with the judge and jury staring at him waiting to predict his future. He had enough on his plate without him getting uptight because I was there too. Now Mandy was in my arms telling me it had gone proper pear-shaped.

"I best get back in there." So she went back into the courtroom. Johnny looked up as she came back in. I started to pace up and down. Shit, this could only have happened to me. Why me? I sat down, put my hands over my face and looked up letting my hands slide down. I had really fucked it up now; I could have curled up and died. All I could hear and see in my head was the Jewellery Thief saying in his deep voice, with the bullet in his hand, looking deep into my eyes. "Son, don't fuck this one up will you." I was fucked now. It echoed round my ears like I was in a wind tunnel.

Now things had gone wrong, terribly wrong. There weren't any more angles I could try and pull off, to put this one right. I was a walking dead man. Waiting to be taken out to the woods and shot in the back of the nut; or taken out to sea with a pillowcase over my head on a boat and thrown out to the sharks somewhere off the coast of Spain. I sat down; I was in bits and shaking.

Within time the case had come to an end as Johnny told the solicitor to put a late plea of guilty in. Mandy looked at Johnny with teary eyes once again. Johnny looked back at her and tried a half hearted smile. Then the judge and jury appeared in court after what had seemed like a lifetime waiting.

"Please stand," a voice said as everyone had come back in to the courtroom to hear the verdict. The judge says, "This man is before me on two counts of murder. He now stands here with a late guilty plea to one of them and not guilty to the other. Would the chairman of the jury please stand. What is your verdict?"

"Guilty, your Honour." Mandy looked at Johnny, smiled and shut her eyes and prayed. Johnny looked back at Mandy. The colour had drained from his face. The judge then told him to sit down. "On the second count do you find this man before you guilty of murder or not guilty?"

"Not guilty." Mandy took a deep breath and sighed in Johnny's direction. Then the judge said his summing up.

"Stand up, Johnny Mansion..." As he did so the two guards next to him took an arm each. "You have been found guilty of one count of murder. The law states that we must find you guilty beyond reasonable doubt and we have found you guilty on that one count as the evidence has been so overwhelming. I have in my mind that you may have killed this other man too, but my hands are tied to the law and the law must find you guilty beyond reasonable doubt and that has not been done today on that count. Only on one count of murder has the evidence been so strong and overwhelming to me that we have gone beyond that doubt to convict you. On that basis you were found guilty. However, you are a danger to life. You have no passion for human life. You will kill people for money; or at the drop of a hat or for friends, as your actions have shown in the evidence I have heard today, in both these counts. I have no doubt in my mind that you must serve life in prison with a recommendation of serving at least 22 years before you are considered for parole or any sort of early release. Now take him down."

The jailers ushered him through the door, slamming it shut behind them, leaving the courtroom in silence. Johnny would be taken to Belmarsh prison that day. Mandy left the courtroom. No one said a word. The two friends or faces from the marines said goodbye then left. The barrister came out and said, "One count wasn't bad. It could have been a lot worse. He will be taken to Belmarsh prison." He then said goodbye adding, "If I can help out any further then I will try." Mandy and I didn't speak all the way home. I didn't know what to say. I didn't have the heart to say anything to her, it wouldn't make any difference now. I had just lost her 100 grand and her brother, so really there wasn't much to say.

Mandy said, "Twenty-two years. He'll be 68 and an old man and for what! A bit of respect and some money, it makes me sick." She said goodbye, kissed and cuddled me, "Thanks for taking me." Then I left feeling numb and empty. I'd just shattered her world for her now, her brother wasn't coming home and now the money was gone. I had to face the Jewellery Thief again. With no excuses I was as good as dead. They had run out of patience and uses for me. I went and got an 8th of cocaine and a bottle of Jack Ds and got wrecked all night 'til the paranoia had gone and I had finally fallen asleep.

Meeting Some of My Old Pals
Plus Being Introduced to The Russian Mafia

I had to move fast, I needed money quickly. I was now in a desperate situation and it was only a matter of time before my time ran out. So it was time to call in all my ace cards and any little favour that was owed to me by other firms who owed me a favour. I had landed right in the shit this time and time was running out. Now that Johnny had been banged up it wouldn't take long for the Jewellery Thief to get wind of what had happened. Who could I turn to in my time of great need without getting too many people involved? Not only had I messed up with Johnny I had now messed up with the 100 grand of Mandy's, and had well burned all my bridges with the Jewellery Thief. Any strings they could or would be able to pull for me had well gone out the window.

I dug out my old diary with all my old and new contacts in it. As I looked down over the numbers, for some reason Old School's number stood out the most. I then called him on the mobile.

"Hello, it's me Cookster. I'm in trouble, mate, and need your help and need to make some money fast."

He said, "Oi mate, don't we all!"

"So can you help?"

"Look, mate, I'm not in to all that anymore."

"Listen, I need your help. Don't give me no, Old School."

"OK! OK! So what's up then that's so important that needs my help so urgently?" I clued Old School up with what had happened. We arranged to meet up after he finished his set at the pirate radio station he was now involved with.

Over a meal at the local Indian restaurant he said, "You're fucked, mate! But yes I can help, but as always I want paying half of everything made just like old times." He knew just the person who could help us and would arrange for us to link up with him in the next few days. This was handy, and I felt relieved for a bit as he knew nearly everyone or anyone that was a face or worth knowing at least.

Old School had worked with this fella before who was going to help me out. They had done some big business back in the day, with exporting large amount of drugs, for him and his Firm. His pal that he would soon introduce me to only turned out to be one of the Russian mafia. They had met when things were going well for Old School, but like all good things, they come to an end… and they did. They had all got nicked, that's when things went a bit pear-shaped between them as everyone started to point the finger at everyone else. Saying they had been grassed up and started to blame each other, but it was Berty Smalls that had done the talking about most of the firms and who had lifted the lid on them all. Well the main players at the time. So the Firm fell apart as no one would trust each other or show any love or bail and definitely no gear moved between hands any more.

They all started pointing the finger at each other and had put a large amount of money on the grass's head. The police offered the fella a new life and even plastic surgery for him to try and stay anonymous. Well someone did get taken away by Old School and hasn't been seen since. So things were left in a bit of a sour way between them all. So for the sake of my life it was time to try rebuilding some old bridges and get a little respect back between them. If it was going to help me and get me out the mess then that was the way forward. I needed to build a firm back-up and one with real people, not with the kind of "messers" that promises the world and comes up with nothing. Saying they can get this and that and know this and that. When the day comes and you have the money on you ready for the deal, they leave you sitting there scratching your arse and playing with your nuts listening to their bollocks on the phone as they have nothing for ya proper 'messers.'

One night Old School and I was on a night out in Stringfellows. We were there to talk about how to get me out this mess and what my options were. Old School had phoned his pal, the Russian who was looking to get back into the business but just needed a contact and a reliable source. We had had the chance to talk to him on the phone to arrange a meeting and would soon meet up in due course on how we could start working together. The Russian had some money and said he was struggling to get some cocaine in large amounts, that's where we came into it. All his contacts had been nicked and were now out the game or lying low but ours were still at large. He said too much had been said already on the phone, he didn't want to bore me with the details so best we arranged a meeting.

Old School said he would introduce me to his Old Russian acquaintance in due course whilst we sat there in Stringfellows looking at the girls strutting their stuff and flashing their bits. We were sitting there watching the strippers when who should walk past our table like a blast from the past but Mr B. He sat down at a table three down from ours. He was with a couple of Cubans and a Columbian fella. He hadn't noticed us sitting there eyeing up the dancers and we hadn't seen him 'til he walked past our table and rejoined the table he was on. Old School sent a bottle of champers over to their table, to get their attention and when he knew it was us who had sent it he invited us over to meet his friends.

"Hi, boys," he said. "Long time no see. How you doing, Old School?" said Mr B as they shook hands. "How you doing, son?" As he looked at me.

"I'm not too bad, Mr B, could be better, seen better days, you know how it is; ducking and diving, wheeling and dealing, swings and roundabouts all that stuff." Mr B laughed.

"You know how things are in this game, Mr B," I said.

"I thought you were out the game nowadays?"

"Well you know, so did I but you know how it is in this game, it's hard to stay away."

"Why didn't you contact me?"

"Well, sometimes you're up and sometimes you're down."

Then Old School looked at me and says, "Well in your case they're always down." They all laughed again. "It seems you always take two steps forward and three steps back." They all laughed at me once more.

"Fuck me," I said, "Am I now the night's entertainment because if I am you can start paying me to dance for ya instead of the girls." They all laugh again some more. Then Mr B introduces me and Old School to his friends.

"This is a good friend of mine," he said pointing to me. "He has known me for years. We've done loads together. So how's life treating you, boy?" Mr B said looking back at me.

"OK, Mr B," I said. I wanted to tell him about my problems, but I had to be careful who I talked to and this wasn't the time or the place. If he knew I had upset Mr Nice then he would be doing the deed of getting rid of me himself, just for some Brownie points. Friends or no friends, this was strictly business to him, nothing personal. He was well happy to see me. Just as I was him. After all I had paid all the money back I owed him, and we had had some good times together. So things were good between us now. He introduced me to the Columbian fella and the Cubans. They said sit down and join us, have a drink on us and relax, the more the merrier.

The Columbian fella said, "A friend of Mr B's is a friend of ours. So why not join us, gentlemen." So Old School and I sat at their table. Old School was giving it plenty of large with the women and the manager of the club, he knew him well telling him to bring more drinks over to us. We all got chatting amongst ourselves. I got chatting to the Columbian.

He said, "I hear you worked for Mr B once and earned some good money for him. As Mr B had said he worked for me a few times. Would you like to work for the big boys again, son? The gangsters work for us and we pay their wages." I took a sip of the drink, looked at the stripper's tits and said, "Some work. What do you have? I mean do you have some?"

"Yes I do, funny you should ask, I have quite a bit."

"Well," I said. "I'll soon be introduced to a Russian fella by Old School who was looking to do something in this line of work again. He has a few quid stashed away behind him and wants to

149

turn it into more, and wants to make some money fast and rebuild his contacts again. Old School, tell him about your mate."

"Why?"

"Just tell him."

"I have a good friend that wants to make some money, so what?" Old School grunts.

"Yes that's right," I said as Old school turned around and the girl started stripping for him.

"Well," the Columbian fella laughs, "We all want to make money, son. The faster the better, but some people aren't clued up enough to be able to do it or they get too greedy and want to rip you off and think they're gangsters. When really they're only pranksters or they go about it in all the wrong way. You see, they get too excited and forget its people's lives we're risking with every drug deal we do. Well if you're serious, boy, you have come to the right table, at the right time, as we are looking ourselves to open the market a bit more. If the Russian is serious then it seems like he could be our answer, for someone to spend big money, to make bigger money. He then said, "What's your name again, son?"

"My name?" I paused and then I looked at Mr B. I hadn't told him my name. So was he trying to catch me out, then I thought for a second. "People call me the Gangsters' Runner round here, but some call me the Cookster. Nice to meet you and this is…" as I point to Old School "…this is Old School."

Mr B winked at me. "You're learning, boy." Real names weren't important here. Only business was important. Now we had started to talk business and I didn't know him from Adam. So it's always best to be a bit cautious at first if not all the time with these sorts of people. You never really know someone 'til you're sitting eating dinner with their family and talking to their kids, that's if they have some that is. That's when you know someone, not just saying hello or being in their company now and then or shaking their hand once when they were introduced to you. So it was best to tread carefully, Mr B's friend or not.

"Yes you can call me the Gangsters' Runner," I said again. Old School shook his hand and turned and watched the strippers some more. They mesmerized him like the boy out of the *Jungle Book* when the snake turns up and starts giving it "trust in me." He couldn't keep his eyes off them. Well we all couldn't at one point.

"Well, my gangsters' runner, nice to meet you, nice to meet you both, fellas."

"And your name is?" I asked looking in his eyes as I spoke. They were cold as ice. You could tell he had killed a few men or had had many men killed on his say-so.

"They call me the Grim Reaper," he said. "As I'm the last thing people see before I have to kill them or have them killed." He then glared at me very hard, to see my reaction and OK yes, I felt a little intimidated by the words I had just heard. Then he smiled slowly and continued, "That's if they think they can have me over, know what I mean, son?" As I looked back at him, I thought you could tell a lot by looking in a man's eyes and seeing his expression. He was telling the truth, this man was no bullshitter; he was a man of his word. He didn't need to blind me with science or baffle me with bullshit; he spoke the truth. A nemesis to society and a natural born killer. Well they all were once you hit bigger leagues. They didn't get there by being nice or by selling a few packets of charley on the street or the local boozer or becoming your friend overnight. These sorts of people weren't your friends at all and would probably never be as they were just interested in business, not friendship. If you were making them a load of money then they were your friends; owe them money for too long without paying and you then become the enemy. The only friend they had was the pound note, they were more like business assets and that's how you should keep them, at arm's length.

He continued with, "Too many people think they can make it to the top and a lot of people die trying, let me tell you. Only a very select few make it to the big time as money, powder and power can confuse some people." He then stopped talking and continued to glare at me with his cold staring snake eyes waiting for my reaction again.

"Well I'm not here to get confused, have you over or get to the top. Those things don't interest me. I'm here to make some good fast money if that's possible and then get out while I can. That's where people also go wrong."

"Sorry?" I said.

"Once you are working with us you work with us, no one else and we tell you which firms to contact to work with us and we tell you when you can get out. Not the other way round, son. Ain't that right, Mr B?" Mr B nodded at me then started talking to one of the strippers. He then says, "Let's talk then, son. You seem like a smart man and we now seem to be singing from the same hymn sheet. You seem to understand me, and what I'm telling you. Tell me what you have to offer me and then I'll tell you what I propose to do for you."

"It's like this; Old school is going to introduce me to a Russian fella who wants to spend 500 grand. Old School..." I said. He turned round from looking at the women and says, "What?"

"Your mate."

"What about him?"

"The Russian fella."

"Yes, he wants to spend some money to make some. That's right about £500,000." He looks back at the stripper, writes his phone number on a fifty pound note and places it in the crack of her arse cheeks, as she bends down and picks her knickers up from the floor in front of him. She then kisses him on the head as we all laugh.

"See you again soon," she says.

"Oh yes, baby, I'm sure you will. Come see me at the end of the night if you like then we can really party."

The Grim Reaper says to me, "Tell me more about him, this Russian."

"He wants to spend some money to make some money that's all there is to tell right now. I guess that's all you need to know as it's me and you doing a bit of work not you and him. Cut the middle man out then that leaves me skint."

He laughs, "You sound like Mr B." The truth is I didn't know that much about the Russian until after our meeting with him. I had only spoken to him once on the phone.

"OK, so the Russian wants to spend £500,000," the Grim Reaper said. "So he will make £300,000 back on his little initial investment."

"OK, seems fair. Tell me more."

"What do you stand to make then?"

"Well it all depends on your prices."

"OK, you can have a key of cocaine for let's say each one at £20,000 sterling. So at that price, with the money you're spending, you stand to make a very tidy amount of money if you sell them on for 30 grand a key that is. Take off what you have to give to the Russian and me," the Columbian fella said, "then you should be a happy man with making that much for yourself."

"Yes," I said. "That's more than enough." I should have tried to get him down a bit on the price, but I was excited with all these big deals and numbers he was talking.

"OK, this is how it will work then," he says to me. "I have a shipment of cocaine ready to be moved from Columbia to Africa and then it will be transported over here by boat. I will add your 15 keys to that and you will be the last drop. It will come to you by boat. If the shipment goes right, then you stand to make some very good money. We all do, all of us on this table. If all goes well you will have just made the biggest contact of your life, my son, and you won't be sitting at my table again with just a fiver in your pocket." How he knew that I don't know, probably just a lucky guess on his part.

"OK, let's do it then. Let's get it sorted." I couldn't wait.

"So we can do this deal and many more if it goes right."

"Yes why not."

I had just been catapulted in to the fucking Colombian fields, so I was now lording it up, sitting there living it large. Living life like a king on lemonade pockets with no cares in the world. Now this had just gone down I was now working with the top boys, the top notch of people. They were at the top of the ladder. You couldn't climb no higher than this lot. I was now in Mr Nice's league of gentlemen. Unless you were growing the shit yourself then this was the top of the food chain. I was excited and realised it wasn't the drugs that gave me the buzz I was looking for. It was the life, the planning, the getting the people, the danger, the money, the women, the scamming and the plotting and the places you went to.

"Let's start making some very good money," as he raised his glass to mine to give it a "Cheers", so I did. "The only problem, son, is that the more you make, the harder it is to hide."

"Well maybe I would like to just do one job and stop."

He laughs. "Son, it ain't like that, you do it until we tell you to stop." I thought to myself, if I tell the Russian fella that he will make £300,000 on his little investment and then the rest is ours, with the money I make I can then give Mandy her 100,000 back in no time. Maybe that might cheer her up a bit for now. With the rest I could open a Swiss bank account or one in Guernsey if I'm still alive and the Jewellery Thief ain't caught up with me by then.

I could get this done and put behind me and now work on the next big thing. But if I did a few jobs with the Columbian boys and Mr B, then who cares about the Jewellery Thief. He would be paid off quicker than I thought possible an hour a go, Johnny out or not.

"The money I make is my problem."

"OK, then we seem to have made ourselves a deal." We shook hands. "This is how it works then, come closer." The fella said with everyone around the table listening. He told the girls dancing to come back later, after the next song. The Columbian fella continued, "Our shipment will come over the water to you by boat. Once the stuff is in English waters it's your responsibility."

"OK once it's here I'll pay you C.O.D. (cash on delivery) as they are getting too hot on chasing money and bringing it over through Customs. It is now nearly as hard as bringing the drugs through themselves. You can only bring 10,000 pounds in cash at a time and they always keep an eye on the paper trail." Me acting like I had been big once.

"So this way it's probably better for now."

"That's OK, not a problem," the Grim Reaper says, "if it makes you feel safe then that's OK. I will arrange so Mr B can pay it on delivery. If that is what you would like."

"Yes."

"Make sure it's there."

"For this one let's do it like this. Until some more trust is built between us," I said even though he was a bit unsure.

"Mr B's here. He will look after it for you and oversee everything. He will make sure that it all goes to plan. Do you understand? Anything you want me to tell you again?"

"No."

"OK, my friend, then you have a deal." We shook hands again then the Grim Reaper ordered some more champagne for us all. As it arrived he said he would get in touch with Mr B when the shipment would be ready to come over. Mr B said that he would contact Old School and me when he got the all clear from the Columbian fella.

"OK enough talk for now. The only thing is you may need a rowing boat and some divers to come out to meet us once we're out in the sea. Can you arrange it?" as he turned to Mr B.

"Yes? OK so all is set then."

Then Mr B and his friends said that they were leaving. The manager of the club thanked them for coming and that it was a pleasure to have them here again and not to leave it so long until they came back to England and visit the club again.

The Colombian fella said, "Tell Peter thanks for a great night," as the girls came over and kissed him goodnight.

"I'll be in touch," the Grim Reaper said to me.

Mr B said bye as we all shook hands and they left the club. "I'll be in touch."

Old School and I sat there and once again discussed all that had just happened in more detail.

"It's time I met your friend. Old School."

"OK."

We talked about what was what, and what the Grim Reaper had said to me. The Cubans hadn't said much, they had just looked at the dancers and then looked over at me every now and then; they were more like Mr B's and the Columbian fella's minders. Left on their table in the ashtray were the butts of big fat Cuban cigars next to an empty bottle of cognac and two half bottles of champagne. One was the bottle that we had kindly sent over, well Old School had as I was still living a footballer's life style on 5 pounds in my pocket. But that was soon to change once the cocaine comes over from Columbia. One of the empty champagne bottles was given by the manager and was still half full. So Old school and I polished off the rest.

They had spent a small fortune with the girls and were all hovering around our table even now they had gone. They must have thought we were loaded too as they all knew that's where the money was and the sniff. They only started to drop by our table every now and then, less frequent than when Mr B and his friends were there. Just the odd girl kept coming over to see if we wanted a dance now. Some of the dancers Old School knew, which was cool, as they had also danced at 'For your eyes only' once or twice. They had made friends with him whilst there, as Old School was well connected to the management team. He knew the girls on a different level not just the stripping level but on more of a personal one. It had been good to see Mr B once again. He was looking well and on form just like old times. Old School and I went back with some of the dancers to their flat back in Kilburn and sat there getting pissed and sniffing up. That's when the girl had told Old School that the fellas that we were on the table with must have spent about a thousand on the girls, with sniff and stripping. "Well they weren't short of a few bob," Old School said.

The next day it was time to meet Old School's friend, the Russian contact and get the money sorted ready for Mr B's say-so. When our shipment would come sailing over, all our troubles would be over. Apart from Johnny's, I guess, as he was still stuck in Belmarsh prison. Thinking about it, it was a stroke of luck me bumping into Mr B and his close pals that night. Once again he seemed to have all the answers to our problems, or should I say my problems.

So Old School and I met up with the Russian fella in Starbucks, Oxford Street. He then got his driver to pick us up and he drove us to an old style freeweights bodybuilding gym in north London so that we could sort out the money.

We walked into the gym with the Russian and his minder. The gym was closed no one was around just me, Old School, the Russian and his minder who waited outside in the car. We clued the Russian up with what was what, once Old School had introduced me as his closest pal. The one who has the contact. The one you talked to briefly on the phone.

"Hi nice to meet you, Privet. And you are?"

"Well around here they call me the Gangsters' Runner." The Russian then moved a bench out the way, removed some of the padded flooring and then under the padded floor lifted up the wooden floor cover. There had been a safe put into the concrete below. He typed in the code and the door lifted up. He put his hands in and pulled out a single sheet of paper. As I looked down in to the safe there were loads, and I mean loads, of Krugerrand and about ten of these bits of paper with an elastic band round them and some very rare stamps. They were used to pay off debts or buy stuff as you can walk where you like with a stamp that might be worth near on £5,000, without anyone knowing what was really going on.

"There you go, my friends."

"What's this?" I said and, "I can feel something very hard in my arse, can you Old School? You ain't trying to fuck me over are you? I'm here to see the money." The deal was nearly ready to go off and he had ordered the stuff now, so in my eyes it was a done deal. Well I had ordered it. So as far as I was concerned, he had called it all on, when on the phone we had chatted to him before our meeting to arrange it all and get the go ahead. So I wanted the money in my hand ready or at least to know it was there for when I needed it.

He laughed. Well I weren't laughing nor was Old School. From where we were standing it looked like he was trying to fuck the both of us over, calling on this lot and now just trying to palm us off with a piece of fine paper. We had now called near on

1million pounds worth of gear on the streets and we were standing there in his gym holding a single sheet of paper and no readies to give to the Grim Reaper. Proper fucked; looking like right donkeys.

So in a Russian accent, Old School turns to me and says, "Show me the way to your anus. Sorry, mate, I thought he was genuine." We are now proper fucked. In a few hours a boat will be coming with Colombian's finest on it. That hasn't been in this town for a long time and we will have to find the money to pay for it.

"If he hasn't got it Old School, he will have to find it."

Old School then turned to the Russian, "I thought we had put the past behind us and we were going to move forward, do some serious work again and forget about the money I owe you." If the Columbian sends the shipment tonight, we were well fucked and I would have to try and sell the lot somewhere else. Either that or I had a lot of explaining to do.

"No. That's the money," the Russian replied.

"What?" I said. "This piece of paper? Come on. You'll have to do better then that to con us, Rusk. We didn't just get off the boat you know. So stop fucking around and wasting my time. Show me the money or take me to it. Then I'll know you understand us, and then we can have this deal on the road and ready for delivery."

"Look," the Russian fella said, "look closely at that. It's not just a piece of paper." So I looked down at the paper he had given me. I turned it over.

"See?" It said sterling on it and had some fancy pictures on it, but what was it? It only turned out to be a fucking bank bond, for £500.000 sterling. Can you believe it and all the time we thought he was having us over. He was being serious and wasn't fucking about.

"I thought you weren't working with amateurs Old School" as he looked at me.

I said, "Look, these are top fellas. So there'll be no problems."

Now you don't get to hold many bonds in your life and at that moment I wish I had a camera with me, as I probably will never get to hold one again. No one will ever believe that I ever held it in the first place, well Old School will as he was there. Well they do exist. It's like getting your first big carp out the water when you're out on the bank fishing and there's no one around to witness it; and when you tell everyone how big it was they all say yeah, yeah but don't really believe ya unless they see it in a photo or for themselves with their own eyes. We had now hit the big time. Fucking bonds, these fellas were big fish not your average drug buyers, just as Old School had said they were. All within a night I had jumped into a small pond with some very big fish.

He said it was as if he had never left and was doing business just like old times before he was a big timer. With this little mob I knew it now but you get to hear loads of stories of people and you never know which ones are true. But right now I believed him as the proof was in the pudding and I was now standing here holding a bank bond. We were now working with the top of the food chain. I was well excited.

I said, "OK, put it back 'til we get the all clear from Mr B and the Colombians are ready."

The Russian said, "You could always change some money into Euros," as the biggest note was about 350 or thereabouts.

"No, bank bonds would do just nicely." Now I had this, it made sense to have a piece of paper instead of bundles of Euros. I was trying to be all cool and calm; trying to conceal my excitement. It's like winning the lottery and just waiting to receive your money. You know it's there but you just can't pull it out your pocket yet.

The Russian fella said to me how he worked with a very connected and heavy Firm so please don't cross him. He looked deep into my eyes when he said it.

"It's OK, don't worry, I know there's history between you and Old School but remember it's us doing business now, me and you. Old School is just making the introduction and believe me, what he owes you will all be paid once we do some more deals like this, mate. So there'll be no dramas there. Things will be OK you'll see, my Russian friend. Trust is a big thing in these circles and with a bit of trust comes loyalty and with that a lot of money."

He smiled. "I trust you."

"So it's about time you showed me some loyalty and get your sniff out and show us some appreciation, I don't just want a gym membership card whilst I'm sitting here. Get your gear out and let's start sniffing."

So he did.

"Don't worry, once we take your money it will be safe with us." Old School winked at me.

"OK," he said as he opened a bag of cocaine. We did a few lines then a few more 'til it was light again. We had been sniffing all night with them, and as we left we could hear the birds going tweet-fucking tweet.

We told the Russian we would call as soon as we needed the money, ready for this deal to go off. He said OK it wasn't going anywhere.

So now it was just a bit of a waiting game 'til everything fell into place. Old School and I left the gym after saying our goodbyes and said we would call again soon, and nice to meet him.

"Likewise," he said, "don't forget; I work for a well connected Firm."

We then left and walked down the stairs from the gym. I joked with Old School and I said I work for a very connected Firm too, you know.

"Ha don't we all eh, Old School," I said being a bit cock sure with myself. Now I knew the deal was all ready to go off and my currencies was now only fucking bank bonds, and we were now working with the top players in the drugs trade.

"Ha," Old School said, "he only works for the Russian mafia, who else do you think would have stolen bank bonds like that?"

"What?" My jaw nearly fell off. It weren't a joke now. I was playing with some very heavy people and the penny had just dropped on how dangerous these people really were. It had just kicked in. It wasn't some fellas I knew from down the pub that if it went wrong I could knock them for a bit 'til I could make a few quid to pay them back for the cocaine. These people were Columbians and the Russian mafia. I didn't need to worry though, this deal was foolproof; we weren't out to rob no one so why worry about it. Russian mafia, Columbians or not, from this deal I would now have £100,000 spare ready for my next plan.

So right about now I had no cares in the world and the Jewellery Thief would be happy with me once again. Once the money was in their hands and it was just lucky on my part that I could help Johnny out. I would be able to sleep at night without worrying someone was coming to kill me. The Russian had a tattoo of a teardrop by the side of his eye. It meant nothing to me but it stood out.

That night Mr B got a call from the Colombians, they told him on the phone they were half way to Africa. Then the Colombians phoned me. I asked can't we pay half now and half later, pushing my luck. He laughed and said that wasn't the deal that had been arranged back at the strip club.

"Come on, my English friend, 60 kilos is small business for us. If you're not interested then I will pull out and you will never hear from me again. I will be just a distant memory of yours. A desperate illusion conjured up by your own debts and desires."

"Listen," I said. "I'm ready to go tonight, so will all the money be there or are you wasting my time? Time is money for me."

"OK, it will all be there, on the drop tonight as promised. This isn't how the payment is normally done," the Colombian said, "next time I will send someone to collect the payment from you first or will talk about laying someone on to you 'til the payment is required."

"Do it this way first. You may understand this is our first deal and I want to do it this way, 'til we have built up a bit of trust between us, just like we said."

"OK, I understand. Then I hope it will all be there once the drop is made. Remember once it's in English waters it's your responsibility, my English friend. Look Mr B has all the details of what's what and how it will all go. So chat with him."

I said thanks as the phone went dead.

The Columbians had told Mr B that the drop would be at Southend at 3.30am as the waters would be still and the tide would be in. So Mr B phoned his diver mate who got his other friend to come with him from the diving club, he was an old boy and seemed a very well educated man. They would all drive down to Southend with 2 divers at 3.30am. He had to row out to their boat from the beach as a motorboat would have been too noisy and would alert people to their whereabouts. The Colombians had got to Africa and met the two Cypriot fellas that they were also dropping cocaine off to. They had asked where they were off to next and he had said to England. They said if they could have their cocaine cheaper then they would drop the gear off in English waters. They would sort the money out once they next met, as they wanted to make a little drop off themselves on the sail over. The Colombian agreed and the two Cypriot fellas sailed to Southend with 60 keys ready for Mr B to collect.

Once they arrived about one mile from the beach they dropped the anchor off a luxury yacht. The bags of cocaine went over the side in position just under the yacht. The bags had been coated in wax like you get on cheese and stamped with a scorpion. They had dropped the bags of drugs into the water for their safety just in case they got stopped whilst they were sitting there waiting for their payment to come. Once they were paid the boat would be out of there. Once we had the parcels then the money would be handed over to the Colombians, well that's what Mr B had told me.

So I met up with the Russian in a Mayfair hotel. I was sat there having coffee when the call came through. He told me to get in the lift so I did and as the doors shut he instantly handed me a brown envelope, he then got out the lift. I pulled the bond out to check and then pushed it back in. I came out the lift grinning to myself and he was gone. I then took it to Mr B in London Conley. He then phoned a friend, who he knew would be into a bit of skullduggery and was a diver, who then called his mate to dive with him and for doing it they would get a £1000 each. Well it was small change in comparison to what we were all getting back. So they were hired.

Mr B picked the two divers up after I had met him with the bond. He then went down to Southend that night with these two divers ready to go out to sea, collect the cocaine and bring it back to the gym for safekeeping. I was working out and Old School was waiting with the Russian watching the boxing on the TV screen in the gym. They were ready to sample the merchandise once it arrived and then get it pressed to sell it on to his contact, then we would all be quids in. We waited for the amatol to arrive so as soon as the cocaine arrived the Russian could give it to his minder who had a good friend who would then press the cocaine with it. In one hour a fella comes to the gym and there it was, 5 tubfulls of amatol.

Mr B and the two divers had driven down to Southend; they all got out the BMW 4x4 and onto the beach. They dragged the rowing boat down to the water, got into it and rowed out to the yacht. Mr B looked at his watch, 3.45, then looked up and out to sea with his binoculars, nothing. Then just as he put them down he saw a flashing light, he got his torch out and they flashed torches back at each other.

"That's it, fellas, let's row towards the light."

When they had reached the yacht two Cypriots greeted them.

"Ahh, my English friends, how are you?"

"Good, where's the Columbians?" Mr B said.

"What took you so long?" one of the Cypriot fellas said as he threw him a line to keep the boat from sailing off and had avoided the question.

"Let's be quick about all this, there are 5 bags just below our boat. So do you have the money for the Grim Reaper?"

Mr B said, "Yes I do but not until the drugs are collected and safe onboard our boat." Then he we would part with the money and they would have a deal. He showed them the bond as he stepped on their boat.

"I'm not going to hand it over 'til the drugs are on the boat and I've tasted them to make sure it is what it is."

"Look, don't fuck about with it; we have our orders from the top boss, the Grim Reaper."

"I know who sent you, but I'm not fucking about. I'm just being sure that what you say you have is what you have, OK? There's nothing wrong in being a bit careful."

"Hurry up then as we ain't got all night out here, it'll be getting light soon, you know." So Mr B turns to the divers and says, "Come on fellas, let's get down there and get the drugs onboard and then we can get the fuck out of here. I don't know about you lot but I'm freezing my nuts off out here. So let's go and get some money in our pockets."

"OK," they said, putting on their masks and air tanks. The two divers then slipped off the side of the boat and dived into the water and within a short time they start coming up with the big bags, then they dive again, two more bags got collected.

Then one diver says, "I'll go down for the last bag, you wait here." The other diver gets up into the boat takes of his mask and wetsuit. They opened a little hole in each of the bags, to find the most pure of purest cocaine, around 96 percent.

Mr B was a very happy man as he sniffed it hard. Then happily he hands the bond over to the two Cypriots who then climb back into their boat ready to go. About a minute after the diver went down for the last parcel a big light comes on with two blue lights and then they hear the mega phone.

"Go," the Cypriot man says to the other one as he starts the engine up and tries to get away.

Another police boat pulls up "Stop, this is the police. Don't move and stay exactly where you are."

Fuck! They had been well caught. The Cypriot guys tried to steer their boat and try to get out of there but the police boat cut them off. The police boat pulled in front of their boat before they had a chance and then a police helicopter hovered over the top of them with their bright light shining down on them just as they tried to speed off. But the helicopter illuminated the whole area around Mr B's rowing boat and the Greek Goddess yacht with its spotlight like it was in the middle of the day. Then another police boat joins them. The diver on the rowing boat tried to get his tanks on again, but before Mr B or he could jump or even kick the rest of the parcels back overboard the police were on them.

Even if they had jumped off the boat they were out in the middle of nowhere. Somewhere off the Southend coast and the water was cold like ice; they wouldn't have got far in just a rowing boat.

The police boat had crept up without anyone knowing. They had all been too busy and concerned with what they were doing. They had been caught bang to rights. Money, drugs and everything; if they had jumped and tried to swim they would probably have frozen or drowned; one of the two as the current was quite strong in that part of the water. The other diver, the oldish fella that was a friend from the diving club was still under water. He looked up and saw the spotlights and the blue light go on; he stayed down until he could no longer see the lights. He knew something had gone badly wrong from the blue lights flashing on the water. It could only mean the Old Bill.

The diver had the last bag in his hands; he thought it best to head to the shore as quickly as he could, before he was caught too.

When they had been arrested Mr B had asked the police officer how they had known they were there. The police told him that someone had used their phone from the Greek Goddess and they had tracked it on the satellite. They had heard them talking about the deal they were doing on the phone. Then when the Cypriots had rung them at Southend to say they had arrived and they were waiting for you to go out to meet them to collect the parcel, they knew what was going down and were on to them. They had wondered what a boat like that would be doing so far in and it could only mean it was dropping something off. So they followed it in and sat waiting for the best time to come and get them, the rest is history.

They were under arrest for exporting drugs and conspiracy to supply them. The Greek Goddess was towed in to shore and they were all placed into an awaiting police van whilst both boats were searched once again. They didn't have a clue they had been grassed up.

Dead Man's Money and The Plan for Johnny

Old school, the Russian and I were waiting for ages for Mr B to contact us. I had done my workout and was getting a bit worried, the boxing the Russian and Old School were watching was coming to an end and the time was nearly 6 in the morning and still no contact. What if they had knocked us? I would now owe the Russian, but he would never do that or would he? Would Mr B do that? My efforts to phone him were fruitless. So we called it a night and all went home after we thought there might be a good reason for him not to answer the phone. We had to convince the Russian that everything was OK. Even though everything wasn't and we would tell him the news in the morning. As no news was good news or so we thought. We were all panicking ourselves a bit, all for nothing.

I tried contacting Mr B in the morning, but once again no answer. I was really worrying now as to lose the Russian's money would be just my luck.

It didn't take long for the news of what had happened to Mr B and the rest of them to get to me as Frank D, Mr B's son had told me once I had gone round Mr B's house to see what was going on. I knocked, no answer, and then I banged on the door.

"Mr B, are you there, mate?" Then Franky D came to the door.

"Franky, hello mate, where is he then, son?"

He told me that he wasn't there and that they were all caught last night out in the waters at Southend. Something to do with a shipment of cocaine he was collecting. He had said the police had come early this morning and had raided the house, leaving the house all ransacked as if it had been robbed.

"Look," as he showed me where they had come into the house. "They were going to arrest me too but they never found anything here at the house, which was lucky and I have moved everything else from the lock up. So they let me go again."

Mr B and the people he was with were all on remand and looking at a lot of bird now he said. I said thanks and left. They had been caught and confessed all to the police including the bond. What was going down?

They were all now on remand in Belmarsh prison awaiting their trail. The same prison where Johnny was being held, but Johnny was to be moved to Woodhill prison very soon.

The story that had gone around in the prison was that the Cypriot fellas had known they were going to get caught and it had been a set-up, well they weren't far wrong but they didn't know for sure. So all Mr B's debt would be wiped clean with other firms that he owed money to, but it was only talk and was far from the truth or so they thought. Now we knew what had really gone on with Mr B and the Cypriot fellas and we had to tell the Russian fella. I told Old School about me going to see Franky D, Mr B's son. He said we needed to go see the Russian as he had left about 16 missed calls on the phone already, wanting to know what's going on. So we got back to him and met him on the golf course.

Well, we blag him that we were still waiting for the deal to go off and that it had just been put off or on hold for a couple of nights 'til it could go off again. As one of our pals had got nicked and we were worried just in case he talked to the police and they were on to us all. So it was best to be safe, well it was sort of true. He agreed but of course he would want the money back 'til the drugs deal could go off and rightly so. So we told him that the Colombians had his money and that it was safe for now and in good hands ready for the all clear when our deal would be able to go off in the next couple of days. That would mean he would have his drugs and be able to make his money back on them, so no problems. He wasn't happy he said he had people waiting on him for the cocaine and it not being here when he thought it would be was starting to make him look silly, soon the buyers might go elsewhere. If they did then he would need his money back as he didn't want to be sitting there with it all for too long when he had a buyer that would take most of it off his hands.

He wore the excuses for now which gave us some much needed time to try sort this mess out. What else could he do? Go over to Colombia and get his money? If we told him the truth he would have wanted paying there and then and wouldn't have let us go 'til it was all there. If he knew it had come on top and the police had the drugs and money we would be fucked and he would have gone mad. He had swallowed what we said for now as he thought it was all under control and had no reason for any alarm bells to ring. He agreed that it was all OK for now after he had spoken to his pals on the phone awaiting the gear. On the phone they were cool 'til the end of the week but after that they needed to move on and get the work off another Firm if the Russian couldn't deliver, which would be bad and very bad for us as he looked at me and Old School. We had a week to sort this out, he said it was all good and wouldn't worry but would be expecting the money or the drugs back very soon.

Well you couldn't blame him getting a bit concerned; it wasn't as if he had just been knocked for a gram. Old school and I had reassured him enough with our bullshit that everything was cool. So at least he thought his money was safe, even if it wasn't in his hand right now.

I then said, "Look you're not working with monkeys here so you won't get monkey business, my friend, OK? Your little £500,000 were peanuts to the people we were working with. So don't worry, everything is cool. Just relax and it will all come through you'll see. Stop being so impatient these sorts of big deals take time to be palled off, you know that. You know you have done deals like this before."

"OK, I understand, but if it doesn't happen soon I want my money back."

If only he knew the truth. Then things would have been a lot different. Right now he weren't even getting a pound back of his money let alone an investment on it, he was getting nothing. He might have been happy with a gram or two but because of the circumstances we now found ourselves in, he was getting nothing right about now; not even a gram of cocaine from us. I also had the Columbians on my back wanting their money too and they were more important right now as they were life threatening. I had to keep them sweet as well as the Russian and the Jewellery Thieves.

Right about now I was in big trouble and there was no one to run to for help. These were the big boys that the gangsters worked for. So I was now juggling with everything from money to people. It's hard enough with a set of balls, let alone juggling with lots of money, people and my own life at the same time.

Within two days The Grim Reaper had made the call to me. For some reason I knew it would be coming soon. I knew it wouldn't be good news once it did come. The news had got out that they had all got nicked. "Bad news," he said as I answered the call.

"I know."

He continued, "What has happened is a bit of bad luck. It could have happened to anyone, but unfortunately it has happened to you. Mr B is now locked up, and it's you that must deal with the consequences and pay off my money, which as you know is £500,000.

The shipment had been delivered on time and as arranged, unfortunately the bust happened in British waters. So as we agreed back at the club that night it would be on my head to pay the money back if anything goes wrong and unfortunately it had. It had gone very wrong indeed.

"Don't worry your money is safe," I lied, "just give me ten days and I'll have it with you, OK? There's no use crying over spilt milk, Mr Reaper."

"I'm taking your word on that, ten days is all you have, no more. I expect it to be in my hands able for me to count every last 50 pound note, otherwise you can keep the money for your funeral." Now that Mr B was locked up all safe and sound, it was me taking all the shit when things went wrong.

"So I hope you ain't juggling with my money by any chance or lying to me are you…?" You wouldn't want me to come over there to get it from you. It would be an experience that you, my friend, will never forget. It will be as painful as I can possibly make it for you. That's if you stay alive long enough to live to tell the tale about it."

"Behave yourself and don't be silly," I said, "we're all friends here. We've got loads of money enough to pay you. It's just a bit tied up right now, but you'll have it in ten days as I said. So don't worry."

Fuck! I had ten fucking days to find their money. I'd need more than a bank loan to sort all this mess out. I had to laugh; where in the world I get this money? I wasn't due to win the lottery, or was I? I was juggling with my life and their money with all the lies I was using to cover everyone's backs and my own.

Soon everything could come crashing down all around me fast and before I knew it I would be carried off in a wooden box and knocking on the pearly white gates; and there's no deals to be made there. I had already made my deal with the Devil by doing the things I was doing and now involved with. Ten days; ten days that's all I had; it had to be a bank job or something along them lines, I was desperate for money now.

Just then Mandy rang, "Hi, Cookster, it's me, Mandy."

"Hi, sweetheart, how are you, darling?"

"I've just spoken to Johnny."

"How's he doing?"

"He's OK, he said he's doing the best he can in there. People are looking after him. He's going to be moved to Woodhill prison this Friday morning; he said it would be nearer for me to be able to come see him." This was it, I thought, my chance to get Johnny out. If I didn't move now then it might be too late and I would never get the opportunity to do it again.

"OK, Mandy, must go, something's cropped up."

"You OK?"

"Yes, sweetheart. OK, you take care, bye-bye."

I had forgotten about the Columbians for now, this had set something better off in my mind. This job could get the Jewellery Thieves sorted at least and put a smile on everyone's faces once again. Then maybe Mr Nice could help me out a bit and have a chat with the Colombians for me. I needed to get Johnny out of there, after our entire plan to get him off from the shootings had gone wrong. I would only have one shot at getting Johnny out this Friday. When he was due to be moved to Woodhill prison in Milton Keynes. We needed to get him out and to somewhere safe. It wouldn't be long before the Jewellery Thieves had found out what had happened and that yes, I had fucked up once again real badly with this and the other stuff that we had tried to do.

I had to move fast and get some people to help me to do this job. I rang Tom the Moose and met him down the Woodcock pub in Borehamwood to ask for his help. While we were there I phoned Old School. I told him that I had a job that had come up and that we would all get well paid if we could pull it off. It was a bluff on my part but I had to try to convince them to help me and to my surprise they all said yes.

The job was to get Johnny out of the nick. Johnny had the contacts for the next job, although he didn't know it. Mandy had told me in Spain whilst we ate at the restaurant that her and Johnny had a stepsister who worked for a security firm. Vans would drive round all day full of money, collecting big amounts in from different companies and banks. Result. I had kept that under my hat 'til now, as it was no use in getting excited about it. It didn't mean anything back then. It was just someone's job. But now it was an opportunity. Once you're in the shit you start looking at everything just to make a pound note. It was now time to get a little team ready to get Johnny out of prison.

The Great Escape
and Taking Johnny to Paradise

The team turned out to be Tom the Moose, Old School (aka DJ mad Al) and a fella we'll call Matt the Mac from the West End. Not forgetting George, the Hairy Fellow and Ray S the one that was in the limo that night and who owned the security at Bagley's night club. George was an old school friend who knew the crack about me but didn't really get involved in much skulduggery until now. As like everyone else he also needed a few quid. He also knew how to drive lorries which was most handy and why we called on him in the first place. He was now the driver of a dustcart that we had nicked from Westminster council in the early hours of the morning. That's all his involvement was in the Firm 'til later on after he had done this little bit of work for us. Ray was an old time career criminal. He knew his stuff and was a good friend of Mr B's too.

He was the one I had met in the limo that time when I was young when he had shown Mr B the guns that he had for sale. He had heard us talking up the Director's Arms and he had said that if I needed any help then to add him in, so I did.

He joined us and had clued us up a bit more on what he knew about. He had allegedly robbed many places and knew how to open the cases from the security vans without letting the dye come out. Learned from doing several jobs with a fella called Bill P. They had got away with a few in the past. Bill P was a real nice fella; he smoked joints like he was sitting with the Indians, sharing the peace pipe round the camp fire every night, in some tepee far out in the Wild West somewhere. Well he was a bit far out man, with all the pot smoking he done, they were all a good bunch of fellas, so Ray was just the right person to get involved for this job.

The Hairy Fella's part was to provide a safe house for us all to meet up and where the plans were all put together. If we were at his house we knew we were safe and no one would come and disturb us while we shared our views and planned and plotted what we were about to do this Friday. I said we should call Matt the Mac; he was called this because he always wore a black mac with a hood. He was up and ready to do any job at anytime and had done a few things for other firms, which had got them to where they were now. He was a tool merchant; he could and would get his hands on most tools as and when they were needed and for the correct price of course.

He had learnt to strip firearms down in the army whilst getting stoned out of his nut with the rest of the squadron. Well that was 'til they kicked him out after he failed a piss test and was told to pack his kit and jog on. This mac he wore had pockets like Mary Poppin's bag or a magician's hat. He could pull out many different tools from them, be it guns, knives or bats from each pocket; a bit like the fella out of *Blade* the movie. He was proper textbook, and if he couldn't baffle you with science then bullshit would do it. He knew a lot about nothing and what he did know had been Googled on the computer first. He was very smart and what he did helped the firm out many times. He had more stories than *Jackanory* to tell you. Now his story was he worked for Malcolm, who we know was a big time minder and debt collector in London and who was good friends with Mr B at one stage. He worked alongside some known and unknown faces in London's underworld, and closely with a fella who was nicknamed The Hands. This guy was his hired help at the time. This hired help; The Hands was his mate, who was a fella called Aggie. A boxer who worked with a fella called Manny C, who was also a face in the underworld. He was also very handy himself with his hands and had done a few rounds in the ring and made a nice few quid out of doing so. They all worked with Mr B at one time or another, but some of his little mob had been killed in a getaway car.

The car that they jumped into after the armed robbery in London they were all involved with, had collided with a lorry whilst the police were chasing them. They were shooting at the police in the chase but the driver they had employed had powdered his nose while waiting for them to come out. When they did jump into the car with the large bags of dough, he had started to panic and become all paranoid and was driving all over the road. They had skidded out the way of the police car and had collided full on with a juggernaut; two of them had been killed instantly apart from Ray and Aggie. The lorry had smashed into the car and crumpled it like it was a toy. The police caught Ray at the scene trying to limp away and Aggie in the car with a big cut on his head and a bit delirious, holding his balaclava in the front of the car with money sprawled out.

Ray and Aggie had done 5 years for their parts in it, all at Pentonville and Wandsworth nick. Whilst in there, Aggie had trained hard in the gym with a few travellers that were well into their boxing. When he come out he went straight back into the ring and won a few fights with Mr Manny C. Which made the Firm some good money, 'til he retired recently. But the word was he could soon be making a comeback. Whilst Ray was inside he still had outstanding debts that needed to get collected in for Mr B so he could then pay it to Malcolm. So Ray got a good contact of his to come up to the nick and then got him introduced to Mattie the Mac and in turn, to some other faces within the Firm to take care of Ray's interests while stuck inside.

So Mattie the Mac was no longer just a foot soldier. He just jumped ranks within the Firm and was now selling keys. He was number two under Mr B's boss which was a fella called Malcolm. He was working for Mr Nice at this time, but it was all kept quiet 'til a lot later on. Malcolm had become Mr Nice's number one over here in England while he was out in Spain because he didn't really come over to England. That meant Matt the Mac had to get the debts in.

Ray's firm had been left behind at this point from him being stuck inside. So Mattie started collecting the debts in until he got to this one fella, Gary the G. He owed about 75 large, he had borrowed it for an investment for some business deal for some property he wanted and promised the Firm interest on its return.

Now this money was the last outstanding debt that was on the list that needed to be collected in by Mattie the Mac to keep the pressure off Ray from Malcolm.

Malcolm's minder, a Greek fella called Hector, was in the same nick giving Ray a hard time from Malcolm. By getting the money in he could use it to buy more drugs with Mr Nice and sell on, keeping the pound sterling rolling in.

Matt had rung this Gary the G fella several times but kept getting his calls jogged on, he was having no joy. Well he was using a withheld number. He had put the word out that he wanted to see this Gary the G in the pubs and clubs. He had told the doormen of every club in the West End that if this Gary G should turn up then they were to call him on the quiet, so he could come down unexpectedly and see him. He had asked them to try to keep him there 'til he could turn up and surprise him and catch him off guard. This too turned out to be fruitless. He was still having no joy and Mr B started to get on his case a bit more saying he wanted the money in to give to Malcolm so the fellas inside would stop the pressure they were giving Ray. Mr B had told him to get in contact with me back then, so I got an address for this Gary the G by going to see his ex-girlfriend who couldn't wait to give his address over because she was still a bit angry over their break up. But he had moved. So I asked a good friend of mine from Borehamwood of his whereabouts. His name is Martin Bones, the fella I spent some great years with, buzzing hard at raves and having the crack with 'til I went all mad on a drug psychotic trip and was nearly sectioned for my own good, back in the 90's.

He was from Stonebridge; he had stayed loyal to me as well as Treeny; they have moved on now and are living a good life. So I asked him if he knew him, he said he knew of him and told me whilst I was in the nick he was running things in the Wood. He told me where his house was and where I could find him; which was either at his home or at the golf club or I may even catch him at a small nightclub called the Hearts and Tarts or Cloysterswood near Standmoore.

So Matt called on me, I told him what I knew and that we should just go to find this Gary the G's drum instead of hanging round the nightclubs in the chance we may bump into him, have a little chat to him face to face. We both went round his house to collect what was outstanding from Ray. Once it was paid everyone would be happy in the Firm again and life in prison would get a lot easier for Ray. Gary the G was a tallish fella with black hair, he used to drive the supermodels around in Hampstead and done other bits and bobs. He was allegedly involved in porn films and held swinger nights back at his pad, to get his money and had made a tidy amount out of it all too. So Mattie the Mac and I got Matt's driver to pick us up from the West End and we went straight to this address we had been given. We pulled up in the Jag; the house was more like a mansion.

Mattie leant across to the driver of the Jag, "Pull up here please, mate." So he did. Mattie the Mac and I got out the back of the Jag, he tells the driver to open the boot as I walk up to the big doors. Mattie then joins me and bangs on it with his fist. With the knock he gave the person inside would have thought that Goliath had just knocked on the door.

"OK, I'm coming," said an old man's voice from inside.

The door opens and Mattie the Mac says, "Hello, mate, are you Gary the G?"

"No I'm his butler. Who are you?" in a slow precise voice, "is he expecting you?"

"Is Gary the G there or not, let's not fuck about."

"No. Who are you?"

"Me, I'm Matt the Mac," just as Mattie pulls a sawn-off shotgun from out of his mac.

The old fella turns to me, "and you are?"

"Me, I'm the fucking invisible man," as now I can see the gun and that meant we were ready for action.

Mattie puts the gun to the butler's chest and says, "That's his car isn't it?" he had seen it before outside Ray's drum once or twice and it had Gary on the number plate.

"So show me where he is."

"I'll just get him."

"Ah so he is here then? Come along, old man, don't fuck about." It's amazing what a shotgun can do; it's like having your whole firm standing behind you.

"Now we'll get him," Mattie said as we walk in with the gun behind the fella. The butler leads us upstairs to Gary the G's bedroom. Mattie tells the butler to knock.

"Mr G, there's some people here to see you."

"Tell them if it's important to come back later. I'm sleeping. I've been out all night clubbing and just got back and I'm tired. So it's best they come back this afternoon when I get my scruples back together."

Mattie whispers to the butler, "Again, Tell him again."

"There are people here to see you, Gary."

"I'm tired. Tell them to go away. I'll sort business out later. Unless it's the Old Bill and if it is tell them to get a fucking warrant and stop wasting my time."

Matt the Mac told the butler to move, as he kicked the door open. We walk in and Gary the G had the covers pulled up over his head. In the bed next to him was a very busty brunette. She looked up at us in amazement as we walked in to the bedroom. She looked a bit scared when she saw the gun. I then looked at her and put my fingers to my lips, she didn't move. Gary then turns round from the noise of the door being kicked open. She then grabbed for the sheet to cover her big naked breasts. Mattie the Mac points the gun into the air and lets off a barrel. BANG, bits of ceiling fall all around us and then he points the barrel at the girl's head as she winces and tries to squirm away.

Mattie says, "You ready to talk business now, mate?" Gary the G turns fully over and sits up a bit more sharpish.

"What the fuck? Who the fuck is this? What the fuck are you two wankers doing in my bedroom? Take that fucking gun away from her head will you?"

The butler then says, "I did tell them, Gary." The cheeky git we thought, as we looked at each other then back at the butler. He didn't tell us nothing.

Gary continues, "What do you want? Fuck this." He pulls the covers off and looks up at the ceiling to see the hole.

"Stay where you are and sit the fuck down unless you want to be splattered all over the wall like fuckin' artex," I said.

"I guess you're fucking awake now, Gary. Now we have your attention, you best start listening."

The bird in the bed is gobsmacked with what is going on and pulls the covers over herself covering her boobs and chin.

He replied, "Who the fuck are you two cunts coming in here uninvited like you own the fucking gaff, looking like something out of *Pulp Fiction*?"

"Me, I'm Matt the Mac," Mattie says.

"And you?" as Gary looks at me. "Yes you, sunshine."

"Me, I'm the fucking invisible man 'cos I'm the last person you'll see before we bury you in your garden underneath your fucking daffodils." I just got a glimpse in to his garden from the window.

"Why are you two cunts here anyway? You can see I'm sleeping. Didn't you hear me say that I'd sort out business later if that's what it's about? What's wrong with the phone, couldn't you ring or something?"

"We're here for the money you owe and I have rung several times but no joy. You keep jogging all my calls on. So we thought it be best to speak to you face to face. I've been looking high and low for you. That's why you now find us here."

"If you phone with a withheld number, then I ain't going to answer. Am I silly, bollocks? It's not rocket science is it? If you two had brains you'd be fucking genius and you wouldn't be standing here with a gun in your hand now would you?" he says. "You two ain't burglars are you?" Which throws us right off the scent for a bit.

"You what?" Mattie removes the gun from the girl's head. Then we both look at each other and back at the G and both at the same time say, "No do we look like fucking burglars to you?"

"Didn't think so, I can still see your faces. So come on, fellas, who sent you?"

"You owe Mattie some money. So if the lady doesn't want to get it, you best start paying your debts off, Gary."

"No I don't."

"Oh yes you do," Mattie said.

"So we're in the fucking pantomime now are we? I say oh no I don't and you say oh yes you do."

"Well you fucking well do now so get your arse out of the bed and get the fucking money before I have to make a mess of ya," as Matt placed the shotgun to the G's chest.

"Look I don't owe you anything. Now piss off out of here before I call someone to come round and take your fucking heads off with an axe. I don't know you two from Adam and you haven't shot me yet. My guess is it ain't going to happen now is it. Not with all these witnesses, and my guess is you only have one shell left."

"Well for your information you do owe money." Mattie says, "it's Ray you owe it to and I'm here to collect it."

"So where's Ray and I'll pay it to him?"

"He's in the nick, so you now owe it to me and I'll make sure Mr B gets it. He'll then give it to Malcolm. Ray is still getting shit from Hector inside the nick because you haven't bothered to pay your debts back, it's long over due."

"Now we're getting somewhere. Is that it?" the G says, "that's why you have come here to wake me up. Butler."

"Yes?"

"Get these two pricks some money out the safe. So they can then piss off out of it and I can get back to sleep. And take out the fucking money for a new ceiling, let them explain that one to Hector, now fuck off, boys, I'm trying to get some sleep." He pulls the girl next to him and pulls the covers around them. "Next time, tell Ray to send someone else round that knows what they're doing."

Well it looked like we only had to knock and ask and we would have been paid the money, but Matt the Mac liked to take things to the extreme. He was a bit of an extremist. Well more like a terrorist.

I had met Mattie some time ago, when he had helped my mum outside a grocery shop when two lads tried to rob her; luckily Mattie had seen these two boys telling my mum to hand over her money from across the road. He sold newspapers for his dad. He had run over to her aid, told the boys to stop and had kicked one of them up the arse and told them to get out of it. He then walked mum home and made sure she got in safely. She was a bit shaken up but asked who he was. He said he was Mattie the Mac and if she ever needed any help in the future to give him a call. Which was a very kind thing to do I thought even though he turned out to be a gunman for the Firm in the end. He left his number and was gone. Mum told me what had happened and I thanked Matt on the phone and took him out for a drink.

I didn't see him again 'til I was working in London for the Firm. I was waiting for a deal to go off so I went to buy a newspaper outside Kings Cross and who should be sitting there selling papers, Mattie the Mac.

"Fuck me, how you doing?"

"Good, mate, well not too good to be honest, there's a door firm round here that keeps bothering me, they are a bit out my league." Well we were a bit younger back then. "They keep asking me for money, they want to take my stall over."

"Who are they? I'll get it sorted it for you."

"How much will that cost me?"

"Nothing, mate, after what you did for my mum, that's no problem, its good to see you again I'll be in touch." I then got into the black cab, collected a bar of cocaine, then got out and jumped on the tube to Camden to get shot of it.

It turned out, this firm were running the doors round here in the clubs. In their spare time they were bullying local business people into paying protection money, but it was them setting up all the trouble themselves in the first place. So they were on a win win basis. That is, until we turned up on the scene to put things right.

I talked to Mr Adams about it all and he said, "Do you know what, son, I'd like to run the doors around here myself." I told him how things were round here and so he lent me two of his biggest minders to come on a little errand for me to get to the root of the problem. So we found out where the office was for this door firm. I walked in with these two big lumps behind me and believe me they were big.

As the minders slammed the office door behind me, the main fella of it looked up and in a deep London accent says, "Hello, fellas, come for some work? Who are you and what can I do for you lot?"

I turned and looked at the two minders then said, "Who are we, well let me introduce myself. I'm Jason and these are my fucking Argonauts," as I pointed to them standing behind me. "I'm going to tell you once and once only; so let's make this short and very sweet; so you listen and listen good, my friend. My pal owns a newspaper stall around here and you say he owes you money. Well he doesn't owe it to you anymore. As he owes it all to me now and I want paying. So stay away from him as all debts he had with you have just been wiped clean."

He interrupts and says, "'old on a minute, fella, obviously you don't know who I am or who you're messing with. I run this Manor and all the clubs in it and if he owes me money then he should pay it to me. The likes of you can mind your own fucking business and get in line and wait 'til he has paid me. So take your Argonauts and go look for the Golden Fleece elsewhere, my son. As you won't find it here."

I replied, "I don't care who you are or who you know. This place is a fucking no-man's land. So here's £50,000 and a pair of new trainers that Mr Adams has kindly given me to give to you. I threw the money and the trainers in a bag on to his desk. Now do yourself a favour, behave yourself and jog along old man and take your no good doormen with you. Mr Adams now runs these manors and the doors in them, so it's time for you to move on out. So take the money and fuck off out of it. Things could get quite heated and messy around here for you from now on, and we don't like bullies. Do you hear me?"

One of the minders says, "Cookster"

"Yes?"

"I'm just stepping outside, son, Mr Adams has rung me."

Then we all look out the window to see Mr Adams' minder pouring petrol all over the Maserati that was parked outside. He then stood there with a box of matches.

"So looking at that, my friend, you best fuck off out of it sharpish before we really get upset and send people down here to shake you and your doormen around a bit 'til you start to see sense. As you can see we ain't fucking about. We're all gangsters round here and we all know where you live. So do the right thing my friend before it all gets well out of hand and you find yourself going missing."

All of a sudden there's a great big bang as the Maserati blows up, the minder walks in.

"Some silly cunt had thrown a fag out their car window on passing and it rolled under the car and before you know it, BOOM."

It had had the result we needed. We all rushed to the window again to see the car on fire. Then to my surprise he took the money and in no time left with help from Mr Adams' mob. That's what happens when you confront the bullies. So it left Mr Adams and his mob to take over and start running things including the clubs in the manors in the right way.

The gangsters had all turned security consultants or film stars, and the Russians, well they had now moved in and been given S.I.A. cards to work the doors, with the help of Mr Nice and Mr Adams. Westminster had changed their badge system for all the bouncers so the old school ones had now changed into doormen. Within no time they too were running parts of London as the Russian mafia don't fuck about. This is now why I could do pretty much what I wanted to do and go in most clubs with a V.I.P. but only with their say-so. Old School who was once again well connected with most of the big named main mobs in England. He would DJ and promote in most of their clubs or work the doors himself.

So, getting back to the job in hand. The plan was to get Johnny out of prison, he would be leaving Bellmarsh prison in a security van this Friday morning about 8.45am.

He had already spent six months on remand, so the police didn't think he was that much of a threat. They didn't have a police escort follow him, which of course was to our advantage. Before the plan could go ahead, we needed to do our homework to find out what gate the van would leave the prison from; to see if there were cameras watching streets or to see what security they had and what we would need to look out for. So Ray and I drove down to Bellmarsh prison and sat there watching and observing every move whilst eating a McDonald's. Then who should walk past but Lewis, Ray looked up.

"There's Lewis, that cunt owes me 250 quid for tick."

"Shit, he owes me 50 too. Let's get him."

Lewis turns round to be confronted with both of us jumping out the motor throwing the McDonald's everywhere as we start running towards him. He is off on his toes running as fast as he can. I give up and lose them both but Ray catches up with him. As I'm walking back to the car I see Ray shouting into the boot of the car.

"There'll be no more fucking tick for you from now on, son. Now move your hands." Lewis was still trying to get back out of the boot, Ray slams it shut and we drive off. Then Ray makes me get out the car and drives off.

The next day Ray pulls up and says, "There you go, there's the fifty he owed you." What he did to get it I'll never know and who cares I had the money now. We then went back to Bellmarsh again to watch the prison.

The prison vans came from round the back. They pulled out from the gates then turned left into a long narrow road that went down the side of the prison. Then they turned right and went onto the main high street. We sat and watched most of the morning, seeing vans come and go; watching and calculating their every move; watching the prison cameras too as we adjusted our mirrors on the car to watch everything that was going on without it looking too obvious.

We decided we would need to hit the van just as it left the prison gates and turned left into the street. This would be the best time to act as the camera would only be able to see the top of the van, and the tracker wouldn't have been activated yet because the prison van would still be in the vicinity of the prison. There was one camera that watched the length of that street and there was a road coming off at a junction just outside the prison. So when the van pulls out of the gates it would then have to turn right. It would have to stop to let cars go and it would be blocking the camera's view of what was going on to the van's left side. That was the time we would strike.

So after a long day just sitting there with Ray, having a laugh and watching every van that came and went past we went back to the Hairy Fella's yard in Lemming road. It had been a constructive day for once. All the things we had observed were written down and taken on board. It's funny that when you were at school you never paid much attention, but when you were on a bit of work you would have got an A plus for your attention span, and the amount you took in and actually remembered. You would have probably been top of the class. That's if there was an exam for skullduggary. Once we discussed the plan to get Johnny out between us all, we found that the only problem we would now have would be the camera.

Old School pointed out to us so how we were going to get past the camera. It would only see the top of the van as it pulled out the prison gates and came out to the road. It would be able to see everything a bit more clearly as the road widened and as the van moved on up a bit.

"That's it!" I said. "We need a woman. Mandy." She was the one men couldn't keep their eyes off. We needed to clue Mandy up with what was going on so she could help us out, so I rang her.

"Mandy, hi sweetheart. It's me, the Cookster."

"Hi, darling, how are you? I was wondering when you would ring me."

"Mandy, could you come over to mine? I need to talk to you."

"OK, let me do my hair, then I'll be over. Why don't you get a bottle? We could make a night of it." Er, of all nights. She now wanted a bottle.

"Umm well it's more business than pleasure, darling. I have a few pals I want you to meet back at my friend's house."

"Oh," she replied, rather half-heartedly, "OK."

By the sound of it, she hadn't had many knock-backs and there was I wanting her so much. But right now I had to knock her back. Because now sitting in my house was some of Britain's most wanted that had the Serous Crime Squad after them. Well Old School and Matt the Mac did and Ray allegedly. She knew some of them but it weren't a quiet night in that it seemed she wanted. This was a means to an end for me to get the Jewellery Thieves off my back once and for all.

The lovely Mandy arrived and knocked on the door. As I opened it I got a waft of her perfume once again, she smelt fantastic.

I kissed her cheeks, "Hi, there's some people here I want you to meet. Some you may already know and some I'll introduce you to." I led her into the room and introduced her to everyone.

"This is Old School."

"Hello, darling," he whistled. "How you doing?"

"I'm, OK thanks." They had met once before when Johnny had done some work for him. "This is Mattie the Mac." He winked at her and smiled like a Cheshire cat.

"This is the Moss, who you already know."

"Hello, darling, nice to see you again, you can sit here," as he stood up. Then he raised his eyebrows with delight. They were eyeing her up like a lion does a piece of meat with their mouths wide open, drooling.

"This is Ray, a good friend of mine and Mr B's."

"Hi, nice to meet you, Mandy." Ray says as he shakes her hand.

"Come on, fellas," I said, "we're here to do some work. Not to chat up the lady. So let's get down to it. Mandy…"

"Yes?"

"We need you to make a distraction in a few days for a camera outside the prison. We need you to wear next to nothing, like a small skirt and a small top, with no bra on, and to walk slowly up the road next to the prison."

"Are you sure this ain't for you lot of perverts?"

I laughed, "No of course it ain't. It's to help get Johnny out."

"Well if you want it to be." Tom said as we all laughed.

"No, this is the distraction we need, Mandy."

"So you want me to dress up as a tart and do this? Don't think so."

"It's for Johnny." After a while she agreed. Anything to get her brother out of there.

So on the first day she walked along that street, our mate the Hairy Fella walked behind to see if the cameras responded which they did… Perverts eh? We laughed but the Hairy Fella said the camera only looked for a bit, then back on the road, then back on Mandy. The camera locked on to the prison van as it left the prison and drove up the road. So how could we slow it down? I knew, have a small dog and keep bending down to stroke it and sure enough, the perverts behind the camera were back at it. Perving over Mandy instead of looking at the road and the prison vans as it should have been. We had it.

On Thursday at about 5.30am the Hairy Fella drove down next to the T-junction and parked up in an old BMW 325i on the left side of the road. Then Ray did the same with another on the right at about 6am. We had bought the BMWs from Johnny's mate, the scrapyard dealer fella for next to nothing. The one that had got clumped in the toilets that night when he had spilled drink on Mandy. The cars were parked one on either side of the road with their boots both facing north. The Hairy Fella and Ray both got out their cars and walked off in opposite directions leaving the two cars open and ready for when the van would come out of the prison gate at 7.30am.

Mandy walks along with the dog like she had for the past 4 days and the camera instantly swings around to her. The gates to the prison slide open and the van leaves the prison gate and turns right. Then just as it starts to move up the road George pulls the dustcart right out in front of it, smashing into the door bending it enough so we could get into the front and stayed there for a bit blocking its path. They beep their horn for him to move back but he ignores them and turns the radio on in the dustcart's cab. That was our cue. Like jack-in-the-boxes, two men leap from the boot of the BMW cars, all in black with balaclavas on and guns at the ready.

They wasted no time at all running to the doors of the prison van pulling their guns on the prison guards.

They shouted, "Out. Out of the front and get those fucking back doors open," as George moved the dustcart back a little.

"Open the fucking back doors now, move it." They did as they were told. Once onboard the van, one of the masked men walked up and down looking into the cells, he saw Johnny.

He turns to a guard, "Open this fucking one, move it." Another balaclaved man pushes the other guard on to the floor at the back and makes him stay face down. The guard then opens the metal door to free Johnny.

He shouts to Johnny, "Move now. Get out, fucking get out." which he then does, a bit unsure with the situation. Some of the prisoners on the van are shouting to get them out too. Some just sit there quietly as they watch the two masked men moving around. Some didn't even look out to see what was going on, they just stared straight ahead.

One of the masked men walks Johnny out from the van. As quickly as possible the other one puts a guard into Johnny's cell and locks him in. As he goes to leave he turns round to see Mr B sitting there all quiet looking straight ahead. He glared at him for what seemed like 5 seconds through the glass to be sure that it was Mr B.

He turned to him, puts the gun to the glass and shouted quickly, "Stand up," to the guard at the back of the van. "Open this one too. Move it." He didn't have the keys so the gun was placed on the glass to the other guard to push the keys under, as they came sliding under the guard picked them up. "Now open it up. Come on I haven't got all day." The guard fumbled with the lock. "Come on, Twinkle bollocks, open it."

This wasn't the plan. We hadn't arranged this and we didn't even know Mr B would be on there, but this was a spur of the moment decision to get him off too. Well we couldn't leave Mr B sitting there after all he had done for us or hadn't done.

"Fucking move," the masked man shouted at Mr B to come out and he then put the other guard in his place.

"Get me off too," everyone was shouting as they moved down the van with Mr B. While this was going on, Tom had come down the other side of the dustcart on a motorbike. He parked it up at the back of the dustcart and then ran over to the masked man with Johnny handing over the crash helmet he had been wearing. Tom then jumps in the BMW and starts it up. The masked man shouts to Johnny to run with him and get on the bike. The bike starts up with Johnny clinging to the back. The masked man shouts to Johnny hang on, he throws the gun into the back of the dustcart and they're away with a screech of tyres. Old School and Johnny are out of there.

Tom the Moose has by then started the BMW up, ready for the other masked man to come running out of the prison van and jump in. The other masked man with Mr B exits the van shouting to Mr B to shut the door to the prison van. Then Mattie the Mac gets out the other side of the dustcart, he grabs the gun off the masked man throwing it into the back of the cart and he gets back into the dustcart. The masked man pushes Mr B onto the backseat of the BMW, which is waiting with its doors open. Once both inside the car the dustcart reverses back up the road and then drives up the street and turns left on to the main road. Tom slams the BMW into gear and we are out of there as we hit the high street. I pull up the 'bally' and make it into a beanie hat.

"Fuck me," Mr B says, as he turns white.

"Yes you better believe it," Tom says. Mr B could see it was me.

"The Cookster, of all people," he said, "that was amazing, mate, done like a true pro on a job." We all laughed. Well I was a true pro in my eyes. I had earned the respect I wanted from Mr B since I was young and he now owed me big time. So the tables had well turned. Old School had Johnny on the bike and had gone to a flat in Colindale. Tom the Moose, Mr B and I were also out of there and we were now on our way back to the Wood. Matt had gone with George and the dustcart to dump the dustcart's rubbish off and to get rid of the guns.

All this had happened before Mandy had reached the top of the road. She turned round to see that the camera was still looking at her. She bends over one last time and strokes the dog, then picks up the dog and walks off round the corner hearing the camera start to buzz a bit as it turns back towards the prison van. It was now too late for them to see anything, as the job had been done. They must have loved watching her walking up the street like that. Whoever was behind the camera would now be getting the sack for not looking at the van when it left the prison. The job had gone off and we had done it. Johnny was free at last.

The camera had now turned back and seen the van sitting there looking as if nothing was wrong until they realised it had sat there for more then half hour and that people were now tooting their horns to get past. So the alarm had been raised.

I must admit it had been mighty uncomfortable hiding in the boot off a BMW. Lucky that we had set the alarms on our watches and had the sleeping bags in the back to make it a bit more comfy. So now I knew what it was like when they throw people in the boot to teach them a little lesson for debts not paid.

It was worth the wait in the boot though, as now Johnny and unexpectedly Mr B were free again. George and Mattie had taken the guns to the tip and buried them under the contents of the dustcart. They had left the cart there as Mr Wong had picked them up and taken them back to his. So they stayed low until things had passed.

We now had to move fast to get Mr B and Johnny out of the country to safety. So we needed the Russian's help again even though we still owed him the money. But we needed him to see if he could get in touch with Murphy who knew a diplomat that could sort out passports for us. So Old School and I meet up with the Russian once again.

"Yes your money is safe, stop going on about it. Look if you haven't had your shipment of drugs by Saturday then I will go to the Columbians and get it myself for you, OK? You're not dealing with amateurs here." Me giving the bullshit once again.

"No but I need to know my money's safe as it's been 3 days now and still nothing, not even a phone call. Then you turn up here wanting some passports."

Old School pulls out his gun and says, "Listen, we've spent your fucking money. Now sit down, shut the fuck up and listen."

"What?" The Russian looked surprised and knew there was nothing he could do at this time. So he did as he was told. I was surprised too as I didn't know Old School was walking around with a gun on him all the time. Old School then shouted at the Russian. "We need to get two people out the country. Can you do it?"

"Of course I can, and my money?"

"I'll get it for you OK, stop spitting your dummy out and going on about your fucking money. Like the Cookster said, the money is in good hands and soon you will have the parcel, but right now you need to shut up and get on with this. Can you do it, or not? Or are we wasting our time with you? Time is money and right now we ain't got a lot of time and very little money." The Russian fella said he would get in touch with Murphy who was nicknamed the 'Viagra man' seeing he could get viagra at 4 quid a pop.

He could do it. He had a friend that was shipping immigrants in and out of London for a small price. They also had connections with this diplomat that could get hold of bent passports, which were shit hot and would see them both through Customs with ease. This was just what we needed and was right up our street. Now we needed to get Johnny and Mr B out the country safely.

The Russian and Murphy got together and within 3 hours the passports were sorted but they had to be picked up in France. So we bought two passports from this diplomat.

The Russian fella asked about his money again when we met, after we had just handed over £2000 for these passports to him and Murphy.

I said, "Look, that night someone got nicked."

"Not my problem," he said.

"Well, mate, look I'll tell you everything. They got nicked with your money and our parcel out in the sea at Southend," not letting him know what Johnny was all about. As far as the Russian knew he was involved with the deal as well. The Russian believed that both of them, Johnny and Mr B were involved in trying to bring the shipment over. Well Mr B was so we weren't lying there. "Now you can see why we need to get them out the country fast. Once they're out we can then sort out the shipment again and your money OK?" That had cheered the Russian up for a bit and made him more attentive to our needs. Now he knew the full picture Murphy was happy, he had just made 500 quid for his share in the passports so he wasn't grumbling for once. We told the Russian to meet us down by the docks at Dover. So we could meet up with Johnny and Mr B and get them on their way with these passports.

The Trip to Barbados and Russian Roulette with an Old Skeleton in the Cupboard

By now Old School had taken Johnny to a safe house, told him to relax for a few hours, have a bath, a shave and to shave his hair off. "I'll get you some clothes and get rid of the bike," he said.

I had taken Mr B to my house for safety too and told him to do the same. By now the photos of them would have been issued by the police and there would now be a manhunt for them to get them back into prison where they belonged and as fast as possible. The plan was to make them look a bit different. I told Mr B I would pick some specs up for him and he would need to keep them on at all times. I said that I would be about 45 minutes and that he should be ready to go by the time I got back, he nodded. So I went straight off to get them and to make a call to Mandy so she knew Johnny was safe and to stay out the way of the police. They would come looking for her now to see if Johnny had been there or contacted her.

Soon it was time to bring Mr B and Johnny together and both down to Dover. So we could get them on the boat and out the country as fast as we could, just after we had their photos done at a passport booth. We could load them on the lorry ready to be taken abroad and the passports from the diplomat would be made up for them over in France ready for them to get to Barbados where they would now have to live their lives. So Old School, the Russian, Mr B and I all met at the Dover docks. Murphy had gone over to France to get the passports off the diplomat and was waiting for Johnny and Mr B's arrival.

As soon as Johnny saw me he said, "What are you doing here, son? Haven't you learnt your lesson, from the last time we met?"

"What am I doing here? Well, me, I'm your saviour. I'm why you're here now, smelling this fresh sea air and not some cunt's farts on the top bunk stuck back in some shitty old prison cell."

"You," he said as he looked at Old School, and said, "Him?"

"Yes, afraid so, mate."

"Him?"

"Yes, me. I'm behind the great escape, Johnny. Me, OK? So get over it." He looked at me, like he was going to kill me at any moment with his bare hands. I was being a bit cheeky and full of myself. Well I had just busted him out of prison and that don't happen everyday, so he should think himself lucky. So why not be a bit cheeky and push my luck a bit even if he was a killer? To my amazement he put out his hand and said thanks. I shook it firmly but nervously and said, "It's been a pleasure." He pulled me close and cuddled me. "There's someone here to see you." I phoned her and Mandy come running down from her car. I knew she would want to see Johnny and say goodbye before he went on the run and I knew he would want to see her too before he went.

She shouts "Johnny" as she runs down. His eyes lit up as she came down the embankment. They cuddled and then she said, "Like your new haircut." We all laughed.

I said, "Before I forget, here put these on." It was some specs, I had picked up two pairs on my travels. They both looked different now. So they should be able to get to where they were going with no problems.

He looked at me and said, "Well, I guess you can see my sister whenever you like, but you keep an eye out for her, son. I don't want her mixed up with any thugs, mugs, gangsters or low lifes. Do you hear me?" I smiled and he shook my hand again, then he shook Old School's hand and thanked him for his part in the escape. "Tell everyone thanks. I won't forget it."

Mandy and Johnny cuddled each other again. "Bye, sis,"

The Russian said, "I'll meet you in France in 6 hours. Murphy should be there soon. So I can get the passport for you and Johnny once they're finished off."

Johnny looked the Russian up and down and said, "I know you, don't I? I know you from somewhere."

"You don't know me, sorry my friend, impossible. I have never seen you before in my life," he says.

"Yes I do," as he looked at the tattoo of the teardrop under the Russian's eye. "I know…"

"You must be mistaken," the Russian interrupts.

"Fuck," Johnny says. "I can't think straight but I know I have seen you before. Were you in the forces? It was a long time ago. I'm sure of it; it will come back to me soon."

"Look you best go," Mandy said.

So the goodbyes were said, and then Johnny and Mr B got on to the lorry. They made themselves comfortable as the lorry drove off and got ready to board the ferry with the help of course from our Customs officer who was on the Firm at the time. The one I had met that time when I had drove the Japanese car down here for it to be parked up with gear for the Liverpool mob. The Russian had had a word with him to make sure the lorry was untouched. Then the Russian himself got on the ferry ready to set off to France and make sure all was well with the passports so they could then go on their way to Barbados.

Old School, Mandy and I went back to Mandy's and opened a bottle of champers. We were all very happy now they were on their way and free at last. It was good times once again. Well at least for now. Old School and I got the shiny buliney out, Peru's finest cocaine the parley white chang the one with the shiny fish scales Finish along the side of it with plenty of oil not the pressed stuff. This wasn't the old disco dust press, this was the real deal that he had just bought off the Customs officer. They had just confiscated a large amount but had only charged the people with 2 keys when really they had been caught with 4, if we had had the money at the time we would have taken the lot off him. Instead of Old School just taking 3 ounces. Well no one would know and if you were sitting in court you aren't going to say there was 4 when you have only been charged with 2. It was a special accession so we all got nutted. I got a call, it was the Jewellery Thief.

"There's someone wants to talk to you."

"Hello who's this?"

"It's me Mr Nice. Son, we haven't heard from you for some time. So how's it all going?

"Well it's going well, Mr Nice, but not the way we thought it would turn out but Johnny is free."

"That's all I wanted to hear, son. I'll let them know. Come out and see me soon."

"OK, Mr Nice, will do." The phone went dead.

That was one thing of my back. Now all I had was the Russian and the Colombians' money to sort out. I only had 4 days left and the Grim Reaper would be on my case phoning for this money. In time the Russian was back from France and with us, he said everything was OK and that they had got across safely and had met Murphy who had passed on the passports and had tried to sell them all viagra too. Johnny said what the fuck do I want fucking viagra for I'm on the run not going straight. It was a joke and it made them all laugh.

That night a call comes through from a Spanish girl. "Señor Cookster, your friends send their best and can't thank you enough for what you have done for them."

"OK, I will come out to see them soon tell them." The phone went dead. The prison van breakout was all on the news but it was too late they were home dry.

Within no time, me, Old School and the Russian had to go out to see them. When we got out there, Johnny had bad news. "I'm afraid Mr B had tried to get over to Morocco to sort out some business but the police had caught him. They tried to charge him for organizing a boatload of puff (Moroccan black cannabis) to go over to England while he was safely in Marco."

They had picked him up on the bent passport coming back and their investigation had led them to a warehouse he had gone to that had about 25 tones of Moroccan black stashed there. They think someone bigger was being watched and had grassed him up and used him as an escape goat. The Moroccan police couldn't prove that he was organising it to come over to England, but they knew somehow that he had been at the warehouse. They had photos of him there looking at shelves stacked full of bars. He was on the run so he was nicked, but no charges of conspiracy were bought against him, which was lucky. They tried to hold him on a charge of association but they just sent him back to England to finish off his bird. So he has now been extradited to England, and is now doing the rest of his time in HMP Woodhill.

So it looked like I had to stay there where no one knew me, which couldn't be bad eh? Sun, sea and sex. Johnny had met up with an old friend out there who had made it big by exporting tobacco and cigarettes. He had bought some big warehouses out in Belgium, Amsterdam and Denmark and was selling cheap fags, tobacco and booze by the vanload and made a small fortune out of doing so. The friend had come out to Barbados to retire leaving trusted people to take care of his business, so Johnny was being well looked after out here by him.

We all went out to a little shack, which was just a tiny hut in the middle of nowhere. We started drinking and having a laugh then Johnny went a bit weird on us all saying, "Let's play a game."

"OK," the Russian, said jokingly, "let's play Russian roulette."

So Johnny then said, "Yes that's a great fucking idea," being all deadly serious. The Russian had come with us, as we still owed him his money.

"Let's make the Russian feel at home," Johnny said.

"What?" I said looking at the Russian, then at Old School.

The Russian said, "It's cool," thinking it was all a big joke and that no one would have a gun on them. They had all gone through Customs clean.

He then said, "You have a revolver with a bullet in it then?"

"I know what it is and how to play it," Johnny said.

"Why would we want to play that, Johnny?" I said.

"Come on, it's fun."

"You're twisted, mate," said Old School who then sat down at the table.

I said, "Shit, not for me, fellas."

"Well come on," the Russian said calling his bluff.

Old School said, "OK, so where's the gun then?" Johnny pulled out the gun and a bullet wrapped in a plastic bag taped under the table. He then got them out and placed one bullet into the gun looking closely at the Russian all the time. There seemed to be some animosity between them but I couldn't work out why. After all, it was his help that got him out here too. But Johnny had the hump with the Russian for some reason. Johnny then put the gun on the table spun the gun round. The Russian fella said, "You don't do it like that. Here, give it to me and I'll show you."

Johnny then said, "I'll give it to you OK." With that Johnny lent across the table snatched the gun up and pulled the trigger several times. The barrel started spinning round as the Russian tried to lean back on his chair to get out the way.

"Fuck," as the Russian tried to pull back on his seat and laughed a nervous sort of laugh as he thought Johnny was joking, getting up out of his chair. Old School and I stare at Johnny in amazement and disbelief as to what is going on as the gun is going click, click. Then went bang as Johnny pulled the trigger back as quickly as he could for one last time. The Russian stumbles over his chair and tries to make a run for it, just as Old School comes to his senses and tries to grab the gun. It was too late the bullet had left the gun's chamber and had come flying out and hit the Russian in the side of the head causing him to fall face down on the floor, dead. We were all gobsmacked at first.

"For fuck's sake, Johnny!" I had shit my pants. "What are you doing? He is one of us, Johnny. You're... you're fucking crazy. Both of you, you and Old School; you two are off your fucking nuts. I thought Old School was the mad one. We're in big trouble now."

"Why? He worked for the fucking Russian mafia," as Old School ripped open the Russian's shirt showing Johnny the tattoos on his chest.

"So it's true then," Johnny said.

"What?"

"Well let me tell you this, fellas. I remembered him well as soon as I saw him. I would never forget the tattoo under his eye; he was the one that shot my mum and my stepfather. I was there and saw this piece of shit let my mum and stepfather have it. He didn't show any mercy. He just turned to me out the window and said, "Go home, son." His mate had just let off a Mac ten all over the car, nearly killing me. I can still see the bullets hitting the floor and rolling around as the end of the gun spat fire. Then this piece of shit came out of nowhere with a revolver and killed the casino owner who was trying to get away. BANG BANG. I can see it all really clearly. He killed my mum and stepdad because he was hired to do so, by someone that had lost at the casino and owed loads of debts to it. So good riddance to the piece of shit. Working for the mafia or not. Fuck him," as he spat on him. "He still killed my mum. So fuck him. I must have been about 20, he was 22 when it happened. I remembered his face and have been waiting for this moment for a long time. Now, boys, he's got it all thanks to you."

"Shit, Johnny. I'm nothing to do with this one, mate," I said.

"You don't know how thankful I am, son," as he looked at me. Shit I had just got the Russian killed.

"I have chatted to everyone to find this man," Johnny said

"No wonder everyone kept their mouth shut about him," I raised my eyes to Johnny.

"Thanks, fellas." Johnny said.

"You're fucked up," Old School replied.

"Shut it," he said.

"I'm out of here," Old School said as we left and went straight back to our hotel, leaving the Russian dead on the floor; with the gun in his hand Johnny had placed after wiping it over so it looked like a suicide.

"Don't worry, Cookster. Death comes to us all, son, sooner or later, just some people get it sooner."

"Well, Johnny mate, I'd like it to be later rather than sooner, if you know what I mean."

He laughs, "Don't worry. That place is never used and only a few of us know about it."

"So that's why you've brought us out here."

"Well you could say that. Didn't think you were one to come and admire the views, son." He laughs again then slapped me on the back. My head was numb with panic. I had sobered up straight away. I had just seen a cold-blooded execution and fuck me it was because of me he had got it. Did I hate it and did it scare me; like a fucking nightmare. Boy was I scared; it left me with an eerie mind for the rest of my days and still haunts me a bit today. Fucked up or what?

"Johnny, why didn't you shoot me that night in the Land Rover?" I asked.

"You were only a kid. Plus, to shoot you in that place was too risky, everyone would have heard the echo of the gun. It would have been too messy in my Land Rover, so think yourself lucky, son, that you're still here to tell the tale. Not many people get away from murder."

To change the subject quickly I said, "I need some money."

"Cookster," he said. "Don't we all need fucking money, son, but after what you have done for me I'm sure we could sort something out."

"Just a loan to get me on my feet again, that's all, Johnny, can you help me?"

"No I can't right now." The police had frozen all his things when he had got nicked. "But you can go see my auntie; she's a security van driver who collects money from the banks in Tottenham." Well there it is.

"What, rob your auntie?"

"No way; you do that, son, and I'll cut you up into little pieces and feed you to the sharks. No just introduce yourself to her. Well Mandy can do that. Go see Mandy and tell her what I have said. She will help you if it's to help me."

"OK, leave it with me."

"You best not hurt my auntie, Cookster, in any way shape or form. Otherwise you can say goodbye. I'll find you, you know that don't you? Even if it takes me a lifetime. Look, I'll send some money over to you once we pull it off." If we do.

He had told me how to do this job so we could then get some quick and easy money together, on the walk back to the hotel. It had calmed my mind a bit after what had just happened.

"OK, give me an address and I'll send it Western Union to you, and if it don't come then you know we must have got caught."

I said bye to Johnny and went back to the hotel.

Old School was asleep by then so I sat on the bed and thought. Well the Russian fella was now out the way. So I didn't owe him any more money. The Jewellery Thieves and Mr Nice were OK and happy, now that Johnny was free they were all paid. Johnny, I guess, well he would always be a fugitive out here. He was well messed up inside. So all I had to deal with was the Columbians now and try to get Mandy and the rest of us some money. Then it would all be OK and I could get back to a normal life, a 9 to 5 without any grief or anyone else getting killed. I soon fell asleep myself.

Old School had a call in the early hours of the morning, which made me stir in my sleep. I could just make it out. It was Johnny. He had sobered up now and said, "I'll give you two grand to go bury that fella with the gun." Meaning the Russian.

"No."

"OK, I'll shoot the Cookster then for knowing about it. See you soon."

So off Old School went. He knew Johnny wasn't fucking around. Within no time we were back in England Old School and me. We thanked Tom the Moose for his help in getting them out and we asked if he was up for another job if we could sort it out. He said let him know when the time came and then count him in.

The Much Needed New Found Cash with Johnny's Stepsister Auntie

Mandy introduced me to her stepsister; Jo, she was a very nice lady in her 40s. We didn't tell her too much of what had been happening or why we were really there. As far as she knew Mandy just wanted to say hi and check she was OK as she hadn't seen her for ages.

"Did you hear the news?"

"Hear what?" Mandy said, acting dumb.

"I heard Johnny escaped from prison. It was all on the news the other week."

"Did he?" We were both acting dumb now. "Where has he gone then? Have they caught him yet?"

"No," she said. "The news people said that he shouldn't be approached and that he's a very dangerous man at large. He was on *Crimewatch* too." Well she wasn't wrong there. He was a very dangerous man indeed and as far as I had seen he was a proper nutcase.

She continued, "They must have it all wrong. He was such a lovely gentlemen when I last saw him. He had just left the Marines then. Well it was all on the news anyhow. I thought you of all people would have known about it."

"No," she said.

"The police have already been round here looking for him and asking questions. They said two men got out of a prison van, one being Johnny and some other big time gangster from London."

"Did they?" Mandy asked. "How did they do it?"

"Not too sure yet; they said something about two gunmen and that there was some sort of breach of security." I had to laugh to myself, I could just see them now looking on the camera at

Mandy, giving it loads of ooh and cor looks at her as she walked up the side road of the prison.

"So how you been?" Mandy asked.

"I'm fine. You?"

"I'm OK," she said. "Sorry how rude of me, this is the Cookster by the way."

"Hi, nice to meet you." Then Mandy asked if she could use her toilet.

"OK, darling, you know where it is."

As luck would have it, Mandy's stepsister was on holiday for a week from work. She had left her security uniform hanging up next to the toilet. So Mandy took it and the helmet hiding it in the car. We had tea and I asked when she would be going back to work. She said that she was off for a week and needed to get things done around the house. We finished our tea and then she said, "Mandy, be very careful, dear, if Johnny tries to contact you. The police will be looking everywhere soon so if he does just be very careful OK?" She didn't want Mandy getting involved in it all as they could nick her for harbouring a wanted criminal. "OK," she said. We said bye and I said it was very nice to have met her then we left.

"Did you get it, Mandy?"

"Yes here it is." All we needed now was a box, but we could get that off the guard. It was now all in place.

It was time to call in the Firm that I had set up once more for the job; Mattie the Mac, Tom the Moose, Ray and Old School. Now Mattie was a small fella in height and the suit just fitted him, which was a result and with the helmet on you could easily mistake him for a guard. So now it was time to do some more surveillance work. We had to find out the time when the van would arrive at the bank. That's when we would make our move. So Old School and I sat on a bench outside Barclays bank, and waited and waited. Within time the van arrived, this was it. We filmed it all on his cell phone, he made out he was texting.

The van pulled up and the passenger got out, walked to the back and banged on the door, then looked into the glass and without delay the box came sliding out. This all took a matter of seconds and then the guard went into the bank. Within 15 minutes he had arrived back out with the box but this time it looked a bit heavier. The box was slipped in the back and the man walked back to the passenger side and got in the van. It drove off to do the same thing somewhere else at another bank.

Thursday evening we were all ready and waiting in place. Mattie was parked up on the corner just a few feet away from where the security van would park up, in a white van all kitted out wearing the security outfit ready to go. Old School was standing by the corner ready for the security van to pull up. Mandy was in a low-cut top without a bra. She crossed the road as the security van pulled up and the passenger got out and started to walk down the side of the van.

Old School pulls the passenger into the awaiting white van, catching the guard by surprise. After he manages to get the man's helmet off he punches him clean out cold. As this is happening Matt the Mac drives the van round the corner with the security guard and gets out. Mattie quickly bangs on the security van's door, the same way he had seen from the phone's video footage. Then all of a sudden, the box is slid out and given to him. Ray was waiting to drive the white van for our getaway. Whilst all this was happening Mandy had walked up to the security van and asked the driver for directions, to take his mind of what was really going on and keep his mind on her tits. She started flirting with him for a bit and he told her the way, oblivious to what had just happened.

Old School was on the floor with the guard in the back of the white van. Mattie the Mac was inside the bank with the box in his hand. He nods at the security camera and bingo, he is through the security doors to the bank, and in past the tills to the main safe. He puts the box on the table, says hi and the girl manager says hi back. Then she looks at him, Mattie wasn't sure what to do so he went to grab for the gun he had hidden in the back of his trousers but then she stands up. She starts to open the safe and pulls 10 bags of notes out and puts them into the box. Mattie was quite excited by this.

He shuts the box says, "Bye darling, have a great weekend."

"You too."

"Don't worry I will." The girl nods and smiles, none the wiser as she lets him out the secure door. Mattie walks out passing the clerks at the desk, through the door, past two customers and through the bank's outer doors. He walks round to the side of our white van and gets in. They then opened the box using the security tag and mechanism on the security guy's belt. The box was opened correctly without spraying us, or the money with dye. Once the box was empty and the money taken out, I get out with the guard and lay him on the floor. Old School, Mattie and Ray drive off leaving me behind with the guard and the empty box on the floor next to him. Then people started to realise what had happened to the fella and had started to crowd round.

I bang on the side of the security van. "Quick, mate."

"Sorry?" he turns to me from Mandy.

"Your fella's on the floor." He is starting to come round by now and is confronted by the crowd. One of them calls for an ambulance as he still has the cut bleeding from his head where Mattie had hit him.

"I've phoned for an ambulance."

"Call the police," someone said. The other security guard took off his seat belt and ran round to the guard lying on the ground. He pushed through the growing crowd of onlookers.

The other guard started to come round.

"You OK, Ricky?" the driver said.

"Did you see anything?" he said to me

"No, mate, just saw him on the floor as I walked past."

"Well the ambulance is on its way, mate, just stay still."

"OK, thanks," he said as I walk off, Mandy then walked off the other way. I got into a cab and Mandy got the bus home.

We had pulled it off and the rest was yesterday's news when it hit the local newspaper. We were all home and dry and it was time to count out the money we had earned. 75 grand, not bad for a day's work eh? After sharing it, we all got about 19,000 each. Not bad but nowhere near enough for me to pay the Columbians off, as they were still hot on my tail. I gave most of my money to Mandy. She said no, but I insisted, after all I had lost her money for her. I felt gutted that we had to hurt the fella but in this line of work someone gets hurt somewhere.

We all put £5000 in a bag and sent Mandy back to Barbados to see Johnny and give him the share of the money that he had requested if we pulled it off. After all I was still in the thick of things and didn't want to piss Johnny off again. So he done well and ended up with £20,000. So it weren't bad. Not quite the 100 grand we had lost trying to get the copper to get Johnny off but it was something. Mandy also had gone back to see her stepsister and put her uniform back for me that we had borrowed. She too was none the wiser that it had gone off until she probably read about it in the local paper the next day. Ray went off and started up his own building business with his share of the money. We still see each other now and then and reminisce about the past and he still sees Mr B too.

The Columbian's Call

I got the call just as he said I would. It was the Grim Reaper, the Columbian fella.

"Hello, my friend, the ten days has come and gone and I am still waiting. So I can only assume you are juggling with my money and that you don't have it. But don't worry, I have sent my collectors over to England. They will be there soon so speak with them. They don't speak too much English and they only understand payments of sterling, which I'm sure you will have once they arrive. So you best have all my money ready, they know what to do if you let me down." The phone went dead.

Now that The Grim Reaper's collectors were coming, I was in big, big trouble and all they understood were payments. There was no trying to get out of it with telling them a little story to try and get some time on my side. Well I had £10,000 now that should keep them at bay, not quite the Full Monty but at least it was better than nothing. I thought £10,000 might buy me a bit more time in order to work out what or how I was able to try and get the rest to them before they killed me or one of my family.

Then out of the blue, I get a call, it was the diver. The one that had got away that night when the drugs deal was going off with Mr B.

"Cookster."

"Yes?"

"You don't know me but I have found you now. I am one of the divers that collected something for you at Southend."

"Sorry who is this? How did you get my number?"

"Look that's not important, let's just say a friend told me it. I'm the diver, the one that got away, before the others all got nicked. I have something that may belong to you."

"What, what's that then?"

"Come to the old warehouse in Goody Street London tomorrow at 6pm behind the old club Bagley's, next to the Cross nightclub."

"OK," I said. "I'll be there."

6pm came, I arrived and the diver was there. He was standing there on his own holding a silver camera box. He gave it to me.

"Here take it. You are alone aren't you?"

"Yes and you?"

"Yes," as he patted me down for listening devices.

"What is it?" I said.

"Open the case."

There it was. 3 keys of Columbian's finest, the Devil's dandruff in its purest form. All wrapped up in an airtight plastic bag with wax around them with a scorpion stamped on to all 3 blocks. My nose was twitching and started to dribble a bit just at the sight of them. "OK, listen Cookster. I have a deal for you. Does anyone else know how many bags there were?"

"Not that I know of, no."

"And has anyone said anything?"

"No, no one, just that you got away and no one has heard from you since."

"Well, tell your friend Mr B I'm fine, so not to worry about me."

I said, "I just knew that whatever came over was the Russian's." I would make my money and share it with everyone from the payment once it was all squared up. But now the Russian was out the way and this belonged to the Columbians or to me and Mr B, but I didn't say that to him.

"OK, I have a deal for you, why don't I take one key and you walk away with two, never to see me again or say we ever met. Or, you can tell the boys and you will probably get nothing as this is now dead man's money. As I understand the Russian is unobtainable for reasons no one seems to know." How did he know that? How could he? Only Old School, Johnny and I knew that. Something wasn't right; he knew too much for my liking.

"It's all up to you." He looked me in the eyes, picked up one bag, turned, walked outside and got into his Rolls Royce and drove off. And to this day I haven't heard or seen of him since, nor has anyone else come to think of it. As far as everyone else was concerned there was only one key there and that was the one that I had told Mr B about on a prison visit. I told him I had seen the diver and Mr B replied, "OK and what?"

"Well he has a key."

"OK. Just sell it just like that." Just like that, mate, 30,000 split.

So I ended up with another £15,000. Now I was getting my money for nothing and my chicks for free so to speak. I now had £20,000 in my reach for the Columbians once they did decide to come over.

I needed another job. There was talk from another firm about a job that would be worth 40 mil. Old School had found out about it just by luck one night.

He was drinking in this pub and the barmaid kept smiling at him. So he flirted back with this woman and managed to get hold of her, she worked behind the bar of a pub in Kentish town. He was waiting to collect some cocaine and they had got talking and he asked if she wanted to come out for a drink after work. She blew him out at first by saying she already had a fella. Then they continued flirting all night and he had given her a sneaky line or two in the men's toilets. She had spilled her heart out about her fella and about how they kept arguing over silly things and how the relationship was going nowhere and the only thing holding them together was this money they would soon get. Old School said, "Look, let's get out of here and you can then let your hair down a bit." She looked at her watch and said, "Wait ten minutes; let me clear the glasses and then I can go."

Old School took her to his mate's nightclub. They were drinking and laughing together and sniffing hard when she told him that she would soon be a millionaire and that's why she hadn't left her boyfriend yet. It was in the pipeline once he had come into the money he was due to get. This made Old School stand up and start listening, wanting to find out more about how she would become a millionaire. He thought maybe she was due for an inheritance. She had said no she wasn't and that it was like this.

Her fella was a security guard. He worked for a big depot that was holding this money there. He had stumbled on it by mistake whist locking up one night. As he closed the door, there was a big sheet covering something large. Being curious he walked in and looked under it. There was a large amount of money being stored in a big warehouse and when I say a large amount of money I mean 100 million. So he had told these local lads about it, and they were intending to rob it from the warehouse, once he gave them the codes and clued them up with all they needed to know.

She was pissed and sniffed up to the max when she had let it all slip out that loads of money was being stored at a warehouse. That was it, that's all Old School needed to hear for him to spring into action and clue me up on it too. This was my answer to sort out all my problems and walk away from them and the Firm like I never existed to some sort of normal life again. The good old 9 to 5 job where it was all work and no play; well if we could get the money it would be no work all play.

Old School acted dumb as if he knew no one when she started throwing a few names of local faces about, that her other half knew in this other firm of local lads who planned to do the robbery. Old School made out that he was far from being connected to anyone; let alone being a face himself. While he sat they're sniffing hard she was all over him like a cheap suit even though she had a fella. I guess it was probably because of the big bag of cocaine that he kept getting out and dishing her line after line whenever she wanted it. She had started flirting with Old School and they had got chatting more and more about this depot now they were all high on the cocaine.

They had gone back to a hotel and sniffed the lot of Old School's bag, the old truth serum. After a few lines it all comes out. She had opened her mouth about it all to Old School, every last detail about it. Old School thought this job would be easy, having her fella as the inside man in this job. Once it was done, he told me that if we were able to pull it off it would no doubt go down in history as the biggest heist in the UK. Bigger than any

1mill airport job and our inside man was all for it. Whether with us or the other local firm of lads, he didn't care as long as he got a cut of the funds he said. Talk was cheap and action spoke volumes. That's why we were doing this job as soon as Old School had heard about it and had spoken to all involved. This job would hit the front page of all the newspapers and he weren't wrong there. We had to move fast and get it done before the other firm acted on it. So we were on it right away, no rest for the wicked eh?

So This One Last Job Would Be Our Retirement Fund

Our man was the security guard of this warehouse; the boyfriend of the girl Old School had now been shagging, unbeknown to him. So Old School and I paid him a visit and told him to behave. The job was now ours and we would pull it off, not these local fellas. And he would do as he was told, otherwise things could now get very unpleasant as we walked the walk and talked the talk too. We would make sure it got done in the next two days.

He was a bit scared at first, but he soon saw the light and played along with it once Old School had a quiet word in his ear. He then went with this fella and saw the other local lads that were planning to do the job telling them that he was an undercover cop and that he had got wind that a warehouse was going to be robbed and that their names had been put forward for it. They denied it and never got involved after that, thanks to Old School putting the frighteners on them.

This girl's fella was our key to get in, the inside man. After all he had clued us up with all the details of this job. The inside man was the front line manger of the security firm, which was looking after the depot. Result. He had been looking after the place for nearly 6 months now and knew the ins and outs. He worked alongside the other main manager who knew that this money was being stored there for a bit. It was arranged that only 6 workers were told to stay and work there the night of the planned robbery, so this money was there for the taking.

It's not what you know; it's who in most things, and that definitely applies in this game. He was the one that had clued us up with everything we needed to know. The other manager of the warehouse had passcodes to get into the shutters; so we needed to get to him for that bit. We needed him to get us where we needed to go and he would know were everyone was at the time we would strike. He knew the layout of the warehouse like the back of his hand. He was our ticket to be driving away in 3 white transit vans full of crisp, new fifty-pound notes.

This was the plan. Our fucking retirement fund. We would be able to walk away now like we never existed, turning our back on a life of crime once and for all. Everyone would be paid and our debts would be a thing of the past. Well mine would. The Columbian's debt would be sorted, and juggling with everyone's money and drugs would be no more. For me it would stop and I would be sitting abroad somewhere hot in some big fancy hotel with my new found funds and family without a care in the world. Sipping at Pina Coladas with stupid umbrellas that hang out the glasses, sitting there in stupid Hawaiian shirts thinking I looked the bollocks with a pair of blacked-out shades with dollar signs mirrored into them. I would now have loads of money, job done. All retired at the age of just 35. Not bad eh? The only juggling I would be seeing would be the real jugglers in a real circus; where the animals and clowns would be under a big white tent.

It's funny, when you have a pocket full of money and a bag of cocaine, the chicks are there for free. When there's no money or sniff there's no chicks about, and you have to spend or sniff all of it with them, trying to impress and get them to stay.

The manager of the warehouse was just leaving the front gate at 3am. As he got in his car and drove towards the front gate he nodded at the security guard to pull the gates back just as our inside man had said he would do. As that happened that was the cue for the 3 white transit vans to pull up with their full beams on, blinding the manager and the security guard.

The manager stopped at the entrance, one of the vans pulled out in front of the manager's car; the others at either side of his car. All of a sudden the doors flew open; one man jumps out of the van in front of the manager's car. Another man jumps out the side of the van and runs over to the security box and puts a gun to the guy who had come out from his hut to try to see what was going on. He too was blinded by the lights and now a hostage. Two more men jump out of the vans. One runs over to the manager's car and forces him to get out, shouting and waving his gun at him as it flickers in the light. "Get out; move it; out now!" he does as he is told, leaving the car still running. The other man gets into the manager's car and reverses back between the gates and parks it up leaving room so the vans could now come in.

The men from the vans were all dressed in white jumpsuits with white Adidas trainers on. They all had white balaclavas on and all were wearing black mirror swimming goggles. They were flashing their 9ml guns to the security guard and manager. The security guard had a gun to his head, "Get on your knees and hands on your head." The other robber runs to the manager and points the gun at him, telling him to open the gates. "Otherwise the security guy gets it," a voice shouts. The manager is told to get up, as they put their hands behind their back and walk them down into the second compound within the depot. Then the 3 vans drive in still with their full beam on, shining on the backs of the men as they walked down to the first hangar.

The manager and the security guard were told to put their hands together and were clingfilmed tight. They walk them to the first hangar as one of the men pulls the manager by the arm to the front shutter of the warehouse; the other leads the security guard. Then the masked man with the manager grunts. "Put the code in to open the doors or the security guard gets it. Open them fucking doors, now," as he pulls back on his gun to cock it.

"OK," he says panicking and he shouts the numbers out as the fella in the ski suit punches the number in the door. It doesn't open and he grunts again as he now moves the gun to the manager's head. "Mess this up again and I'll be messing you up." This time it works as the big warehouse doors slide into action.

The manager says, "Just don't harm us. I have two sons."

"Well so do I. Do as you're told and no one will need to get hurt. By the way, we know you have two sons. So, do as we tell you, and like I said know one will get hurt. They too will be safe." The doors open and there it was, bundles of money piled up in a neat stack. Not quite 100 mill's worth but there was a fair few quid piled there.

"Where's the rest of the money?"

"There's more in the other hangar but there are three workers, two girls and a man in there." He shouts back at them nervously.

The other masked man runs back to the van and drives it to the first shutters, starts loading the money into bags and into the deep trolleys that were used as rubbish bins. He then wheels them onto the van. The other masked man with the manager walks him to the other shutter with the security guard. He then shouts to him once again and he does as he is told, the code is put in and it opens. They walk through into the main warehouse and just like the fella of the woman Old School was shagging had told him, there it was a massive pile of used notes; stacked waist height and about 83 notes long. There were four people counting the money, stack after stack of used notes all in front of them. Fuck me, Christmas had come round early this year.

"Right everyone listen up," the workers turned round to see the robbers, "don't move, don't do anything unless you're told to do so; just stay still. No one will get hurt."

There were a few gasps as they saw the manager and the security guard with guns placed to their heads being ushered through the door. "We are here for the money, not to hurt anyone. So just do as you're told. We don't want any dead heroes OK?"

The manager said, "Do it please, do as they tell you."

The masked man shouts at them, "Empty those big warehouse bins and start loading that lot into them," as he points at the money and the trolleys, "and then roll them onto the van. OK, move it." The other shutter was pulled up and another white van pulled up outside, ready to have the money loaded onto it. The other man tells the security guard to help them before running back to the other van to move it to the side of the warehouse ready to be loaded up. "Move it, come on, come on we ain't got all night you know, let's go, let's go." As he looked at his watch. Once the three vans were full of cash there was still a big lump of money left.

"All done, let's get out of here; we can't get any more if we tried; OK fill your pockets."

"What?"

"Fill your pockets full," the masked man that was in charge shouted to them. So they all filled their pockets with as much of it as possible. The two masked men then walked everyone into the tea-room and locked the door. They ran back to the vans, slammed the back doors and got in.

The other van was now parked next to the gate entrance with the engine running ready and waiting for the others to catch up with him. The last van had most of the money on it and was loaded and ready to leave. So the fella that had been helping the other robber was told to lie down on the ground and to shut his eyes. The robber got into the van and drove towards the others. They all drove out the gates one after the other, they were gone and so was the money.

No one had got hurt. The police found them the next day when the workers had arrived. They had seen the gates wide open and no security guard in the security box so phoned the police. It was a job well done; it couldn't have been done better. With such poise, timing and planning you would have thought the Special Forces had pulled this off. Who dares win and all that. They had dared and for now they were the winners having 40 million or so on board their vans.

The vans were now heading off to a hiding place, an old farmhouse in Shelley lanes just down from the Mop and Broom pub to be hidden in an old barn, buried under the stacks of hay until they could be moved on again. The weight of the vans pushed down on the suspension as they moved along. They pulled off the motorway into a little secluded part of the road by the A1 and pulled up to a stop. One of the men ran over to the bushes, grabbed some number plates and put some magnetic strips with advertising on to the side of the vans. The vans now had their real number plates back on. Then he gathered up everyone's guns, put them in the bag and hid them amongst the brambles. He jumped back in the van and the first two started to drive off leaving the one with the most money in it, stuck spinning its wheels in the mud, going nowhere fast.

"Fuck, now what?" one of the drivers said to his mate.

"Shall I get some of the dough out from the back then?"

"And stick it where?"

"We could bury some."

"No, no get out and push the van forward and back. Move." One of the men got out and pushed the van forward to free it from the ditch. It didn't budge.

"Fuck, now what?" the man shouted to the driver, who was looking out the window revving the van up.

"We're fucked. Try once more. If not…" then all of a sudden it jerked forward and it was out the ditch and ready to go. He jumped in, covered in mud, and they sped off to the hiding place to meet the others. They were soon in the getaway cars heading off to London.

While all this was going on, The Grim Reaper was losing the plot over in Columbia and was on the phone shouting that this gangster's runner had taken him for a ride. He said that he had called some very dangerous men. It was taking too long.

"It's been 12 days now and not even a call and no show of my money. He has taken my kindness for weakness. He hasn't paid any money and I'm tired of asking him for it. You know what to do, you will stay in England and find him and do whatever necessary to get my money or kill one of his family, then him if he hasn't got it. I will ring him one last time tomorrow to find out what's happening and where he will be. You two will find him; I don't want you to stop until you find him." He then puts the phone down.

I get a call.

"It's me, the Grim Reaper."

"Yes?"

"Listen to me very carefully as this maybe the last thing you ever hear. You can keep all my money; hope it pays for yours and your family's funeral."

"Chill out and don't do anything silly just yet; I have your money." Well we had fucking shit loads of it now. We were all self-made millionaires with this lot, if the truth were known, entrepreneurs, fucking charley large bollocks. "Listen, Mr Ripper, your money is here, stop getting excited. I'm just trying to get it sorted for you."

"You're late. The only sorting will be you getting sorted once my men find you. My men are already in England, coming to see you. Your time is up and whoever gets in their way will suffer the consequences."

"Look the money is here." The phone goes dead before I had a chance to tell him.

"What's that all about?" Old School says.

"It's the Columbian; he wants his money."

"Fuck him. He'll just have to wait 'til we can think of a way to get this lot cleaned and over to him, if he won't answer his phone then it's his own fault. We'll just pay his men when we see them, no drama."

We laugh; we were over the moon with this lot and had no worries now. The job had hit the news; it went down in history as one of the biggest robberies done on British soil. So now we had shit loads of used notes, but nowhere to spend it as every bank and every place was put on manager alert and on the lookout for these stolen used notes. There was too much to count, but the paper confirmed how much was there for us. Not being able to spend it just yet was like being all dressed up but having nowhere to go. Here we were rich beyond our wildest dreams but still with lemonade pockets. Well we'd spent the money we had all collected in our pockets just to see us through.

The Grim Reaper had sent two hitmen over from Columbia to come get me, and anyone else that stood in their way. I found out that they'd been looking for me in London already. They had blown up the Firm's Lexus and killed the driver. When he had come out and pushed the alarm it had blown to bits. This had happened outside the hotel that we had all been to just hours before. It was just a smoking piece of mangled metal and in no time there were police and firemen everywhere. This was a close call. They also turned up in a club in London where we all used to hang out after hours. Where all our wheeling and dealing was done and where we would all relax and sniff hard all night long at Colombian's finest 'til the early hours of the morning. Lucky for me, we weren't there at this time when they had arrived otherwise I would be a dead man myself and someone else close to me or the Firm would be telling this story. If only I could talk to them without them killing me.

These two Columbian hitmen had turned up about an hour after we had left this club. They had pulled up in a brand spanking new Porsche Carrera. They had got out, all nice and gentlemanly like, walked to the front door of the club and tried to walk straight in and past the doormen.

"Hold up, mate," the doorman said to the hitmen, "you have to pay and be searched like the rest of them, so if you'll just line up."

"Sorry," one of them said to the doorman.

The doorman asked, "What do you want in here?" The Colombians asked the two doormen nicely if they could come in and look for me in the club as they had been told I would be in there. Who by I don't know and never found out, maybe by the driver of the Lexus who was now dead. The Grim Reaper was a very intelligent man and knew a lot of people so it wouldn't be long before someone knew where we all were or where I might have been.

"They ain't here and if you want to look in there for them you'll need some ID and pay. There's the queue, so queue up quietly like the rest of them." Thinking they could be the police, looking so smart and with all the questions they were asking. One of the hitmen laughs at the doorman. They both pulled back their moleskin jackets and pull out two Mac tens each.

"Does this look like I'll need fucking ID to you? Now get out my fucking way or get on your fucking knees." The bouncers run for their lives diving for cover once they saw the tools being produced. They knew they meant business. They locked themselves in the room next to where the girl was collecting money. The girl collecting the money ducked down and got under the counter as they walked in and shot the club to bits. Bullets were falling on to the floor and all around them. The club was almost empty. Luckily it had only just opened. Once their guns were empty they said, "We're here for the person they call the Gangster's Runner, do you know where we can find him?" The barman dropped a glass in shock and shook his head in disbelief as none of the bullets had hit him. I knew they had been to the club as one of the bouncers inside had phoned me and told me that two Columbian nutters were there and weren't very friendly. He told me that they asked to see a fella called the Gangster's Runner and that they had shot the place to bits and did I know him.

"Who?" I said, "The Gangster's Runner, well I have heard of him. Tell them I have the money for them." But once they had come out of hiding it was too late. The hitmen had left.

I was now on my way to Spain with Old School to try to get this money cleaned. So I couldn't do anything right now for them even if I wanted to. We needed someone in the know who could launder it and make it clean again and with the police sniffing around after the robbery it was best we were out the country and getting the money cleaned fast. The only people with that sort of contacts were Mr Nice and the Jewellery Thief. I should have just left someone with a few quid to pay the Colombians off but I didn't believe they would come until I heard about their antics from others that had witnessed the wrath of the Grim Reaper. I thought they would just wait 'til we got back but they meant business. They weren't fucking about and had waited too long already.

I had pre-warned a bouncer at the strip club the Columbians had gone to next, to tell the two that I would be back sometime soon as I was out the country right now. So the bouncer gave the two Columbian hitmen the message. They said, "OK we'll be back," and turned and walked away, followed by the bouncers back to the Porsche with no problems at all. Until they started up the engine, reversed the Porsche back fast and skidded round to face the door again. At the same time one of them leant out of the passenger window, pulled out an uzi, spraying the whole door with bullets and letting every bouncer that was outside on the door have it. They then sped off as fast as they could leaving two dead doormen on the floor and others fighting for their lives. They weren't messing about.

When the bouncer had phoned me telling me the news, I phoned the Jewellery Thief telling him about the two men sent to look for me and the carnage they had left behind. I also filled him in about the warehouse job and that we needed his help, as he knew the best laundry men to get rid of the money. He had access to some off shore accounts in the Cayman Islands and in Jersey ready for us to be able to use to put the clean money through.

The vans were now hidden in the old farmhouse barn and covered over with bundles of hay. We had all taken some money out to see us through before Old School had left for Spain to see the Jewellery Thief. Mattie the Mac had given some bird some money to help sort her out as she had a few problems and debts of her own. And she had gone to the bank to put it in and before she could say her name the Serious Crime Squad was all around her in the bank like a rash. Lucky for us and Mattie the Mac, she didn't divulge any info about anything. Well she didn't know anything really just that Mattie had lent her a few grand. Not knowing where it had come from she had blagged where the money had come, which had kept them at bay for now. So we were all safe but treading on ice. One false move and the police would have us. Even though she had been pulled in and questioned about how the money had come in to her possession. So had the woman that Old School had been shagging and her ex fella too, but they too had kept quiet thinking they would get some money out of it. But Old School and I had other plans for the money and it didn't include any of them.

So we arrived in Spain, Carlos drove Old School and me from the airport once again to Diamonds nightclub in a convertible Mercedes. This time I was over the moon, everything was on good terms. We were all charley large and I had proved my worth to the Firm once again. Mattie the Mac took Mandy to hide somewhere safe from the police now others were getting pulled in for questioning about the depot robbery. I said it was best they stayed out the way as the Columbians were looking for me too and would try to find them. So I told Mattie to stay at the Savoy hotel. I thought it was a good place for them both to keep out the way until we had got back from Spain. So then I could pay them off and everything would be all cool again. Mandy and Mattie could chill out there ready for us to tell Mattie what to do with the vans.

We told the Jewellery Thief and Mr Nice everything. Trying to get Johnny off; the escape with Johnny and Mr B. Also about the job with the vans that were now loaded up with money waiting for our next move. They were well clued up with what had been going on in London and knew the situation we were in.

The Jewellery Thief turned to Mr Nice and said, "Well what do you think?"

He smiled and said, "Look, fellas, the only man I know that could launder this amount of money and move it around without any questions would be my friend the Arab. He owns some oil companies over in Dubai and this money could move about without any questions or the authorities being alerted."

"So he's our man," I said. "Can we arrange a meeting then?" as I looked at the fellas in front of me.

"OK, but it will cost you 1m." I looked at Old School, he nodded.

So I said, "Get this fella on the phone then as we have near on 40 million," and that was without counting it all and just going by what the papers had said about the robbery.

He picked up the phone and rang him. We all sat there in silence for a bit on the edge of our seats hoping and waiting. Mr Nice talked in Arabic for a short time, and then he put the phone down and looked at us. I thought he wouldn't entertain it at first.

"OK, fellas, he's interested and will be with us in two days." Then he put out his hand for me and Old School to shake.

"OK," I said and then he smiled. We were all over the moon and everyone was friends again.

The Jewellery Thief said, "Here I believe this belongs to you," as he handed me the bullet with my name on it. I had well and truly redeemed myself and I was now sitting there with Old School and the big players that were involved in world distribution of drugs with near on 40 million or more, nicely stashed away. Mr Nice had just made himself another million pounds without moving a muscle to share with the Jewellery Thief and his Dubai friend who I had nicknamed the Money

Mover. As he would be the man able to move our money around without a paper trail being made from it and then be able to make it dribble into a bank account in Russia without anyone noticing. Ready for us to then transfer it to Switzerland, back into Gibraltar then once it was all clean back into the Bank of England with no questions being asked.

Unbeknown to us, the Columbian hitmen had been following Mattie on the hunch that he would soon lead them to me. So now they had turned up at the Savoy hotel and found out what number Mattie and Mandy were staying in. They walked into the lift joining a woman who was in there already. They looked very menacing but smart and clean cut. They grunted at her, "Second floor please." As the lift came to rest on the 2nd floor they walked out quickly but quietly, past every room 'til they got to room number four and listened against the door. I had rung Mattie by this time to tell him the good news, that the money could be cleaned and that we had to wait just two days for it to happen. It would have to be loaded into speedboats down in Devon and shipped over to an oilrig where it would then be collected by helicopter by this Arab man. Mattie asked about him so I told him how he is the man that could shift this large amount of money without questions being asked, so it was all good. Just then the Columbians pulled out guns from their jacket pockets and knocked on the door. Mandy started to walk towards the door then looked back at Matt; he nodded but was only nodding to me on the phone as we chatted. Mandy thought he nodded to her to open the door as he continued to speak with me. A hitman placed the end of the silencer of the gun to the door. Mandy continued to walk towards the door, the gunman looked down on the floor to see the shadow coming closer. Mattie shouted but it was too late, the Columbian squeezed the trigger. The bullet shot through the door and hit Mandy, throwing her several feet onto the floor. The hitman kicked open the door.

"Shit!"

"What Mattie; Mattie what's going on?"

"They're here and they have just shot Mandy."

"Who have? Mattie what's going on?" Mattie goes quiet. I shout, "Mattie, Mattie."

Then the Colombian walked into the room "Don't fuck about."

"Don't shoot me."

"Where is he?" as he places the gun to Mattie's head.

"The one they call the Gangster's Runner."

"Who's that then?" As the other one then walks into the room, stepping over Mandy who is lying on the floor holding her stomach bleeding to death. Her eyes fixed just staring in disbelief at what was going on. He then shuts the door looking left and right down the hallway as he does so.

"We have come to get the money off the Gangster's Runner."

"Who?"

I shout down the phone, "Mattie, Mattie!" The hitman then slowly put the phone to Mattie's mouth watching his movements very carefully.

"What's that all about Mattie?" I say down the phone, "What's going on?"

"There's a man here holding a shooter at my head and they say they want to speak with some fella called the Gangster's Runner, ring any bells mate? So who the fuck's the Gangster's Runner?" Mattie starts to panic. The hitman takes the phone out of Mattie's hand.

I turn to the Jewellery Thief. "The Columbians have just shot Mandy."

"Give them one of the vans," Mr Nice said. "Do it or they'll kill everyone 'til you're dead. Get them a van and get rid of them, they don't fuck about, son, as you now know. They'll kill you and everyone that knows you if you don't."

"OK, Mattie," I calmly speak into the phone.

"Yes?" the Colombian hitman's voice comes back.

"Listen, give them a van. One van."

"OK. I'll tell him to," the hitman said.

He then pushes the cancel button as I shout "Mattie" down the phone. "Shit" as I turn back to everyone I was standing next to. "Fuck, fuck, fuck."

The hitman took the gun away from Mattie's head and said, "You must give us a van." The Colombian hitman lets go of the phone; it hits the floor and bounces on the deep pile carpet.

"I have to give you your money?" This had just saved Mattie's life.

"Yes you must." They walked out the room past Mandy who muttered to Mattie, "Tell the Cookster I love him." The hitmen pushed Mattie through the fire exit door, triggering the alarm. People were starting to run to the room after hearing the noise the Colombians had made from kicking the door open. The fire alarm had now gone off as they had left out the fire exit door. The hotel manager and security see Mandy lying on the floor; someone shouts, "Quick, call an ambulance." They glance out of the window but the Columbian hitmen and Mattie had got to the bottom of the fire exit and were gone. As they pushed Mattie out they concealed their guns and walked round and out onto the street. He was then pushed into the back seat of the Chrysler and one of the men drives off and the other was in the back with Mattie.

As they drive off the ambulance and a police car come screaming round the corner.

"Get down." Mattie is forced down with the Colombian in the back. He also lies low as the police go past them.

"Listen, I don't know this Gangster's Runner but I do have the money for you, if that's what you want."

"Take us to the money. That's all we're here for and then you will live. Your friend on the phone said you must give us a van."

"Yes that's where the money will be."

"If you are lying to me, make no mistakes you are dead, just like your lady friend." Mattie gives the driver directions to the old farmhouse. They get to the barn and all get out. The two hitmen then pull their guns out once again and tell Mattie to walk in front of them towards the barn, once there, they put them away. Mattie starts to then pull the bundles of hay down around from one of the vans. He opens the back door to one of them.

"There you go, fellas," they all glance into the back of the van. "Is that enough for you?" The smaller of the two said, "Yes that will be OK. So where are the keys?" Mattie from being all pleased with himself now just handing over all this money to them was once more panicking again and the smile had just been wiped clean off his face.

"Keys?" he panicked again as the other hitman pulled out his gun.

"Yes the keys."

"What fucking keys?" The gun had been produced once again, so he knew he was in trouble.

"To the van."

"Oh, I'll just get them." Mattie said and ran to the well. He moves one of the old bricks to the side to where they had been stashed. The Columbian that had pulled his gun out gets into the van. The other tells Mattie to turn round, put his hands on his head and to start walking as he places the gun on the back of his head. Mattie starts to walk towards the trees.

"Keep walking and don't turn around otherwise I will let you have it right here and now. I want you to forget everything you have just seen." Mattie didn't waste any time at all and started walking before he could hear the rest of what was being said. His bum was twitching like a rabbit's nose. He had tears in his eyes as he walked forward thinking this was the last thing he would see or do. The hitman puts the gun away and gets in the Chrysler. He drives off with the other guy following in the van leaving Mattie still walking with his hands on his head. He walks a bit further and then makes a dart for it and starts to run towards the trees, he was breathing heavily thinking he had just got away from them, but they were long gone. He jumps the fence and lays down waiting. He waits for about 20minutes but nothing.

He walks in a big circle bringing him back to the farmhouse by the barn where the vans were. He sees that the Columbians had gone and pukes up. He didn't know they'd let him go. Mattie was very lucky to be alive; he had seen their faces and had seen them shoot Mandy too. They had kept him alive, as we had been over generous with the money, by letting them take a whole vanload of cash. They had more than I owed them; they had a lot more. They had been paid ten fold. They had told Matt to tell me not to cross them again and if I wanted to do business again then to call the Grim Reaper. Once they had gone Mattie started to get cold feet and took one of the other vans himself as he was now stranded at the barn and had no way of getting out of there. He took the van with the least money in it. He didn't have any other way of getting back from the farmhouse.

He drove back to the hotel where Mandy had been shot, but the police were everywhere. So then he drove down to South Mimms service area just off the A1 and thought it would be best to stay in a room there 'til he could find out whether Mandy had made it or not. So he parked the van up and climbed in the back. He grabbed some sports bags that were lying in the back and emptied them of spanners. He filled the bags to the brim with bundles of money 'til they couldn't hold anymore, zipped them up and climbed back into the driver's seat. He pulls the bags full of money out and over to the front seat; looking all around he got out the van and walked into the reception area to book a room.

He checks in, caked in mud where he had run across the field to hide himself. He gets to his room, drops the bags to the floor, strips off and walks straight into the shower. After that he wraps the clean soft towel around him and lets himself fall onto the bed and lies there for a few minutes. Then he gets his phone out and orders two hookers to come to the room to keep him occupied, knowing he could be staying here for a long time. Mattie knew if he went home he would have got nicked as the police would now want to talk to him being the last one to see Mandy alive and he would be on the hotel's cameras.

The hookers arrived and Mattie ordered some wine and a bottle of Jack Daniels so they could all get a bit more acquainted. Mattie then got on the phone and ordered an 8th of charley off Lee Knock Knock as he was known back then, who soon arrived, took it out of his pockets and was given the money. Then he had a line with Mattie and the girls before leaving. Once the girls saw that, and said, "I have some E's too."

"Well, girls, don't be shy," Mattie said. "Get them out then, darling."

"What these?" as she pointed to her tits.

"No, silly, the E's, you can get them out later." So they all started sniffing and taking the E's. They then all started to get a bit friendly, kissing and fondling each other, and then the two girls said, "Before we go any further we need some money."

"Don't worry, girls; all is OK; I have shit loads, darling," Mattie says and he bends down and undoes the zip to his bag and pulls bundles of fifty pound notes out the bag and throws it all over the bed much to the girls' delight.

"Don't tell me you've just robbed a bank," she says jokingly.

"Well something like that," Mattie said, "but I won't bore you with the details."

"Shit," as she picks up one of the bundles and examines it more closely.

Mattie throws them a bundle each and throws the blonde one the phone, "Tell the agency not to wait up for you girls as you're staying here all night with me and we'll be shagging all night long." They all laugh at him and he laughs back, all the while being deadly serious and a bit drunk now.

"So now you've seen the money, let's see what you two look like. But you can start with a little dance first, then get your clothes off and let's see what I've spent my money on," he walked over to the side and sniffed another line. "Then we can get this party really started."

They couldn't believe the amount of money they had just seen. He had just thrown bundles of it around like it was Monopoly money. He had more money than sense. So the blonde girl picked up the phone and phoned the agency. They start to kiss him and take his and their clothes off, so Mattie could start shagging the arses off them both in any which way he could; with them on the bed and with the money spread out all around them and the drugs just lying there all out over the side for anyone to see if they walked in on them. But right now they didn't care as they were all smashed. By now he was well off his nut on the drink and drugs. Well they all were.

See what stress can do to you? It can make you go wild and behave in a very strange way indeed, being nearly killed and seeing one of his friends killed had sent him a bit wild. A bit of post-traumatic stress disorder on a small scale. Which had now turned him into a liability. He just didn't care anymore and his actions were now showing it, he was so nutted from the drugs and the night's activities with these girls.

Within four hours a police patrol car comes crawling into the hotel car park. Mattie and the girls are lying there giggling and getting down and dirty as the girls took it in turns to do the wild thing. The police pull up and see the white van; noticing that it looked dirtier than your usual dirty van. It was caked in mud from driving down and around where it had been stashed back at the farmhouse. The police stopped next to it and did a check on the van. One of them gets out and starts to walk around it checking it over. Then the radio comes back with it being all legal and OK. The police officer goes to get back into the police car but glances into the back of the van before he does. He goes back to the car and opens the door, he pauses. Turning back looking to the van again he closes the police car door and takes a second look at the van. To his surprise he is confronted with a pile of the stolen money and is straight back on the radio again. The two officers had the Serious Crime Squad all over the place in no time.

Some police officers had now gone into the service area and put an announcement out to all the staff what they were here for and that they should evacuate the building with as little fuss as possible. Then established what room Mattie the Mac was in once the rest of the guests had been ushered out. They didn't want to take any risks as Mattie may be armed. The police had crowbarred open the back of the van. It opened and one of them whistled as the other one picked up a few bundles. This was it for Mattie the Mac, armed response had kicked off his door and found him with the bags of money that were the same as the ones from the van and he was in the bed with the two hookers out of his nut. They had caught him with money everywhere and the empty bag of cocaine he had got earlier.

He was arrested instantly, taken to Paddington police station and was questioned for six hours about the robbery on the warehouse once he had come down off the drugs. The girls were questioned for three hours and then let go with no charge. They'd just said that they had met up with a client that had loads of money in two sports bags, that's all they knew about him really. I guess it gave a new meaning to being caught with your pants down. The Serious Crime Squad and MI5 were now offering him all sorts of deals and telling him he was going down for a long time. They wanted him to bubble the men who had done the depot robbery and to say how they had done it. He finally cracked when they said they could offer him a deal, which would mean a lesser sentence for him. He said, once his lawyer was present that the only deal he would make is that if he got four years less he would tell them where the other van was being kept with the money, but would say no comment about everything else. The police knew he had more to tell but thinking about what he had said they agreed to a deal.

"Tell us where the money is then and you have yourself a deal," was the final demand. The old farmhouse was crawling with forensic officers and CID. The other van had now been discovered just as Mattie said it would be by the police. They found it hidden under the hay where it had been concealed. They were happy but still wanted to know where the rest of the money was but Mattie never divulged that. It was now with the Columbians. So now the Serious Crime Squad was all over us. Once again we were all skint, right now maybe looking at a lot of bird for all our troubles unbeknown to Old School and me, as we were out in Spain taking care of our business and living it large. We had shown the paper article to Mr Nice who was now our best mate in the whole world. Now that he knew we had much more than a few quid. So he was laying money out on use like it was going out of fashion thinking he would soon be making another 1m.

I had told the Jewellery Thief that we would be back when the Arab was ready to start work on this money for us. We had to get back to England to find out if Mandy and Mattie were OK and to sort out about moving the money to Devon. Mr Nice said that would be a good idea, after all we were sniffing all his gear on tick, like it was the next best thing since sliced bread and for once he didn't mind. After all he thought we were now millionaires and could afford to live like this. We didn't have a clue we had just been made into two bobs once again and the only money we had now was just a few Euros what we had tucked away in our pockets. So before long Old School and I were back in England.

We had now found out that Mattie the Mac had been caught with all the money and that Mandy had died at hospital from the bullet wound, even after several attempts to bring her back to life. Mattie the Mac's ex-girlfriend had left a message on my mobile saying that she hadn't heard from him and he normally rings on a Friday to talk to his little girl. She wanted to know why Mattie was there on telly being taken from the police van to court. Mattie the Mac was being held on remand at Pentonville prison on charges of helping people to escape from prison and for his part in both the robberies. The papers were saying that the rest of the money was still out there, not knowing that the Colombians had taken it. She also said that Mandy had been taken to Queen's hospital but didn't make it. Old School and I went there to say that we were her family; well I was all she had apart from her stepsister and Johnny. He was now a fugitive stuck out in Barbados on the run and to come back over here to England would be too risky especially with everything that was now going on.

So the hospital and the police let us in to see Mandy. She was cold but still looked like an angel lying there all peaceful. I had to hold back the tears as Old School kissed her on the forehead and said let's go. I left the hospital feeling empty, knowing that this sort of life we were all mixed up in led to this in one way or another. We now had to try and sort out the arrangements for her funeral. Even though the Serious Crime Squad had come down to see Mandy and do their investigation on her body.

We drove off to a car park overlooking London and sat there numb. For me it was like running into a brick wall. The last thing Johnny had said to me, before he went on the run to Barbados was take care of my sister and let no punk or mug near her. Now look what had I done? I had ended up getting her killed.

"You need to tell Johnny," Old School said. He had to know, he had a right to know after all it was his sister and Mandy would have wanted him to know even if he couldn't be there for her funeral for reasons out of his control.

"He must know. It's better coming from your lips, than to find out from someone else, Cookster." I just looked at Old School with a blank expression on my face. "You have to tell him, mate."

"No way; not me."

"You need to speak with him before Mr Nice tells him she's been shot. We can't make the arrangements for her funeral or bury her body if you don't tell him. Just in case he has some last request for her."

Old School and I phoned all the people to let them know about Mandy's funeral apart from Johnny. So now it was time to tell him.

"Old School, you tell him, mate."

"No way, you're on your own on this one," he said. "It must come from you and you only."

"No he'll kill me."

"Yes, he'll definitely kill you." Old School pondered. I was supposed to be looking out for her not getting her killed.

"It's best coming from you, mate."

"Not me. Look you know him from old."

"Why me? Please don't fuck about just do it, mate." Old School looked at me. He wasn't impressed. Then he leaned forward and picked up the phone and rang Johnny. Beep beep the phone went, as the pips connected on the phone. We couldn't contact Johnny directly so we had to phone one of Johnny's mate's phones in Barbados before we could get him on the phone.

"Hi, it's a friend. Can I speak to Johnny?"

"Who's this then?"

"Tell him it's Old School." It went quiet for a bit.

"Hi."

"Johnny, is that you, mate?"

"Go ahead, Old School."

"Johnny, how's it all going, me old mate?"

"How are you and my sister doing and the rest of the Firm?"
It went quiet on the phone for what seemed like a whole minute
as Old School looked at me again. I was now pacing up and down
the car park full of nerves. I then got in and turned and said, "Go
on tell him."

"Old School son, you there?" Johnny said.

"Yes, mate, I'm here."

"Well tell me the news then. How is she?"

"Johnny, this is hard for me, mate, and I know it's going to be
even harder for you. She…"

"She's what, Old School? Pregnant? Got herself mixed up
with some idiot or arsehole? I did warn the Cookster about all
that stuff. So I hope he hasn't let me down."

"No." Old School looked at me again and I nodded at him
and mouthed go on tell him. "Johnny, she's dead, mate."

"You what? She with some mug."

"No, Johnny, she's dead, mate."

"Oh no; no way, mate; not my little sister; no she ain't Old
School."

"Johnny… She's dead…sorry, mate."

"When? How? Who? I'll kill him. Old School, you just show
me this man! Tell me, Old School, that she isn't."

"I can't, Johnny. She is… I'm real sorry."

"How?"

"By a gunman, mate, came into the Savoy hotel and let her
have it. Don't think he meant to give to her though."

"Who fucking cares whether he meant to or not, Old School!"
Johnny shouted down the phone. "I'll tear his fucking heart out.
So where the fuck's the Cookster? What is he doing about it all?
He should have been looking out for her."

"She's dead and due to be buried in five days' time at Romans
Church. We're going to bury her. Cookster is sorting out the
arrangements. Is there any request from you for her? Any special
thing you would like me to sort out for her?"

"Yes one thing, bring me this man's heart. Cut it out, son, and
mail it to me and whilst you're there find the Cookster and keep
an eye on him. I want to know where he is at all times. Do you

hear me, Old School? I want to talk to him, he's got a lot of explaining to do."

"We had to tell you, Johnny." Then Johnny puts the phone down.

"Shit man," Old School says. "That was the hardest thing I have had to do in my life. It's harder than killing someone, Cookster. At least you can walk away and keep it to yourself and forget about it without having to explain every detail. When you have to tell someone else that a person close to you is dead well... It's hard. There's nothing you can say to put it right or make that person feel any better, everyone is left with a empty heart."

"Don't worry, Old School," I said. "Everything will be OK, don't fucking worry!"

"It's hard for all of us. She was a good girl; she didn't need to be involved in all this."

"We're all in a big mess now and all skint once again. Thanks to your mate Mattie the fucking Mac now there's no fucking money. Try telling that one to Mr Nice. Now we have sniffed most of his gear and he ain't going to get a dino from us, not even a fucking pound coin, son, and when we tell him there's no money he is going to hit the roof. Matt the Mac is banged up; the Russian's dead; Mandy's dead; there's no money for us either. Mr B is banged up and the Serious Crime Squad is all around us and we're going to meet some fella who thinks he is going to move nearly 40m pounds. When there ain't even 10 pounds left of it. Johnny wants this man's heart torn out and all you can say or tell me is not to worry... It'll be OK. Well it's not fucking OK is it? Wake up and smell the fucking coffee Cookster."

"Don't worry, Old School," I said again with water in my eyes. I really missed Mandy too and it was hurting knowing she wouldn't be around no more. "It's OK, Old School."

I pulled him near and we hugged each other.

"It's OK for you, Cookster, you've now paid the Colombians off and the Russian is now out the way. So you're OK. You have had your money, son, but me? I'm fucking skint again and will have to answer to the Russian mafia once they find me. When they come looking for my pal at his gym and find out he's dead. So you're fucking lucky, son, not me. I could be the next one going in the ground."

"Look, I'm not, mate. I have to now answer to Johnny and he will kill me off like he did the Russian."

"Well right now you fucking deserve it. You know how crazy he can get."

"Yes I do, mate, how has this happened? I miss her too you know. Let's get a grip here; it will all work out in the end."

I tried to reassure him and myself that things would be OK even though they were trouble and we were in a big mess, one that seemed it couldn't be fixed.

"Come on, let's pull ourselves together and get the funeral ready for Mandy." I got down on my knees and prayed that everything would work out and I would be out of this way of life very soon.

The Day We Buried Mandy
and Put Johnny to Rest

It was a hot day; Old School and I had turned up at Romans church to meet and greet everyone that had arrived for the funeral. People from all different Manors, from south to east to west to north London, to Manchester to Liverpool to Essex, Bristol and Scotland, even Ireland. You name it, they were there. Even a couple of Italians turned up to pay their respects to Mandy and to make sure the funeral went as well as it could go for Johnny.

There were bundles of flowers scattered everywhere. So many you could have set up your own floristry business with the amount that had been sent. A lot of the people that were there only knew Johnny, but had come to give support and make sure it went as well as it could go. There were known and unknown faces present, villains and criminals all around us. The Jewellery Thieves and Mr Nice had paid for the funeral and sent flowers and cards over to be put on Mandy's grave. They had apologized to us but said it is best they stayed out of the limelight. They knew it was best while things were as they were, sometimes it's best to be heard and not seen especially if you were still active in the criminal world.

Mr Nice had sealed the deal with the Arab man. For a while he wasn't a very happy man once he had found out the news. He calmed down once he knew everything was OK and understood that sometimes things could go wrong.

He just said, "With you, Cookster, I knew it was too good to be true." Even though Old School and I had sniffed away about 3 ounces of his gear without paying for it but he was cool about that too, which was a result. We said we would pay him out the money we had once it was all sorted but there wasn't any now as we were waiting for the deal to go down over in Spain. We had ticked gram after gram after gram off him while we were out there, thinking we had loads of money and him thinking the same.

There were many other Firm members at the funeral too. Johnny's stepsister including other gangsters that didn't want their names, or nicknames mentioned in this book which I understood and respected. The world's a small place when you work in these circles, it's surprising who knows who, or who's connected to whom and how quiet it is all kept. Until something like this happens then they all come together and they can become a force not to be reckoned with. Me, Old School, Ray, Jerry, Tom and the Hairy Fella carried Mandy's coffin off the hearse and into the church. People had said their bits on how Mandy was such a nice girl and how sometimes the good ones go first. I thought that always meant that we're all going to be around forever if we didn't get out of these circles. We hadn't been no angels.

It was time to go outside to the freshly dug grave ready to lower Mandy's coffin down into it and for the priest to say his bit. We were all standing there and some of us threw some flowers into the grave. The weather was on her side that day, as the sun's rays reflected off of my Armani shades I started to have flashbacks.

They started to come to my mind of when I first met Mandy at the party or our trip to Spain; me holding her hand walking back from somewhere, holding her close. I could even smell her perfume once again. I remember Johnny saying to me, "You best look after her," before he left Dover and went on the run with Mr B. Then out of the corner of my eye I could see a Bentley slowly pulling up the drive, which turned my attention away from my thoughts.

As my eyes focused on it, watching it come closer and closer up the drive I could just make out Wong. I was happy he had come and then a big figured man with dark shades on got out the back of the car. George opened the back door… Fuck me, I had worked out that the big dark man sitting in the back was only Johnny. George the dustcart driver had been with Wong all this time. I hadn't seen him since he had driven the dustcart on Johnny and Mr B's big escape. I could have slipped down into the coffin with Mandy right there and then as he was going to kill me anyway for sure, once he found out the truth that it was all my doing that had got his little sis' killed.

Johnny had put the phone down after the call from Old School telling him about Mandy. Then he had phoned Wong in Chinatown straight away to get him a passport so he could come over. Wong was well connected with the Triad firm called the Snake Head. They were bringing over Chinese people to sell pirate copied new released films on DVDs by the hundreds. They were all over here on false passports with false names too so he had one made up for Johnny.

Mr Nice had found out what had happened to Mandy and that everything with the money had gone very pear-shaped, he thought it best that Johnny should come over and say his goodbyes to Mandy properly. Once the passport was in place he then got on a plane out from Barbados to England. He had Wong pick him up from the airport and laid low at Wong's restaurant in Chinatown. The Serious Crime Squad would have a field day; they were on to him and all of us and had followed him back to England to Mandy's funeral.

They were watching our every move, unbeknown to us ready for the best time to try and catch us all out. Wong and Johnny came over to all of us as the vicar continued with ashes to ashes, dust-to-dust. People nodded at Johnny as he pushed his way through the crowed, they mouthed sorry and hi and a few shook his hand not knowing he was on the run. Johnny threw a white rose on to the coffin with a photo of him and Mandy when they were young with their mum and dad, followed by a photo of their stepdad too.

George just sat there in the Bentley waiting as the photo and rose landed on top of Mandy's coffin in what seemed like slow motion. Like a pack of hungry wolves the Serious Crime Squad and the swat team erupted from out of the church and from behind the hearse and a few parked cars and headstones. Even some of the church workers and the hearse driver turned out to be undercover coppers.

"Stay where you are; nobody move! This is the police." They were here for Johnny and anyone else they could pull in. They had a hunch that he would show up.

"Johnny Mancinni, you're under arrest stay where you are." All the people there were confused and some villains ran back to their cars and were out of there. Some ran off in the other directions. One of the officers grabbed Johnny; Johnny pulled the long dark coat off, leaving the copper just holding the coat as he let it fall to the floor. He looked at me then jumped over Mandy's grave. He made a run for it past me and said, "You're a dead man, son," and off into the graveyard. I tried to stop one of the officers who also jumped the grave and gave chase, but he managed to find his feet again and was in hot pursuit chasing Johnny once again.

I guess it gave a new meaning to running through the shadows of death. Other villains tried to get in the way of the S.W.A.T team to give Johnny a head start, as they were gaining distance on him. One of the S.W.A.T team was running down towards Johnny hoping to block his path. Wong ran back to the Bentley and started it up ready to try and get Johnny out of there. Just as Johnny managed to get on to the pathway the officer that had cut him off was now holding the gun at Johnny.

"Johnny Mancinni, don't move or I will shoot, don't move, Johnny." Johnny paused for a second then ran straight for him. Before the police officer had a chance to do anything Johnny grabbed the gun, twisted it out the way of the line of fire and twisted it up into the officer's jaw breaking his jaw, then twisted it again hitting him to the floor. Then Johnny turns the gun round to face the officer on the floor, now with the gun in his hand. He goes to fire just as the rest of the S.W.A.T. team catches up, they open fire on Johnny.

He falls in slow motion to his knees, dropping the gun. Wong, Old School and I run over to see Johnny lying on the floor. The S.W.A.T. team and the Serious Crime Squad were all around him. They were calling for ambulances to come and telling us there was nothing to see and to stand back. I could see Johnny lying there with three bullet holes in him that were pouring out blood. He then looks through the crowd to me with a deep cold stare; he stops and comes to a rest and stops moving his head.

"He's dead," the officer says, as he touches his neck to check a pulse. I look up to the sky and then do a cross across my body. Me, Old School and everyone else turned round and started heading out of the cemetery as quickly as we could.

"Come here, we need you all for questioning, nobody leaves," a loud voice was heard. The others had all done the same in the commotion and left sharpish and we had to get out of there. We needed to get out of there to avoid any questions from the local police or Scotland Yard as they had also been there watching, hoping to find out some more clues about the 100 million that had gone missing. Three men were still at large that had been involved, and 32million was still missing according to the police, and hadn't been found yet.

Back to Some Sort of Normal Life

Everyone had left the police to do their job at the graveyard. We had all gone back to our lives. Wong had gone back to Leicester Square with George to build his empire by getting people to sell the DVDs that had been copied in their millions and brought here to England to be sold. Old School said bye to me and had gone out to Barbados to look after Johnny's Bar. Johnny had bought himself a bar while on the run out there. It was doing well so now Old School made himself the new owner, with the say-so from the Jewellery Thief and Mr Nice. Mr Nice had shares in it and Old School would now pay a percentage of the profits to Mr Nice who would then share with The Jewellery Thief any money made from the Firm with their ill-gotten gains. The money would then go through the bar's books for a bit until it could then go to an offshore account.

One evening as I left the Emporium nightclub in London, three police cars came skidding up and the police had me on the floor for all to see. Scotland Yard interrogated me for three days about the robbery; the escape on the prison van; the bank job; Mandy's murder; for conspiracy and helping to supply cocaine from the deal that went on in Southend. Not forgetting the 100 mil that had gone missing for the depot job. They were wasting their time with me and they didn't have any real evidence that they could stick. Desperate to try and get anything from me or anyone else as what they had wouldn't stand up in court; just a lot of circumstantial evidence but no facts.

Their questions always got the same answer… No comment; I didn't see that happen that way or anyway at all; I was asleep or I wasn't there in the first place, and if I was, whatever was happening was all being done without my knowledge. After three days of no comments they decided to let me go without charge, but a warning saying that they had their eye on me and I would be inside for any little thing they could get on me.

So I was a free man. Thanks to my good brief recommended and paid for by the Jewellery Thieves. Also thanks to the police C.P. lawyer as he said there wasn't enough to hold me or put anything on me at the moment. So they had to let me go, as they never had factual evidence only fabrication and hearsay, which wasn't enough, so I was free.

I walked out of Paddington station a free man. Never to smuggle or juggle again, just walk away from it all like I never existed. A great weight had been lifted off my shoulders. I jumped into a black cab and was out of there, the Columbians were paid, the Russian was dead, Old School was happy and in Barbados running Johnny's bar. Mandy was dead sadly and Mattie the Mac was now banged up in Wormwood scrubs. Mr B was also banged up in Springhill and Johnny... he was dead too. So what else could I do? I walked away from the Firm leaving them all to their own devices. I had left the Firm with £29,000 in my pocket that I had got from a key of cocaine that had been sold. The one the diver had turned up with all unexpectedly at the warehouse. It turned out to be a nice little earner in the end.

My Thoughts

I ask the cab to pull in here. I got out and told him to wait; I walked into the chip shop and got some chips, got back into the black cab and drove off through London back to Borehamwood thinking to myself.

*

Mattie the Mac ended up getting 20 years instead of 22 years once he was pulled in and found guilty at Snersbrock Crown Court. He had done the deal with the police and told them where the other van was with the money. They had offered him a deal before his interview and instead of grassing everyone up about the jobs they had all done at the depot he thought it best to just tell them where the money was. He said that it was he that had busted Johnny and Mr B from the prison van. The others had run off to some place in Germany, well that's what he said. They wanted names of everyone, but he said he would only uncover where the van was with the money. After them bringing Mattie from his cell again and again for questioning they finally gave up and accepted that the van was all they were going to get.

They had other leads now in the case; well he was going down anyway. It didn't matter to him or me now they had caught at least one of them and got back most of the money. The police would then slack off a bit trying to find the others that were allegedly involved; they had the money and a suspect so they were happy for now.

So it worked out well for both of them. He had done it to give the others a chance, even if he had lost all our money it didn't matter and it seems he did the right thing at the time. He never did give names to the police; he kept his mouth shut about everything else and everyone else. He should be out in nine years, if he gets granted parole.

Old School. He went out to Barbados and continued with his DJ'ing and started promoting his raves in different clubs all over England. Even doing Watford some nights and I would still go over there now and then when I had gone over to see DJ Luck when he was there doing the circuit within all the clubs. After all the drama had calmed down here in England, Old School had gone out to Barbados to hide from the Russian mafia. The word on the street was they were now looking for him, to find out where their Russian friend was. People had said they had seen him with Old School and that was the last time they saw him. Unbeknown to them their friend was dead and buried.

Johnny had shot him when we were out there at the shack in Barbados and it had all gone a bit pear-shaped. We had all gone back to the hotel and I was shitting my pants at what we had just seen Johnny do. If they knew Old School was involved they would have dug a hole for him too. As soon as they saw him they would have buried him right there next to the friend, as life expectancy is very short in this game. Johnny had bought the club after he met up with an old time friend of his who was a semi-retired smuggler. He was now organising container shipments to come to England from France and Belgium with one million pound's worth of tobacco, sprits, beers and Viagra in them.

They worked with someone that owned a big warehouse full of pallets of cheap booze, cigars and fags. Ironically it was called the Eastenders warehouse. It gave a new meaning to the booze cruise and if Customs had caught them they would have to say that 50 alcoholics all chipped in for Christmas for the container. Whether they believed it or not it was a gamble. Or you could say that you were intending to have happy hour back at your house and the Viagra was because you had to invite the whole escort agency over.

The Smuggling of the booze and cigarettes was all done in their spare time. Johnny could still pull strings over in Liverpool and in London. Even though he was out there on the run in Barbados with the help of a fella called Malcolm that Mr Nice knew very well. Old School was helping him out and they were making a fortune between them.

Johnny was earning from the shipments and the contacts he was making, he had bought this old bar and done it out and refurnished it. He had called it Johnny's Bar, it is still there today and doing very well indeed. It would have been a little nest egg for him and Mandy. If they were both still here, one nest egg that she unfortunately never got to see. She got shot and he was shot too by the old Bill so you could say what goes around comes around. Now Old School is the new owner of Johnny's Bar, fancy that eh? He still pops over to England every now and then to see me. He does the odd gig in London and Manchester, playing and M.C.ing in some very posh clubs in Bristol, filling in slots for some pirate radio stations sometimes too when he can. George is running the bar in Barbados for him and has now become his right-hand man. George, yes the dustcart driver, my old school friend. He likes to go back out to Barbados every now and then to keep out the way of the Serious Crime Squad and Scotland Yard and the Russian mafia. Or anyone else he might have upset along the way.

When the great escape was done, George had stayed with Wong and helped him, now he helps Old School out until he returns. Old School works with some of the most dangerous men in England, now he has taken over Johnny's. He had met most of them.

Tom the Moose is still probably sitting in the Woodcock pub helping to run things in B'wood in between taking care of the ladies and staying out of the nick. Telling the men or some of them how it is, or at least keeping them under manors, making sure they're doing as their told when they're told. That is when they're not all trying to fight with him.

He is doing his thing here and there and making himself and most of the firms a bit of pocket money in between running errands for the bigger firms in London and Manchester allegedly. He is still out there with a face known as The Hairy Fella. They are the dynamic duo. They do what they want, when they want with help from some old faces that are well known in and out of

London and wouldn't mind sticking their neck out for them as long as they continued to make money.

The diver that came to me with a case full of cocaine has never been seen or heard of again. He has disappeared into thin air and as far as I can tell he has kept the secret of the cocaine to himself. He must have changed his name by deed poll. He just walked away like he never existed.

Mandy got shot by the Columbian hitmen and was buried in the Romans church 2003. R.I.P. Her stone is still there today and I still go to see it and talk to her about good and bad times, and leave some flowers from me and a white rose from Johnny. I always say how I wish I could change things and that I knew how she felt about me but it's too late. Mattie had said she told him she loved me. I wish I hadn't got involved in the Firm at all but it's too late for all that. Now it's easy to say once you're not involved but you try getting out when you're in the thick of things. She would still be with us today if it weren't for me. How I wish I could have got to know her just that little bit more. She will be greatly missed by us all and all the underworld members too.

Johnny the hitman got shot by S.O. 19 at Mandy's funeral and was buried 10 days later next to her. The police had to explain what had happened and did a full report, which made it to the papers. Not many people turned up to Johnny's funeral as the Serious Crime Squad were still at large trying to piece everything together. The faces and villains knew it would be too much of a risk to be there, but they paid their respects in a local church and signed a book. Those who wanted to made their peace with Johnny. Some of the Sicily mob had also turned up to this send-off at the church as he had done some work for them. The Jewellery Thieves did come over and attend Johnny's funeral, as well as two police officers and myself and the CID fella that had been following the Firm and Johnny for the last ten years and could now retire on the day he went to the funeral. That's all that were there on that day when we put Johnny to rest. Mr Nice didn't come to England unless it was very necessary.

Mr Wong went back to Chinatown and started working with George when George wasn't helping Old School out in Barbados in the bar. George and Mr Nice were now working very closely with the Triads and our mate called Jerry, the one that had helped watch the cameras movements outside Belmarsh prison. Between them all they had all built up a big empire in England, selling counterfeit DVDs all over here in England in the markets or any way they can. Getting their scouts to go into the pubs or building sites or anywhere else. Wong still works closely with the Jewellery Thieves and rubs shoulders with most of the firms here in London. He still has his connections with Mr Nice and his big connections to the cartel and the Liverpool firms. Connections with the firms in China, Japan, Malaysia, Russia and Colombia are still as strong as ever. Mr Wong is in with the Italians now the Godfather has been nicked and most of the Italian cartel along with the Rodrigo's brothers allegedly.

Mr B was arrested trying to get to Marco from Barbados with the fake passport as he was trying to arrange a shipment of puff to come from Marco to England. They had some money to play with whilst being out there on the run and he got four years from the judge at St Albans Crown Court for his part in the deal at Southend and one year for his escape, all to run concurrent. He is now in Woodhill prison serving his time with the two Cypriot men and one of the divers.

They were all charged with conspiracy, for the importation of large quantities of cocaine and they all received a maximum ten years each between then, but to run simultaneously. So in the end they would all serve a four-year sentence and some six from the judge, for a first time offence. They were caught with 11 keys of cocaine in total, which the police estimated it to be worth on the streets near on three million pounds. They are now on the back end of a four-year sentence and should be released in a year's time, if they all get their parole that is. The Cypriots got the brunt of the sentence and are still serving a long time. They are now serving their time in Springhill Open Prison. They're able to pull strings with some of the firms, even from inside the prison, as they're working with the prison guards because some of them are now on the pay roll and bringing in parcels for them.

Some of the gear that had been confiscated by the police had turned out to be moody and it seems they had been set up with the Cypriots. They had swapped some of the gear over as they were going to take the money and run. They had bubbled the shipment up and had turned Judas and would have split the money with the Columbians once they had got away. Mr B got nicked with the 11 keys of moody gear as one of the Cubans owed a lot of money and this was the only way he could pay it back by giving the Cypriots moody gear. Only five keys of it were good Mr B even had tested that night but it hadn't turned out the way they planned. He hadn't handed the money over first so they couldn't get out of them knowing Mr B would soon be nicked. So it had all backfired and they had all got caught and were all doing their bird.

Me; I walked away from it all. Never to smuggle or juggle again, or so I thought. I had the key of cocaine from the diver that had been taken to a good friend of mine to be sold and the money split. All that was all well out of my league now. The Columbians were paid and I never heard from them again, thank fuck, nor did I see or bump into their hitmen. Last I knew they were being banged up over in Columbia for the murder of Mandy and some Cuban boss that they had killed. He had owed them money that they tried to stick Mr B up with it so they didn't have to pay. The word on the street was their racket had come well on top, as the police were now sniffing round them all, so much so, that a top member of their firm had now been caught in Liverpool.

Mr Nice had now allegedly been able to take over a coca leaf field over in Columbia now these arrests had been made. I'm sure someone upstairs was well looking after me and the rest of our Firm, or lady luck must well like us or fancy me. Me, Old School and some of the old faces meet up now and again which is not very often now days. But when we do, we now sit with the top firms at most clubs around London and other parts of the country now Mr Nice is in a much better position. We now sit at their tables that would cost £1000 a night for the normal Joe Blogs and no less than £250 for a bottle of Champagne. Laid on for us by the club managers that we were now protecting and were well looking after. After all it was our doormen looking after their clubs and their interests for now. So why not show a bit of respect every now and then. That meant we weren't sitting with the aftershave man in the toilets sniffing hard at Columbian's finest. As many people still are doing today, when you come out after your line in the cubicle.

Jimmy the aftershave man is standing there trying to fleece you for a £1 for a stick of fucking chewing gum and another quid just to wash and wipe your hands. So you're being robbed and he ain't even wearing a mask. How much would it be if you want him to wipe your arse?

Them days were long gone. Our toilets were in the back room now. So no more being crammed in a cubicle and people thinking you're gay when you both come out wiping your nose and sniffing hard, checking each other's nose for loose bits that hadn't been sniffed up yet by the greedy nostrils. No more sniffing off the dirty toilet seat or of the back of the cistern or flicking it with a card at the side of a wrap for use. It was now off the manager's desk or off a few nice women's tits that were invited to come into the office with us from the dance floor. I picked up the Jack Daniels from the table and took a sip. I looked to my left and then to my right, here I was sitting at a £2000 a night table at the Mayfair nightclub with Old School and Ray, Aggie and the most dangerous men in England. Once again all I had in my pocket was a tenner and a head full of good and bad memories. Not bad eh for a gentlemen that always showed the upmost respect to those that had earned it, and a fella who was in the wrong place at the wrong time? But it don't come good for everyone. I'm just a lucky guy I guess. I still missed the gorgeous Mandy even now she'd been dead for 3 years. Well they say the good die young. So looks like we will all be around for ages yet. I then said, "Listen, fellas, I'm going to go," even though they wanted me to stay.

One of the dangerous men was Many C a prizefighter that I had been with in Woodhill prison back in the day. He said stay, he was the one that had clued me up with saying the cocaine was a disease, the more you take the more you want and you just go round and round in circles cashing the pound note. He was in there for shooting someone so they say. I stood up, shook all their hands and said I would love to stay but I got to get back to the family.

Old School said "Cookie" in a deep London accent as he joined the table, "Where you going son?" I hugged him and said, "I'm going home, mate."

"Goodbye, I love you, son," Old School said.

I got Vivien's coat and left the table and made my way through the minders and the bouncers and out through the VIP lounge bit into the main club area. Everyone was dancing and rushing of their tits from the E's, coke and speed. The doormen were all now working it back in to the clubs as we had taken it off people and sold it back into the clubs. So it was 100% profit for us all. Vivien and I made our way through the club dance floor and out the door. The bouncers said goodbye as they paid their respects to Vivien and me before we left. They said, "You're welcome here anytime, Cookster, and you sweetheart," as they spoke to the sophisticated Vivien. "Whenever you like you just come to the front and ask one of us, and we'll walk you in. No paying, no problems. We'll take care of you, and make sure you have a good night."

"Thanks, fellas; give my best to your families." I then shook their hands.

"No problems, Cookster, for you anything, mate," as what I had done back in the day had given them the jobs they all now had. We left the club never to see them again or the most dangerous men in the U.K.

Well I did see Old School and them once or twice. When we would meet up out the blue and out of ear and eyes shot of others, but it was all kept hush hush. The Serious Crime Squad, MI5 and FBI and other agents were still at large pulling in big firms and names. Breaking down different rackets and bagging up different mobsters and villains of all different sorts all around the world. Like the big mafia bosses, the Columbian's firm and the cartel, and a few faces from Italy. So it was best to keep quiet about our meetings and business and not be all in the same place at the same time. They could try and get us all nicked by association or set us all up with an entrapment eventually. So I got to see the Firm less and less. I stopped going to the clubs and pubs in London and Borehamwood as the Met police had now put a stop to that as they had put me on pub watch, even though I hadn't got in trouble in any pubs. Weird I know but at least it saved me a few quid.

I did recently read about some of the Firm in magazines and papers that I was involved with whilst coming out the gym. Allegedly, some of them had tried to do a 1-millon pound deal with a football director in London. Enough said, as talk is cheap and actions speak volumes. I did get a call on holiday in Spain though when I was out there relaxing with Mr Nice. He had invited me out there to try and get me back into the Firm once again, but more about that one later. As that could be:

"A nice little earner"

As Mr Nice always said: "Life is easy, son; it's living the life that's hard." That's why some people need to be educated in the ways of the Firm. As we're all gangsters 'round here."

The only place you'll be ending up is in prison, or someone will take you out the game as they will take you out to the trees and put a bullet in the back of your nut if you're not careful. Get out while you can or you'll end up OD'ing to death on the drugs if you keep sniffing that shit like your life depends on it. Drugs are for mugs, but for an old dog like me it's a means to an end. It pays the bills but for you lot you still have choices to make, just make the right ones. My advice for you lot is to get out why you still can.